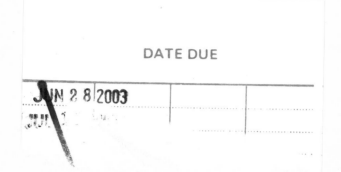

DATE DUE

JUN 2 8 2003		

SAFE
IN HEAVEN
DEAD

SAFE
IN HEAVEN
DEAD

A NOVEL

Samuel Ligon

HarperCollins*Publishers*

SAFE IN HEAVEN DEAD. Copyright © 2003 by Samuel Ligon. All rights reserved. Printed in the United States of America. No part of this book may be used or reproduced in any manner whatsoever without written permission except in the case of brief quotations embodied in critical articles and reviews. For information, address HarperCollins Publishers Inc., 10 East 53rd Street, New York, NY 10022.

HarperCollins books may be purchased for educational, business, or sales promotional use. For information, please write: Special Markets Department, HarperCollins Publishers Inc., 10 East 53rd Street, New York, NY 10022.

FIRST EDITION

Designed by Nancy Singer

Printed on acid-free paper

Library of Congress Cataloging-in-Publication Data is available upon request.

ISBN 0-06-009910-0

03 04 05 06 07 ❖/RRD 10 9 8 7 6 5 4 3 2 1

For Kim

Poor! I wish I was free
of that slaving meat wheel
and safe in heaven dead

—Jack Kerouac,
from "211th Chorus,"
Mexico City Blues

SAFE
IN HEAVEN
DEAD

ONE

JANUARY 6

Robert Elgin died on the street, knocked down and run over by a Second Avenue bus while pursuing a woman he thought he could not live without. He'd been considering settling quietly in a small town in New England or the Southwest or someplace else—doing the dishes, mowing the lawn, shuttling his lost children to ballet and music lessons, attending adult education classes in anthropology and history at the local university, a comeback to the world of hardware stores and county fairs and voter registration and car repairs.

His last words were "Carla, wait! I'm not finished." She was across the street, walking away from him. He was thirty-nine years old, fifteen pounds overweight. He was running out of money.

One of his shoes, a black tasseled loafer, flew into the lap of an elderly woman in a wheelchair as she was rolled down the sidewalk by her nurse. The old woman picked up the shoe and held it away from herself, examining it, then handed it over her shoulder to the nurse, who dropped it into a wire mesh trash basket.

The cops hadn't arrived yet, the ambulance would be a meat-wagon.

Traffic snarled, and the horns started blaring.

TWO

SEPTEMBER/OCTOBER

He was staying in a small, pricey hotel in Murray Hill, fresh flowers all over the lobby, in the elevator, on tables outside the elevator, in arrangements littering his suite. He came on smooth and quiet at first—not that you ever can tell—opening the door and extending his hand: "Carla, is it?" he says, as if we hadn't talked on the phone twenty minutes ago, and I smile and tilt my head, look down, demure, a girlfriend being taken to the country club to meet the family. "What a lovely apartment," I say.

And right away, he's got nothing to say; he's stuck, looking down at the floor, not that this is so unusual. I take his hand and lead him to the couch, trying to weigh out how he wants to play it: straight to bed? confessions? mild humiliation? hoping it's straight to bed.

"How about a drink?" he says.

He places me on the couch and opens a bottle of wine in the kitchen area across the room. I smile wholesomely. They need to believe that you love your job.

He hands me my glass and sits in the armchair opposite the couch, then looks down, Mister Timid, which is fine by me, though that doesn't mean he won't turn into a sadist later. In which case I walk.

"Well," he says, behind a nervous laugh, "I thought we'd go out to dinner."

"I'd love to," I say. "Maybe dancing afterward."

"Great," he says. "I mean, we've got all night, right?"

"Pretty much," I say. It's obvious he's never done this before. Once the appointment starts you never discuss money or time; it's already been settled. He's waiting for something else from me. I feel like a streetwalker negotiating prices. "We've got all kinds of time," I say, looking at my watch. "Eight hours, I guess." Like I'm not sure.

He's still waiting.

"Teddy gave you the terms," I say, "right?"

He gives me a sharp look, the first sign that there's something burning inside.

"Uh-huh," he says, dragging out the sounds in his throat. "But let's not ruin it."

I play with my hair stupidly. "Are you kidding?" I say, crinkling up my forehead. "Nothing's going to be *rui*ned. We're going to have a great time tonight." Or maybe you will, I think. Me? I've got a Faulkner seminar in the morning for which I am unprepared, the prof, Nabaum, an old fuck who hates my guts and will most likely be on my dissertation committee, who gave me a B on my first paper, subtitled "Or why biographers should be executed," who is completing the second of his planned three volumes on Edith Wharton, entitled *Edith Wharton: A Life,* who hates books, who hates teaching, who hates people, who is setting traps for me left and right, hoping I go up in flames. Nabaum.

The man across from me holds his face in his hands, thumbs at his earlobes, pinkies pulling at the corner of his eyes, and says, as if he's suddenly back in the room with me, "We'll meet at Gotham, over on Twelfth Street. How's that?"

"Good choice," I say, but I'm thinking, *Meet? Aren't we already together?*

"Are you sure?" he says. "Maybe you should choose."

"No," I say, wondering just how much of a pain in the ass this guy's going to be. Too passive can be as bad as too aggressive. "Gotham is very good—one of my favorite restaurants."

"Are you sure?" he says again.

"William," I say. "I really want you to have a good time tonight. You having a good time is what will make me happy."

He looks at the ceiling. "All right," he says. "But will you do me one favor?"

"Sure," I say, thinking, that's what you're paying me for.

"Call me Robert," he says.

"No problem."

He sighs, unsure, seems to be trying to decide something, then says, "And my last name's Elgin, not Oliver."

So it's confessions.

And then, before ushering me out, he gives the instructions: that I am to install myself at the bar at Gotham; that I am to say, if asked, that, yes, I have a reservation, under the name of Oliver, but to divulge this information to no one but the maître d'; that I am to sip my drink and—though he doesn't say this in so many words, I understand the fantasy—display my legs, my smile, my cleavage, and, most important, my conversational and flirting talents to any and all comers; and, of course, it also goes without saying that I am to be Elgin's prize. I don't bother to tell him that the fantasy is flawed, that Gotham isn't a pick-up place where you meet someone at the bar, have dinner, and then go home and fuck. You don't get far in this business questioning verisimil-itude, though: you figure out what's required, you deliver, you take the money.

So I have a club soda and wait at the bar, wondering if I can some-how finish the novel later tonight and then be a good girl in Nabaum's seminar without any sleep. Elgin shows maybe an hour later, hair gelled back shiny, red tie white shirt black suit gold watch—the uni-form—all very expensive, and stands to the side of the crowded bar, watching me in the glass. He's not bad looking, and here, in public, the shy uncertainty he exhibited in his suite has vanished. He's giving off the power vibe, like so many of my clients who want to be pissed on or slapped or made to lick the toilet rim when we get back to the room, something I just will not get into: if you don't draw lines, peo-ple start to look so ugly that you can end up hating even yourself. Two bankers to my right try to impress me with banking jargon—"high exposure to the ingress of foreign suppliers"—and NYPD brass to my left smoke cigars and talk *street*, shooter this, player that, niggers, actors, perps and vics, the fucking mayor, the fucking Port Authority. All these big, bad powerful men, it's enough to make a girl crave some protection.

When one of the bankers goes to the bathroom, I smile at the other one, shortish, tight curly hair, a hundred-dollar manicure. "How you doing?" he says. "You waiting for someone?"

"No one in particular," I say, perky, conscious of my audience across the room.

He smiles, showing me his big square horse's teeth. "That's great," he says. "We're in from Detroit; we'd love it if someone could show us the town."

"Detroit?" I say, turning on the radiance and touching his hand. "Oh, my God. I grew up in Flint."

Elgin secures a seat down the bar, his eyes in the mirror fixed on me. "Flint, huh?"

"My dad works at Buick," I say, touching his hand again. "Do you work for GM?"

His head bobs up and down on his shoulders. He swirls the ice in his drink, looks down at it, and his head keeps bobbing.

"My dad's UAW," I tell him. "Are you?"

He smiles up at me, his head cocked down over his whiskey. "Nah," he says.

The bartender places a martini in front of me, up, olives. "From the gentleman at the end of the bar." He points to Elgin. I raise the glass in a thank-you toast, while GM's eyes rake my chest. Men are so transparent and easy to manipulate it's a wonder they ever ruled their bowel movements, let alone the world.

"I'm a designer," GM 1 says as GM 2 returns to his seat.

"An *interior* designer?" I ask, the stupid-girl-confused look on my face.

"No," he laughs. "Auto."

"Oh," I say, laughing with him. "Of course. GM, right?"

GM 2 says, "Who's your friend?" presenting me with what he must believe is his smoky, seductive look.

"Oh, I'm sorry," GM 1 says. "I don't even know. I'm Dan Pangle," he says, giving me his hand.

"Carla," I say.

"Dan Howard," the other one says, shooting his hand out.

"The two Dans," I say to general merriment, Elgin smiling down the bar at me, the first smile I've seen on him.

"Carla here's from Flint," Dan says.

"Really," Dan says, and Dan says, "Home of the Halo Burger."

"Are you a designer, too?" I ask.

"Yep," Dan says. "What about you?" He squinches up his right eye. "Let me guess—a model, right?"

"Close," I say. I lean in to create a conspiratorial aura, which they bend into. "These guys behind me are cops," I say, "so keep it to yourself . . ." I place my index finger to my lips and wink naughtily. "I'm a terrorist," I whisper, and I hang with them for a second, searching their faces, before pulling away and sipping my martini.

"No, really," Dan says.

"No, really," I say.

They're still leaning in, craving the conspiracy and a look down the front of my dress.

"Come on," Dan says.

"Come on," I say.

Elgin moves down the bar, positioning himself on the stool next to the far Dan.

Near Dan straightens and says, "Carla here said she could show us the town."

I look past the Dans and say to Elgin, "Haven't I seen you on television?"

He points his finger to his chest, eyes wide, a who-me look. Both Dans turn.

"No," Elgin says. "Not me."

"You look like that guy on *The Young and the Restless*. The broker guy. What's his name?" The men panic a little. "Dan, what's his name?" The Dans shake their heads, far Dan giving Elgin his back.

"Lance," Elgin says. "His name's Lance."

"That's right," I say. "Lance."

"It's funny, too," Elgin says, "because my name's Vance."

"That is funny," far Dan says.

"Nice to meet you, Vance," I say. "Carla." As I reach my arm between the Dans the maître d' arrives to tell them their table is ready.

"You want to join us?" near Dan asks me.

"No, thanks," I say, letting my eyes linger on Elgin—I am clearly and ridiculously smitten—before finally tearing myself away to smile at Dan.

Far Dan follows the maître d'. Near Dan grieves, examines his manicure. "Maybe later tonight?" he says.

"I'm sorry, Dan. I can't."

"That's cool," he says, pulling himself away. "Nice talking to you."

"Yes," I say. "Good-bye."

"You're the one who should be on *The Young and the Restless*," Elgin says, assuming near Dan's seat.

"Don't I know it," I say.

"Robert Elgin," he says, sticking out his hand.

I'm forever shaking men's hands. And other things.

"Temple Drake," I say.

"I thought your name was Carla."

"Oh," I say. "That's right. Carla."

He gives me a half grin, the left side of his mouth curling up, as he turns to the bar and gestures to the bartender for another round. "So, how long you been doing this?" he asks, still showing me his profile.

So many of them want the statistical rundown. It's enough to make me think I'm giving off that not-so-fresh feeling. "Not so long," I say. "And I'm clean, if you're worried about AIDS."

"I'm not worried about AIDS," he says. "How many days a week you work?"

One out of five gives me some variation of this interview, thinking, I guess, that we're having a conversation, or that they'll get a glimpse into some mysterious dark underworld, or that I'm a virgin, for goodness sake. The drinks arrive. Elgin tips the bartender a twenty. "How many days a week do *you* work?" I ask him.

"None," he says, holding up his drink to toast.

We touch glasses, and after we drink he lays this warm open ministerial smile on me that pisses me off out of all proportion.

"I'm not tragic," I say, "if that's what you're looking for," thinking, you trust-fund fuck.

"No," he says, hurt and concerned. "I thought nothing like that. I actually envy you your job."

Typical male anonymous sex fantasy, I think, but he reads it in my face, and says, "Not the sex, exactly, and certainly not the people you must find yourself with."

"You'd be surprised," I say. "Most are pretty damn successful. What you'd call high achievers," and I can't believe I'm defending my clients.

"Of course," he says. "I didn't mean—" He holds up his hands in surrender. "I'm sorry. That's not what I mean. I mean, at your rate, I'm sure you must get the best."

"You know, Robert," I say. "You're making me feel like a whore."

"No, that's not what I mean," he says, the color coming up on his neck and cheeks. "All I meant was that there's nothing fake about your job."

"Are you kidding me?" I say.

"No," he sputters. "It's just that the terms are so clear."

His eyes are so desperate for me to agree, to be there with him, that I drop out of the conversation and go back on the job. "You're right," I say, taking his hand. "You are absolutely right." I must be out of my mind to talk like this, practically chasing the money away, but I've walked away before and will, I'm sure, again. I rub his palm with my thumbs, and it feels like the guy's about to break into pieces.

"All I'm saying is that you probably don't have any illusions about what you are."

Jesus.

He puts his other hand over my own, looks up at me, the panic in his eyes again. "That sounds horrible. That's not what I mean."

"Right," I say. "But what I am isn't based on the two days a week that I work."

"Yes," he says. "Exactly. Good point." He looks at me, searching, not at my boobs, either, and says, "So what are you?"

I laugh. I honestly laugh. "I don't *know*," I say, playing it dumb. "What are you?"

He nods a few times, *yes, yes,* squints past me, our hands still tangled, and, like, fifteen seconds go by.

"Well?" I say, and he keeps nodding, squinting over my shoulder, like, *It's coming to me, it's coming to me.*

"What it is," he finally says, still nodding, still looking past me— and I find myself nodding along with him, trying to help him pump out the words—"is that I think—and this is weird, this is like, hard to believe—but it's like. Okay. This: I might be dead," he says, still not looking at me, and the nodding becomes more rapid, deeper, an agreement with the words: "I think I'm dead."

"Oh, really," I say, trying to pull him back. "And how did you die?"

"Surrender," he says, nodding, but more slowly now, a definite confirmation. "It must have been in my sleep."

"You look too good to be dead," I tell him, and I giggle stupidly.

"Thank you," he says.

He is completely vacant.

And I'm thinking, Careful. Be very careful with this one.

≡

After only a few hours in New York, Elgin felt that he would never be clean again, a permanent grime lining the whites of his fingernails, a sooty, sticky film coating his skin, the heavy humidity a stew of disease molecules to be waded through. The air-conditioning in his room at the Ambassador Hotel didn't work properly, and he noticed a few stray pubic hairs in the graying sheets of his bed, but he was so tired that first night—the flight down to Miami, Barbados, then back to Miami, the train up to New York, days without rest—that he didn't even bother to shower, and slept a full twelve hours without dreaming. In the morning, he woke to the dinginess of his room, the dead air and mildew, and for a moment it seemed as if none of it had really happened.

The pipes in the shower groaned, but he'd only be here for one more night, maybe two, three tops—until he got himself established. He walked over to Sixth Avenue and headed up toward the park. He'd never been to New York, had never known anyone from New York, but he found that he knew things about it—from movies and television and books—that everything he'd need would be somewhere up around the park. He carried the money with him, slung over his shoulder in a red-and-white duffel bag, some towels and T-shirts and toiletries on top covering the taped-up garbage bag.

There was nothing else to do with it. He certainly couldn't leave it in the room of that shit hole motel. Movies instructed to leave it in a locker at the train station, but he hadn't seen any lockers the night before, and wouldn't have left it there anyway. Wasn't that exactly where the cops were always lurking, waiting to nab you? In his two front pockets and his wallet, he carried five thousand dollars, less his train ticket and the hotel.

He'd just have to deal with the paranoia. Once he had the clothes, the watch, the personal organizer, the shoes, the haircut, the briefcase, he'd become less vulnerable, but the question was in what order to make the purchases. And then where to put them.

The street was packed with purpose. At eleven in the morning it didn't seem possible for this many people to be out trying to get some-where. Aside from the deliveries and the shoppers and tourists, most of the people seemed to be on their way to work, women in suits, men in suits, many carrying thin leather briefcases that couldn't hold more than a legal pad and a bottle of aspirin. Elgin noticed that a lot of the men were in shirtsleeves, which meant that their jackets were back at the office. So just where were they going? Very irresponsible, Elgin thought, very inefficient, to let these people wander the streets when they should be working, until he realized that his watch had stopped. It was lunchtime.

He bought a cup of coffee and kept moving, mapping out places he'd need to know. One thing about New York you didn't get from the movies was the smell. At ninety degrees, the grates in the sidewalk seemed to belch a stinking plume of boiling piss, spoiled milk, rotten vegetables, and diesel exhaust.

He reached the bottom of the park and headed east toward Fifth and the Plaza Hotel. A big gold statue of a general on a horse—Sher-man, it looked like—gleamed in the midday sun. It occurred to Elgin that he would need a good hotel for the tourist guides and concierge service that would allow him to figure out everything else, but he couldn't go into one looking like this, and then, also, there was the problem of having no credit cards, and the suspicion paying with cash might arouse.

He felt stuck, then shook it off, part of the paralysis of the last few months. He wasn't going to be a victim to fear or weakness anymore, which would only mark him anyway. He was going to take intelligent, calculated risks, act as if he deserved everything he had and was going to get, and he was going to survive.

He bought a leather briefcase and overnight bag, a gold watch, a lightweight, charcoal suit, white shirt and tie, new shoes, a fountain pen, a three-pack of boxers, some socks, and hauled it all back to his room, where he ordered a pizza for dinner. He was out of there tomorrow, on to a better room, another step forward. He needed some kind of semipermanent lodging, hidden somewhere in the city, where he could disappear and figure out what he was supposed to do next. But there would have to be a transition hotel first, a far nicer hotel, until he could determine where he should be. He wondered if anyone was looking for him yet, if anyone knew. Laura, of course, would assume he was still at the Holiday Inn out by the Palace, which the Holiday Inn would assume as well since he hadn't checked out, and had left most of his clothes there, along with his briefcase and a do-not-disturb sign on the doorknob. Actually, Laura probably wouldn't assume anything; she'd be too busy suffering, on the phone with her therapist, with Carrie's therapist, with a member of the support group, with some asshole from the church. He'd taken the rest of the week off work, so Pearson might not know anything yet, unless the bank had gotten suspicious and called Klister or McCabe, but why would the bank do that after the fact? It seemed likely that no one knew anything. He hadn't vanished. He hadn't disappeared. Not yet. He was still at the Holiday Inn in Pontiac, less than thirty miles from home. What did any of them suppose he was doing there, alone in his hotel room? Carrie or Tommy would probably be the ones to wake Laura up—"Why hasn't Daddy called?" or "When can we see Dad?"—if she was capable of being woken up or caring as to his whereabouts, which seemed doubtful at this point. He didn't want to think about his kids right now, since he couldn't contact them without giving away his location. He couldn't do anything for them, anyway. That would have to come later, when things sorted themselves out.

The good news was that he hadn't hurt that little bastard, Corey Newkirk. Or was that good news? Maybe that would come later, too. He hoped not. Or, maybe he hoped so. He wasn't really sure. But, as it stood, the one thing he could say to the cops or the judge was that he'd never hurt that little bastard, Corey. That should be worth something. Or maybe that was the problem.

≡

So, he wants to talk during dinner, seems to have recovered from his near-death experience, and I'm really quite good at this, making a man feel important, as if what he says is of the greatest interest and intelligence, sort of like a Mother Teresa for rich men's self-esteem. He tells me about his kids, which is rare from a client, how great they are, how much he misses them, even shows me a picture, which I study, commenting on their beauty. But that's it for the personal stuff; everything else is current events, the NFL, politics, the stock market, which I'm well prepared for, having read the *Times* and *Wall Street Journal* before our appointment. And then he says, "What about you? What's your story?" as if he's told me anything about himself, and I smile, and say, "What do you want my story to be?"

He rolls his eyes, says, "Come on. Jesus. I'm not looking for any big secrets."

"I'm just an average girl," I say, "out for a good time."

"Yeah?" he says. "What's a good time?"

"Being with you," I say. "Going back to your place. Having a glass of wine. Maybe fooling around a little."

"Okay," he says, holding up his hand. "I get it." He signals the waiter and asks for the check. "All I want to know is how you fill up time," he says, "what you find to *do* with your time."

"Well," I say, looking up at the ceiling, "I enjoy shopping, movies, working out, needlepoint, museums," and then I look right at him. "But, mostly shopping and working out."

"Okay," he says, "I'll tell *you* something. I mean this is our first date, our getting to know each other session, so I'll start," and I'm thinking, *first* date, part of me following the money, and mildly entertained by the guy, but another part unsure of how much effort he'll require, and, of course, wondering if he'll go psycho on me.

"When I was a kid, seven or eight," he says, "I got this idea that I could make myself invisible."

He looks into my eyes, monitoring my reactions. "Okay," I say. "Go on."

He chews on his thumbnail, examines his palm, then says, "We were members of this pretty conservative church in Western Michigan—Dutch Reformed country—and while this church wasn't quite fundamentalist—I mean, there was no bullshit about dancing or cards or that kind of thing—some of that Dutch stuff must have worn off, because of the region or something. Anyway, one day the preacher's up there talking about faith and how faith can do anything, can get you anything, like, if you just believe hard enough, God will answer any prayer—withered limbs healed, riches and prosperity, that sort of thing, but what he keeps hammering is the word *anything*. So, I wrack my mind for what it is I want: a five-dollar bill rolled into the Sunday paper, a new bike, a hundred-count box of Bazooka, and then, like a bolt of lightning, like a message from God himself, I know what I want: to be able to turn myself invisible."

The waiter arrives with the check. Elgin doesn't bother totaling it, just lays three hundreds in the little book, a 50 percent tip, minimum.

"So," he says, "I start working on my faith, start believing as hard as I can believe—that God exists, I guess, or that he's there with me, listening to me, waiting to grant my wish, but I can't think that because it's selfish, so I hide that wish far away and trick myself into thinking that I'm just filled with holy belief. I walk around for a couple of days believing in God with everything I have, looking for good deeds to do, being obedient, kind to my sister, taking out the trash, I don't know, and after like three days, I'm in bed, right before sleep, and I actually hear God say to me, in this faint, wispy, but unmistakably Godlike voice, 'Robert, you can become invisible now,' and I sit straight up in bed, wide awake, just thrilled, of course, and I say, 'Thank you, Lord. Thank you, Jesus,' and while I'm not sure of the mechanism that will turn me invisible, I just figure I have to wish it, to believe it, to have faith, and it will happen."

He takes a drink of water, eyes still attached to mine over the glass. I wear my mesmerized mask.

"So the next morning at the bus stop, I will myself invisible, pick up a chunk of busted concrete, and sidearm it at the taillight of the first car that goes by."

He smiles at me with his whole face, his eyes bright and skin glow-ing, and he says, "And, of course I didn't run. The car stops and one of the neighbors, Mrs. Bigler, jumps out, and says, 'Robert Elgin, just what do you think you're doing!'

So maybe that is his real name, I think, and I say, "Well, what *were* you doing?"

"I don't know," he says, waving me off. "But, anyway, I'm a little stunned when she says my name, then figure she's just guessing that I must be the invisible boy who threw the rock, because no other kids wait at my stop. And, of course she walks right to me and grabs my arm and drags me up the hill to my house, and I say, 'How did you see me?' and she says, 'Your mother is going to be furious with you,' which she was, and then all the questions in my little chair in the kitchen: 'What would possess you to *do* such a thing, Robert? You could have hurt Mrs. Bigler *terribly*. You could have caused a *horrible* accident.'

"And I couldn't really answer, just apologized and said I wouldn't do it again, and my mother said, 'You'd better believe you'll never do it again,' and walked me over to Mrs. Bigler's house to apologize and say that I would pay for the taillight myself. I spent the rest of the day in my room, wondering how I'd been so stupid as to allow myself to be tricked by the minister, wondering how anyone could believe in a god who so clearly did not exist."

He looks at me, waiting. It's confessions, all right.

"I felt entirely betrayed," he says, and I say, "Didn't you wonder if maybe the invisible power didn't work because you were using it for"—and I post the air quotation marks—"evil? Or pettiness? Or some kind of cheap transaction—faith for invisibility—that God wouldn't go for?"

"It doesn't matter," he says, "because, as sure as I'd been the day before that God existed, I was equally sure—and I mean, positive—that He didn't exist when I didn't turn invisible."

"But, now," I say, "don't you think that the faith wasn't ever real, or wasn't pure or something, that you were just using it for selfish gain, or that maybe God is more mysterious or complicated than that, that He wouldn't allow you to test faith so cheaply, or that the whole point of faith is not being sure, not having the concrete evidence?"

"Oh, sure," he says. "But that's not the point."

"What is the point?" I ask, surprised that I care.

"I don't know," he says. "I just couldn't believe after that. I knew the whole thing was a hoax. Around the same time, the church, in some crazy progressive mode, brought in a Christian rock band for the kids. They wore these hilarious white jumpsuits with fringe on them and sang groovy songs about Jesus. My mother dropped me off, and in the middle of the show, the singer starts talking about the devil, about how this friend of his who had lost her way began *dabbling* with the Ouija board one night, and how that very night—get this—she felt the hand of the devil strangling her in the shower, which left actual satanic thumbprints on her throat, and how this other friend, who had taken up with a pack of drug-addled hippies, was found by his parents with his insides *literally and completely* burned out of him—by the devil, of course. Well, I was just a kid. These stories scared the living shit out of me. And I tried to believe in God again, selfishly again, just for protection against the devil, but what I found was that the devil seemed a lot more real to me than God, a lot more believable."

He smiles a sad smile, shakes his head in a sort of *crazy, huh?* gesture, hangs five seconds of silence and then says, "You ready to go?"

"Wait a minute," I say, because I've got to be sure of something before I leave with him. I mean, I'm thinking the guy's probably incapable of hurting anyone but himself, but you have to be careful, especially since he got through Teddy's screening with a fake name, so I say, "Do you believe in that stuff now?"

"What stuff?" he says.

"You know," I say, "about the devil being more real than God?"

"No," he says. "Not at all."

"What do you believe?"

He shrugs. "I don't know," he says. "What?" He smiles with his whole face again. "Oh, man," he says, "I didn't mean to freak you out, or offend you or anything. It was just—"

"I'm not freaked out," I say. "Or offended."

"No," he says. "You know what it is? Until a few weeks ago, I had a completely different life—a real life, I guess, whatever that means."

He squints, or cringes, apologetically.

"And, now, what I find myself doing is picking through it, because I'm sort of on hold, waiting to know what it is I'm supposed to *do*. And I was thinking this morning about that one night when I knew I could become invisible, and how great that one night was. And that's all, really. I mean, I'm not satanic or anything."

"All right," I say. I haven't seen a guy this desperately sincere since high school, junior high, maybe. "I know what you're saying," and the scary thing is that I think I do—the thing about different lives.

"Look," he says, "let's just—we don't have to go back to my place. I mean, I already paid the agency and everything, so, you know, obviously you'll get paid."

No kidding.

"Why don't we just meet for lunch or something."

I post a radiant smile, thinking, this is too good to be true, thinking I can go home and finish *Sanctuary* for tomorrow's seminar. "You know it will cost you," I say, squinting a little, real sorry and everything, "right?"

"Sure," he says. "No problem."

"I could call the agency and arrange the hourly rate, or an afternoon rate, or something. But, if you want to pay cash again, you'll have to go there first. Next Wednesday works for me."

"All right," he says. "That's fine," and he walks me out of the place, hails a cab, puts me inside, and hands the driver a fifty, doesn't even try to kiss me. I feel like I've won the lottery. I never do the hourly, but for lunch, and for talk, I can make an exception. The guy's like a cash machine.

$$\equiv$$

For five thousand bucks, Elgin got a new Social Security card down in Chinatown, which allowed him to get a safe deposit box for the cash—in midtown, since he still wasn't sure where he was going to be. He must have asked twenty cabbies for help with the ID, riding around all morning, before Vladimir said he could help him for a thousand bucks. Elgin handed ten hundreds over the seatback. Vladimir raised his eyebrows, studied Elgin in the mirror. "You a cop?" he said. "You INS?"

"No," Elgin said, thinking that if this actually worked, it was yet another way that the movies had furthered his criminal development.

"You look like cop," Vladimir said, still holding the money.

"I do not," Elgin said. "Come on. I want to do this as fast as I can."

"Okay, okay," Vladimir said. "First I telephone."

He pulled over to a bank of pay phones, turned off the cab, and made the call. When he returned, he twisted around and studied Elgin. "You sure you not cop?" he said.

"No!" Elgin said. "Come on."

"Show me wallet."

Elgin handed his wallet over the seat, and said, "If I were an undercover cop, do you think I'd carry a badge in my wallet?"

"No," Vladimir said. He examined the wallet. "Okay," he said. "I vouch for you, but not in this clothes. You look too rich."

Elgin peeled off ten more hundreds and handed them over. "Come on," he said. "Let's do it now."

The place was on Mott Street over a grocery store, the sidewalk out front jammed with mostly unidentifiable vegetables. A wispy Asian man in faded jeans and a Betty Boop T-shirt opened the door and led them into a room with a round table and folding chairs. "This the guy," Vladimir said.

The other man didn't speak. His thin black hair hung down over one eye as he regarded Elgin. He pointed to a chair. The room smelled of stale sweat and rot. Elgin sat.

"What you want?" the thin man said, still standing.

"I need identification," Elgin said, trying to keep his voice calm and even.

"No' a green card," the man said, the fierceness in his eyes and set jaw reminding Elgin of pictures he'd seen of the Viet Cong.

"No," he said. "Social Security, I guess."

The man stood over Elgin, his hands splayed out on the rickety table. "Fi' thousan'," he said.

"I only have three."

"Booshit!" the man said.

Why was he haggling with this guy? Christ, he'd pay ten thousand, twenty thousand. "You can have my watch," Elgin said, slipping it off his wrist and handing it to the skinny killer, who examined it, face and back. He nodded and left the room. Adrenaline pumped through Elgin's limbs and stomach. He felt like a professional criminal.

"I tol' you about this clothes," Vladimir said. "You should of let me talk. I could of get it for five hunred."

Elgin shrugged.

Twenty minutes later, Vladimir drove Elgin to the DMV, where he found he had to have proof of address to get a driver's license. "Come on," Elgin said to the fat, bored, civil servant. He was feeling confident from his earlier negotiation with the Viet Cong assassin. Even if he had been ripped off, he'd gotten what he needed. "Here," he whispered, sliding ten hundreds across the counter. "For your kids. Just help me out, okay?"

The civil servant looked left and right without moving her head, then slid the money toward herself. "You still have to have an address," she said.

"I'll tell it to you," he said, "okay?"

She nodded. "Give me your old license," she said.

"My wallet got stolen," Elgin said, wondering just how stupid this woman could be. "I don't have anything, except Social Security."

"Let me look you up on the computer," she said.

"Oh," Elgin said. "Okay." He slid another pile of hundreds across the counter. "I don't think I'll be there," he said.

"You've never had a license," she said.

"Right," Elgin said. It was amazing how well bribery worked. It seemed you could buy anything. Not that you wanted to push it.

"You'll have to take both tests," she said. "Written and driving."

"I don't have a car," Elgin said.

"Well," the woman said, "state identification then."

"Fine," Elgin said. "Great." He got his picture taken as William Oliver, the name the skinny Viet Cong assassin—or whoever had made the Social Security card—had given him. Elgin wondered how many other fake William Olivers existed. He walked out of the DMV elated by his criminal successes of the day. Only four days out of Michigan and he was a new man.

He panicked a little on his way back to the Ambassador Hotel, though, wondering if the money would still be under the bed, in the duffel bag where he'd left it, but it was, and he took that and his few other belongings and checked into the Hyatt near Grand Central. In the clean, expensive-smelling room, he sat on the bed and felt himself letting go, filling with relief that he was still alive, still free to come and go as he pleased, and then he thought of his daughter, his son, who were still in Michigan, and that little bastard Corey, and guilt pressed against his chest, flattening his lungs, it seemed, and he said aloud, "No," and, "I won't," and, "I will," and then washed his face and hands and went down to the bar and got drunk.

In the morning, before the guilt could penetrate his hangover, Elgin made a list of what had to be done, of activity that would fill the day. He needed a more permanent place and he needed clothes and he needed the safe deposit box. He needed a P. O. box, too, and maybe he needed to start establishing credit under his new identity, so he could fill up his wallet with cards, but how could he do that without a bank account? How did the phony Social Security card even work? He didn't want to risk an account with fake ID. But the New York ID was real. And what about income tax returns? Maybe he'd better not have a P. O. box, or start establishing credit. No, in fact, what suddenly became obvious to him was that he had to talk to his kids as soon as possible, and that meant getting out of New York so the call couldn't be traced anywhere close to him, and that meant getting a suitbag and filling it up, along with the overnight bag, and flying out to Portland, Oregon, and making a phone call.

After buying two more suits, he paid cash for his ticket to a travel agent across the street from his new safe deposit, and caught a six o'clock flight out of Newark, with a layover in Chicago. Eating a hot dog at O'Hare, he was tempted by the phone banks, but then decided that if he didn't call from Portland, something horrible would happen. Plus, he didn't want to talk to the kids from a pay phone. And what if someone recognized him in Chicago, only a few hundred miles from home? Jesus, but he was stupid. And what did William Oliver do for a living? He should have stayed in New York and planned this out better. He went into the bathroom and locked himself into a stall. Men came and went, farting and pissing and talking too loud, washing their hands and faces, a few shaving, or changing clothes, while Elgin tried to construct a life.

William Oliver was in advertising, Elgin decided, which seemed like something anyone could do: "You know the little hot dog that dances with the butler? then the old lady in an evening gown? and then the two kids in pajamas, and the mom and dad in formal wear? everybody finally chasing the flying dog around the fancy mansion party? That's one of mine." Sloan Agency, Madison Avenue. He was divorced, had two kids, had attended Penn State, grew up in Pennsylvania, corrected people when they called him "Bill." When he was a kid, his father had beaten him regularly, until he turned sixteen and laid the old man out one night. No, that seemed too clichéd. Until he turned sixteen and ran away to Chicago. His mother was a hopeless but lovable alcoholic who died in a car accident, cold, stone sober, on her way home from the grocery store, where she'd picked up ingredients for William's birthday cake. Or, maybe not. Maybe they were just a regular family, bland and television normal.

After what seemed like an hour of planning William Oliver's past, Elgin walked out into the terminal to find that only twenty minutes had gone by. He bought an overpriced cheap watch in a gift shop, picked up a few magazines and a prepaid calling card, wondering what Oliver's wife had looked like, and how they met, and what went wrong in their marriage, named the kids Tucker and Sue, no, Danny and Sue, and finally boarded his connecting flight, half hoping a seatmate would start up a conversation so he could work on his past, half dreading it, but certain that someone on the plane would be from Oakland County and recognize him.

But no one spoke to him, no one recognized him. Maybe it wasn't a divorce. Maybe William Oliver's wife had died. Recently. A long and brutal illness. Maybe the kids were away with her parents, his in-laws. But what kind of an asshole father would that make him? Why wouldn't he have the kids?

Elgin should have stayed. He should have stayed.

The woman in front of him reclined her seat into his lap. He put his knees up against the seatback and pushed. He wasn't used to the money yet, stupid for not flying first class.

"Do you mind?" the woman in front of him said, turning and looking over her seat.

"I don't mind," Elgin said.

Maybe it was just temporary for Oliver. Maybe the in-laws were just helping out for a little while.

"What were you thinking?" the judge would ask Elgin, a cop would ask, a detective, the woman in the seat in front of him, and he'd say, "I was thinking of getting the hell out of there."

In the movie, the judge would be bald and severe, high up on the bench above him. "You didn't possibly think you could get away with this, did you?"

The camera's behind and above the judge, looking down on the shrinking Elgin.

"And now you have to go to jail, where you will most certainly be raped every day, sometimes three times a day, eight times a day, all day, for the rest of your life."

"Nobody got hurt," tiny Elgin squeaks.

"Young man, of course they did. You just ran away, abandoning your children, your wife, your family, that little bastard Corey. That's what you always do, never finishing anything, abandoning every-thing."

Close-up on Elgin's face, twitching. Then, the transformation: he lowers his brow, sets his jaw, a breeze blowing through his hair; he's the hero after all. "Fuck off," he says. "Send me to jail."

Gasps, applause, gaveling.

Close-up on his daughter, Carrie, a single tear poised at the corner of one eye, then trickling down her cheek.

The music swells.

≡

Lunch is at the Russian Tea Room, not good food, but an out-of-towner's outdated idea of the scene. Teddy calls with the location, and says, "He didn't ask for a dining discount, so I just charged him a dou-ble platinum hourly. You can't call to confirm, but if he doesn't show, so what? I mean, I know your tip, and everything—"

"I'm not sure he gets the tipping aspect yet," I say.

"What, he doesn't tip?"

"He just has to be educated."

Teddy's not bad, a little dopey, but he seems to be genuinely concerned about "us girls." I've thought about going independent, setting up a website, and doing my own screening, and, yeah, it would mean a lot more money, but I just can't be bothered with it right now, and it seems like too much of a commitment to the business, and I don't really want to deal with setting up the security and dealing with those types. And it's not as if I'd post my picture on the Web.

Elgin's waiting out front when I arrive. "Hey," he says, beaming. "Great to see you."

I kiss his cheek, and he flinches a little. "You're so sweet," I tell him.

Once we're seated, he orders a bottle of Pouilly-Fuisse. He's jumpy and excited until it arrives, fiddling around with his silverware, smiling at me and looking away, ignoring my attempts to engage him in conversation, but after the wine is poured, and the sommelier gone, he says, "I got something for you," and he hands me a blue box, which could only contain jewelry.

"Oh, my," I say, "what's this?" but my eyes must pop out of my head when I open it. I've been given jewelry before by clients, but nothing like this. It's a delicate necklace, a light chain with a small cluster of diamonds and sapphires between every third or fourth link, must have cost thousands. "It's beautiful, Robert," I tell him, and it is, not a bit gaudy or ostentatious. "Help me put it on."

He stands behind me and clasps it, while I hold my hair up off my neck, and then he kisses my cheek. Other diners glance our way, one old couple watching the entire show, reliving their romantic youth, or something. The whole thing's a little embarrassing—how earnest he is, how expensive *it* is, how false the act is. But, still, I feel a little off balance by the whole thing, am even considering keeping it instead of cashing it in, Elgin babbling on about how the sapphires accent my eyes, when my worst nightmare finally arrives: Deanna something or other approaches the table, and before even reaching us, says, "Stacey, is that you? I didn't recognize you at first."

"Hey, Deanna," I say, trying to suppress tremors, pissed off at my reaction, then pretending these two worlds aren't about to collide. "This is Robert—"

"Oliver," he says, offering his hand. "Robert Oliver."

"Nice to meet you," she says, smiling, then faces me, and says, "I just didn't recognize you all dressed up like that. You look great."

"Thanks, Deanna," I say, wishing she'd drop dead on the spot. "I love your dress," I say. "Where'd you get it?"

"Oh, I think up in Boston."

"You look beautiful in it . . ." in a sort of dumpy Dworkinian kind of way.

"Thanks," she says.

Elgin wears a mannequin's smile.

Deanna says, "I tried to catch you after class,"

—Fuck—

"but you always bolt out of there so fast."

A high-pitched tittering erupts from my mouth, making it worse.

"I just wanted to say that I think you were absolutely right about Temple being a flat character—what did you say? an avatar of Faulkner's notion of threatening female sexuality."

"I said Benbow's," I say, smiling hard.

"And Little Belle, too. Whatever, but that whole idea of female desire as a corrupting and destructive force might be true for the time and world of the novel, but for every single female character—except the desexed and therefore harmless Miss Jenny—to be ruined by her sexuality, or lack thereof, to be completely dominated and defined by it, and, crucially, to ruin the men, and, therefore all civilization, I mean, I couldn't believe Nabaum didn't see it—"

"Deanna's a friend from school," I say to Elgin, who opens his eyes wide, nodding.

"Oh, I'm sorry," she says. "I just thought you made a lot of good points, that were, like, basically ignored by Nabaum, or worse, ridiculed, and I just wanted to tell you that I agree."

"Well, thanks, Deanna," I say, trying to dismiss the bitch.

"And that whole thing about prostitution," she continues, piss shivers running up my spine, "and all the men being impotent, or killed for not being impotent, and then Miss Reba being empowered by prostitution, but still being controlled by or afraid of the impotent man . . ."

"Yeah," I say. "I got a little long winded. But listen, why don't we talk about it next week after class."

"Okay," she says, "I'm *sorry*. But that thing about the shrimp. I mean, how could Nabaum *not* see that—probably because he's gay or something, though you'd think a gay man *would* think that. But you *know* Faulkner had to see it."

Elgin says, "What about the shrimp, *Stacey?*"

I give him a tight-lipped smile. "Let's talk about it later, baby."

"Oh, I'm sorry," Deanna says again. "I'm ruining your lunch."

"Not at all," Elgin says.

"We're just on a tight schedule," I say. "Let's talk next week."

"I am so sorry," Deanna says again. "Pleasure to meet you," she says to Elgin, who nods, beaming. "'Bye, Stacey," she says, and she walks away.

I have waited for this to happen since I started in the business, but after almost six months, and the city so huge, and always going places a grad student could never afford, I was beginning to feel invulnerable, safe. At least the revelation didn't go the other way, but that thought makes me hate myself a little, like, Oh, I actually do care what those fuckers think, or that what I'm doing is somehow wrong, or that I give a fuck about their rules. But I have to figure this out by myself, when I'm not on the job. Elgin's looking at me, smiling, I'm sure, waiting, just a client, a nobody to me. I flash him a guilty smile, like, oops, you caught me.

"So, what about the shrimp," he says, "*Stacey?* What didn't old Nabaum see?"

"If you must know," I tell him, "I commented on what I thought was obvious: that the shrimp dripping on the sidewalk, week after week as Benbow carried it home to his wife, and which he described as the reason for leaving his wife, was a metaphor for *vaginal* secretion, for *vaginal* lubrication, indicating arousal, I guess, another sign of female desire ruining men, or men's fear of it."

Elgin doesn't flinch, for once. I smile, the anger still alive in me. I have certainly never talked to a client like this before. I thought *vaginal secretions* would shut him down, but apparently not.

"I'll have to read it," he says. "What's the title?"

"*Sanctuary*," I say. "You'll love it. It's a nice little story about, well, I guess you've already heard what it's about, sort of, and the rape scene is just to die for. You'll *love* that. I mean, all men love rape scenes, right? Or are they primarily for women?"

The playfulness fades a little from his eyes, but he tries to keep the smile up. "Okay," he says, nodding, "maybe I'll read it."

"The great thing about the rape," I continue, "is first trying to figure out who will do it—because you know it's coming—and then trying to figure out who, in fact, did it—because there's so much confusion—and then, once you know the who, and think you have the actual event understood, you get thrown off again later trying to figure out how he did it—because, well, I don't want to ruin the book."

The waiter arrives to take our order. Elgin's face is bloodless. I've certainly touched a nerve, but I am so pissed off, that after the waiter leaves, I say, "The other thing about the rape is that—" and he cuts me off with his hand like a stop sign, the forced smile still on his face, and says, "I don't want to hear about the rape right now. I mean, don't ruin the book. Okay?"

"Of course," I say. We both drink. He sits hunched over the table, looking around the room. I take another drink, the anger dissipated. Now Elgin's got a little tremor, which makes me feel okay, and I'm wondering if all this identity crap is because he *is* a rapist, wanted in forty states, or something, then dismiss that thought and wonder if he could actually believe I'm accusing him of some McKinnion bullshit about all men being rapists, or if he's just hurt that I came on so strong, if he's fucking in love with me or something, I mean, the necklace and everything, but he looks so goddamn pathetically sad that I think it's something else, something bad, something I don't want to know about, and he looks so dejected for an unguarded second that I just start giving it away. "So, yeah, I'm a student," I say. "Kind of a cliché, right?"

He claws his way back to me. "What do you mean?" he says.

"I don't know," I say. "It seems like some kind of porn fantasy."

"No," he says. "No, it doesn't."

The salads arrive. Elgin picks up his fork. I launch into a discussion from the morning paper about a recent study suggesting that the Internet is eroding social skills and leading to possibly greater antisocial behavior. Elgin "hms," and "ums," raises his eyebrows in a gosh-isn't-that-interesting sort of way, and the fucker's hurt radiates off him like a stink under the vacancy, so that once the salad plates are cleared, I actually surrender and tell him that I'm a doctoral student up at Columbia, at which point he starts to come around a little, starts asking questions, which I actually answer, a real conversation until we finally determine that we both attended the University of Michigan, though more than ten years apart, that we had some professors in common, most notably a blind English prof named Sanders whom we both found tremendously stimulating and provocative, and that we both grew up in Michigan. Oh, how darling and intimate. And then he actually has the balls to ask if he can see me again, and that snaps me right out of it. "Of course you can," I tell him. "You know how to reach me."

"Right," he says. "I'll make an appointment."

Which I always have the option to refuse, his twenty-thousand-dollar necklace around my throat no collar.

And in the cab, I feel a little shitty for laying into him, feel a little pity for his weakness and hurt, but that's it—a little. And then it's gone.

≡

When Elgin arrived in Portland, he checked in to the airport Sheraton, but it was far too late to call the kids. The antiseptic sterility of another hotel room was oppressive. There was nothing to do, no one to talk to. Like so much else in his life, like so many of his recent perceptions of the world, the noise and images from the TV struck him as patently idiotic. Had he always perceived people and the world as cruel and idiotic, and merely covered that part of himself with something else, some other persona? Or had he been capable of something more, some generosity of spirit, some fucking compassion?

He watched a hospital show in which a mother loses her six-month-old daughter to crib death, and felt such an outpouring of emotion for the woman—for the *character* played by the *actress*—that he almost started to cry, swallowing hard against the lump in his throat, an idiot, completely manipulated. He turned off the TV. He turned off the light. He sat up in bed, pushing the heels of his hands against his eyeballs, bringing orange and yellowish blobs into his vision, concentrating on the blobs, imprinting the blobs into his mind for sleep.

At four A.M., seven in Michigan, Elgin called and got the machine. It was Sunday. Laura never slept past six-thirty. And she wouldn't wake the kids to take them somewhere at this hour. Unless there was an early morning, pre-service, prayer meeting, the kids bullied by threats of the devil. She had really gone over the edge with *that* shit. He hung up the phone, couldn't speak to the machine. But he couldn't wait around in the room, either. He'd been awake for hours, doing nothing. He took a cab into the city. He had to be around people for a while. He had to keep moving.

It rained off and on, a light mist, all morning. The hills around Portland were lush, so lush as to be on the verge of rot. In town, he picked up a couple of detective novels, drank coffee, ate lunch, bought a pair of black tasseled loafers at Nordstrom's. Being quiet and away from people he knew, it was amazing just how much everyone around him talked. Yap, yap, yap—and then I did this, and then I did that, and then I did this, all the false camaraderie and authoritative pronouncements nauseating. He had to get away from them. He couldn't think of one adult he wanted to talk or listen to.

He got back to the hotel and took another shower, stalling. Finally, at two, he called again, hoping Carrie would answer, but Laura picked up on the second ring.

"Hey," Elgin said, as if he were on a business trip, just checking in, after a night with a prostitute, far too much enthusiasm in his voice, "how you doing?"

"Oh," Laura said, "it's you. We just got back from church. Can I call you back?"

"Well—"

"Room 302, right?"

Had she not tried to reach him once in the last week? Surely the Holiday Inn realized he was gone. He'd only prepaid through Friday.

"No," he said. "I'm out of town. A conference. I've been trying to reach you all week."

Silence. "Well, *we've* been busy."

What, snake handling?

"I'd really like to speak to Carrie," Elgin said. "Tommy, too."

"You know what Pat said about that. Carrie still has the association problem. It's better in a structured environment."

The idiot Pat. It was incomprehensible to him how Laura could buy into that bullshit. And even worse was the fact that he'd surrendered, finally just stopped fighting it. "Well," Elgin said, trying to sound calm and reasonable, "hadn't we better try to work through that? Pat must think Carrie's relationship with her father is important."

"Oh, of course," Laura said. "And *you've* certainly been reaching out. I mean, you missed our Thursday, when we could have had the benefit of professional assistance, then Carrie's appointment, so I know how hard *you're* trying."

"I told you, Laura. I'm out of town. I tried to call."

"What, once? Twice? And you didn't know last weekend you were going out of town?"

"No, I didn't."

"Not that you were missed at Carrie's appointment. I mean, at least there were no scenes, no cues to Carrie. Pat thought we made greater progress without you there."

"Great," Elgin said, embalming himself in a catatonic calm—just get what you want, get what you want, whatever that was. "So, Carrie's doing well, then?"

She sighed deeply. "You don't get it, do you?"

Wrap yourself like a mummy in calm. And ignore the roiling underneath.

"She's not going to be *all right*. She's not going to be *okay*."

It was the same ground, the same hole they'd been digging for months, their necks tethered to a pole, walking around and around it, shouting at each other's backs, digging the rut with their plodding, idiotic shuffle.

"She'll never be the *same*, Robert, no matter how much you'd like to think—"

He held the phone away from his face, the narcotic calm nearly blinding. What had happened to Laura? What had happened to him? What had happened? Since she was little, two or three, Carrie and Robert had recited nursery rhymes, at one point her favorite being Dapple Gray, which Elgin found himself silently reciting now, as Laura ran through her monologue. *"I had a little pony/his name was Dapple Gray/ I lent him to a lady/Who rode him miles away/ She whipped him/She slashed him/She rode him through the mire/I would not lend my pony now/For all that lady's hire."*

"Do you hear me? Did you hear what I said?"

Elgin brought the phone back to his face. "Yes," he said.

"So Thursday, then? Or, would you rather try group?"

"I'm—" The gravity of his situation was settling into his blood, corkscrewing through his organs. Could he put the money back, and have the theft go undetected? And do what, then? He couldn't imagine doing anything. Except having money. And being away.

"Robert, will you answer me?"

"Can I talk to Carrie?"

"She's not here. She's at a church function."

Oh, Jesus. This was not who they were. They'd never been to church until a few months ago, and then, when Laura got religion, part of the overall transformation, Robert had made an effort, tried to humor her, but the people were fucking insane, the same pukes as when he was a kid. And now Carrie being forced to go on Christian hay rides, or painting murals in church hallways. Reciting Bible verses, for Christ's sake.

"So, Wednesday or Thursday?"

And Friday would be a potluck dinner at the church. And Monday would find him sucking some politician's cock, or vice versa. No, no, no. That life was over. Once and for all. "I won't be back by then," he said.

"What, a two-week conference?"

"I have to go to Washington," he said, "for McCabe, to meet with some people from the party."

"Of course," she said, even more snotty bitchiness leaching into her voice. "Of course you do."

"Look, you're the one that asked me to leave the house—" that forced him to leave. It was all Laura's fault. But, even as he held the thought, he knew it wasn't true.

"Robert, you were holding her back, and you know it. You certainly weren't doing anything to help."

"Yeah, well," Robert said, "and you were doing far too much."

"Well, at least one of us is strong. God only gives us what we can handle."

"Oh, bullshit," Robert said.

"Look, we'll talk when you get back, okay? Good-bye." And she hung up the phone.

Elgin held the receiver in his lap, waiting for a dial tone. The phone wouldn't be any good anyway. But he could send Carrie a letter, at least let her know that he cared and was thinking of her. Tommy, too. The Portland postmark wouldn't hurt him, either.

That night in his dark room, pushing the heels of his hands into his eyes to bring up the yellow blobs, Elgin understood just how alone he was, and for the first time in a week, he did not try to push the sense of isolation away, but embraced it, thinking he could cauterize it. Yes, he had abandoned his children, but that was only temporary, and would be remedied later. Somehow. In the meantime, there was not one person in the whole world, in the whole universe, who he could talk to, or who knew who he was now—William Oliver, with no past, no context, no human encumbrance. It was as if he were dead, and that night, in his black hotel room, sitting up in bed and pushing against his eyeballs, he mourned himself, pathetically.

THREE

MAY/JUNE

It was an election year and McCabe was untouchable. Property taxes had been rolled back twice in three years, and the county still projected a $50 million surplus, the entire state, with the exception of Detroit and the UP, awash in cash, especially Oakland County: *"The third wealthiest county in the nation,"* proclaimed one version of newly embossed official stationery, *"Donald McCabe, Executive,"* a statement littering the county website and other official signs and plaques, as well. McCabe didn't just want to beat Sarjenski, though. He wanted to humiliate him, to destroy him. And everybody who was anybody, or who wanted to stay or become anybody would have to play a role in the annihilation. That meant bringing in the unions, implying, promising, or negotiating future favors. If McCabe was going to make a run at Lansing and the governor's office in two years, he had to show that he could trounce a Democratic opponent now in the county executive's race, no big deal in Republican Oakland County, but if he could really destroy him, with union support and endorsements, especially the cops' union, The Police Officers' Association of Oakland County, or POAOC, that would be something else.

Elgin got the call at home from Klister, the county party leader and McCabe's campaign manager.

"It's Buddy," Laura said, handing him the phone.

Elgin winced, recoiled, and Laura shrugged, like, it's not my fault, and finally dropped the phone in his lap, on top of his newspaper.

"Bobble!" Tommy screamed from his bed upstairs, the only place they still let him have his bottle. "Water bobble!"

Laura looked at Elgin, cocked her head, waiting.

Elgin held the phone out toward her. What did she expect him to do?

"Fine," Laura said, narrowing her eyes. She started out of the room. "I'll go, then. Again. Why should I do anything else?"

As if he didn't have enough problems. And Klister had probably heard it all, the dropped phone, the snotty tone, Klister always looking for the soft spots.

"Hey, Buddy," Elgin said into the phone. "What's up?"

"We're at the Printer's," he said. "Don wants you here."

So the rumors were true, and Pearson, his boss, was on the way out, or simply irrelevant. "Now?" Elgin said, stupidly. It was after eight.

"No," Buddy said. "Whenever you can make the fucking time."

Elgin grunt-laughed. Two years ago he would have been honored—called to the Printer's at night—would have believed he was being brought in on the plotting, recognized for his superior political mind; he would not have even considered the possibility of contamination by secrets and intimacy. "I'll be right over," he said, and Buddy said, "Right," and hung up.

Elgin walked to the kitchen, poured a finger of scotch into a juice glass and knocked it back. If nothing went wrong—and everything could—McCabe would be elected governor in two and a half years, and Elgin would either be a part of it, or wouldn't be able to walk far enough. If everything went wrong, he would be part of the failure, and there would be nowhere *to* walk. Once you were tapped you were trapped. Elgin poured another finger of scotch, wondering when and how he'd become so weak and afraid. And of what? Mortgage payments? Car loans? The job he knew? People switched careers all the time. And those who didn't, or couldn't; well, people trapped themselves, he knew that much. He drank, trying to stir up some excitement for a game he no longer cared about and didn't know how to quit.

Upstairs, Laura was singing to Tommy, petting his sweaty head. "Get the Motrin," she said when Elgin poked his head in. "He's spiking." She'd already given Tylenol, the bottle still open on his bedside table.

Elgin measured the medicine in the kids' bathroom, then sat on

Tommy's bed and handed him the dispenser, touching his forehead. "Here you go, buddy," he said. "Drink this down."

Tommy was prone to febrile seizures, had endured five of them, but the doctor said it was nothing to worry about, that it was harder on the parents than the kid. The last one, just before his second birthday, had been six months ago, on a Saturday, when Laura and Carrie were at swimming lessons. Elgin found him facedown on the playroom floor, pale blue and covered in sweat, a rigid tremor running through him. He picked up his son, the electricity still vibrating through his twitching body, and murmured, "It's okay, it's okay, it's okay," though clearly it wasn't, though clearly Tommy was entirely unreachable, Elgin's words more a prayer than a statement. And when the wave of the seizure passed, Tommy, who was so sturdy and tough, flopped in Elgin's arms, couldn't hold his head up, appeared half dead, his eyes glazed, and he seemed not to recognize his father or not to care, a horrible surrender, a horrible absence. Elgin held him while he slept, afraid to put him in his crib—like lowering him into a coffin—afraid to let go. It was the only seizure he had seen, and he didn't want to see another one.

Laura kept singing, lulling the boy, petting him, his eyes looking up at her with fevered adoration.

Elgin waited in the hall.

"I have to go," he said when she came out. "The Printer's."

Laura shook her head, walked the medicine dispensers to the bathroom to rinse them out, Elgin following.

She knew nothing anymore of what he did. Just that she disapproved, that she was above it all somehow. Her own father had been a judge in Oakland County, with all the favors that go along with that position, powerful in the party, and she had learned to know nothing of that as well.

"I'm sorry," he said to the top of her head through the mirror. "I have to go."

She kept rinsing and rinsing, not looking up. "So go," she said. "Go, already."

And he did.

Outside, across what was left of McKechrin's field, the big boxes of the new subdivision rose up off the scraped and flattened land in various states of completion, some framed skeletons, others nearly finished four-thousand-square-foot monstrosities. Another Oakland County uglification project, brought to you by the development company of Harold Roan, deputy county executive.

When McKechrin's grandson got busted with a kilo of heroin in Ypsi, the old man had no choice, he'd explained to Elgin, but to sell the parcel. Half a million for nine acres and Junior's legal defense. And the kid would end up in Jackson anyway.

The Printer's was a dilapidated two-story building on 11 Mile Road off Woodward in Royal Oak, no sign marking it as a business establishment, if in fact it was one. Elgin was buzzed in and climbed the dim, littered stairs to the second floor. He walked through a narrow maze of boxes, some sealed, others open, filled with newly printed contracts, palm cards, campaign propaganda, and God knew what else. He could hear Buddy Klister laughing and McCabe talking in a high voice. The conference room was in back, and consisted of four card tables lined up in the standard conference table rectangle, surrounded by an assortment of seating: torn cloth office chairs, a couple of metal folding chairs, and, at the head of the table, the Printer's throne, a high-backed Naugahyde boardroom chair on casters. The cracked plaster walls would be lined with tables piled with more boxes and other loose junk, the six huge double-hung windows spray-painted black.

Years ago, when he'd first come here with Laura's father to be introduced and anointed, Elgin had been thrilled by the seediness of it all. He'd been working at a liquor store, playing in a mediocre cover band that was self-destructing, trying to figure out what to do with himself. Two years out of college, he was still hanging out at the old haunts in Ann Arbor, newly married, in love with his wife and mildly, ignorantly indignant about his perception of corruption in Washington—Reagan and the fired air traffic controllers and all the lost jobs in Michigan—oblivious to all the niggling corruption greasing the immediate transactions and interactions around him. They were living in a rented farmhouse on some property outside of Dexter with a barn out back that he'd converted into a studio for Laura, with a kiln and two pottery wheels and a wood-burning stove. Laura's parents came for dinner one night and when the discussion turned to layoffs at Chrysler, Elgin mentioned that he'd become interested in labor relations, that he was thinking about the program at Cornell, suggesting, he hoped, that he wouldn't be at the liquor store for the rest of his life.

The old man said, "Why don't you try it out first, see if you're interested?"

Elgin shrugged.

The following morning, the old man drove him to the Printer's, explaining county labor relations in the car, how you worked for the county executive's office, negotiating contracts with the nine county unions, handling grievances, right in the rough and tumble. It sounded a hell of a lot better than the liquor store. He'd be a peon at first, of course, not much more than a clerk, but it was a place to start, the old man explained. Elgin figured he'd check it out until he figured out what he really wanted to become—until he figured out whatever it was he was supposed to *do* with his life.

"So this is where I have to apply?" Elgin asked when they pulled up to the Printer's run-down building.

"No," the old man said, laughing. "That will come later. There's a civil service test and an application, but you're going to meet the Printer first."

The old man led him up the stairs.

"I'm in back, you fat bastard," they heard from somewhere down a long hallway crowded with boxes and windows that appeared to have never been washed.

"Kevin," the old man said, leading Elgin into the cluttered conference room. "This is my son-in-law, Robert Elgin."

The Printer had a computer opened up, parts all over the table. "These fucking things," he said. He smiled at Elgin, studied him. "Sit down, kid," he said. "How you doing, Ed?" he said to the old man. "Get yourself some coffee, some for the kid."

The old man disappeared.

The Printer sat back in his chair, lit a cigarette, studied Elgin some more. "Do you know how these things work?" he asked, indicating the computer parts spread out before him.

"Not really," Elgin said, and the Printer said, "Well, what good are you?"

"I don't know," Elgin said. "I—"

"Relax, kid," the Printer said. "I'm only kidding. One thing, though," he said. "Get a haircut, would you?"

"Okay," Elgin said. Dick, he thought.

"You want to see something funny?" the Printer said. He spun in his chair and rolled to another table, where he picked up an 8 x 10 photograph, then rolled himself back and slid the picture to Elgin. It was a head shot of a man who appeared to be around Elgin's age.

"What do you think about this guy?" the Printer said.

Elgin studied the picture, panicking a little, unsure of what he was supposed to be looking for, unsure of what role to play in this weird interview, if that's what it was. The man in the photo had pale skin, covered with acne, thinning hair, and eyes too close together, the knot in his tie the size of an apple, a dopey, hesitant smile on his face.

"So?" the Printer said, and Elgin said, "Uh, nice," wondering just what quality the Printer was testing in him.

"Nice?" the Printer said. "Would you vote for this clown?"

"I don't know," Elgin said. He'd never voted in his life. The process seemed like an exercise in futility, or, worse, willing participation in a sham perpetrated against yourself by some vague, unidentifiable evil.

The Printer tapped the picture, the cigarette burning between his fingers. "What do you see here?"

Elgin scrambled for the right answer.

"Don't try so fucking hard," the Printer said. "Is he smart? Do you trust him?"

"No," Elgin said.

"That's correct," the Printer said. "He's stupid, right?"

"He looks a little dull."

"Right," the Printer said, laughing. "A little dull. He's a fucking moron."

Ed walked in with three cups of coffee in white ceramic cups decorated with Republican elephants. "Jesus," he said, looking down at the picture. "Is that Banks?"

"Yeah," the Printer said, laughing. "The early days. Back before he was executive of Monroe County even. Fucking douche bag," he said, still laughing.

Elgin studied the picture again. "Frederick Banks?" he asked.

"You got it," the Printer said. "Congressman Banks. He represent you?"

Elgin shook his head. "We live over in Dexter." He looked at the picture again. Frederick Banks had been a congressman from Michigan for as long as Elgin could remember.

"Good thing," the Printer said. "Like all of them, he mainly represents himself."

"Robert," Laura's father said, pointing to the picture. "Banks here was the Printer's first big win. Made his reputation."

"Started it, anyway," the Printer said. "And just look at him. He called this morning. Needed some help with a little thing, needed to embarrass someone, a rival, yank his pants down in public, if you know what I mean. So stupid, this guy. I just had to pull the old picture out."

Elgin didn't know what to say. He was supposed to be impressed, he realized that much, so he sat in his chair grinning like an idiot.

"Well," the Printer said, putting his hand over the photo and sliding it toward himself, "if I can do something for a guy as stupid as that, I can probably help out a smart young man like yourself, son-in-law of a friend, etcetera, etcetera." He squinted at Elgin, who kept the grin on, then turned to Laura's father. "I'll talk to McCabe," he said. "I'm sure there's something open over in Labor Relations."

"Appreciate it, Kevin," the old man said, and the Printer said, "Yeah, yeah, yeah."

In the car, after they'd left, Elgin said, "So, what does he do exactly?"

"He prints things."

"No," Elgin said. "But does he work for the county or the state? I mean, does he work in government?"

"No," the old man said, laughing. "They work for him."

"Why?"

"Because he likes it. Because he's good at it. Because that's where the power is and he grabbed it and held on."

"Oh," Elgin said. He felt stupid and smart. Smart because he'd always known it was a scam, politics, the lies, all of it, stupid because he knew nothing about how that world worked, who pulled the strings, why, how. The Printer liked him, though, was bringing him in to that hidden world, the real world behind all the bullshit. He'd know things other people didn't know, be a keeper of secrets. And for a little while—no, for quite some time—the indoctrination and subsequent status as an insider was thrilling, kept him engaged in his new life.

Now, fourteen years later, and the assistant to the director of Labor Relations, Elgin approached the Printer's conference room, wondering what they wanted from him, wondering what they'd smear all over him.

"'Bout time," Klister said when Elgin walked in.

McCabe, the county executive, stood from his place at the foot of the table and shook Elgin's hand, gestured to a seat to his left, across from Klister's. "Thanks for coming, Robert," he said.

The Printer reclined in his throne, grinning, his fingers laced over his gut, feet propped on the table. He pulled a pack of cigarettes from his breast pocket and tossed them toward Elgin. "You getting *any* pussy?" he said.

"Not really," Elgin said, and he smiled in spite of himself. Under his white flat-top, the Printer's eyes suggested mischief, a conspiracy of amusement, as if to say, *Isn't this whole fucking situation, the whole fucking world, just hilarious? And you and I are the only ones who really get it.* Elgin had seen those eyes convey other messages, as well, plenty of times, becoming small and somehow pointed, and then they said, *You will do exactly what I tell you to, you stupid fuck, or I will make you regret it.*

"Get him a drink, Killer," the Printer said to Klister.

Elgin pulled a cigarette from the pack. This was the only place he still smoked, something else for Laura to bitch about later.

The Printer tossed him a book of matches. Klister put a half glass of scotch in front of him.

"Everything good, Bobby?" the Printer asked, pulling his feet down and leaning toward Elgin on propped elbows.

Elgin lit the cigarette, nodding. "Sure," he said. "Everything's fine."

"We're talking about the cops," the Printer said. "This next round of negotiations."

"Their contract's not up for another year," Elgin said. "Thirteen months."

"We're thinking about a nice quiet settlement," McCabe said, and the Printer said, "A timely settlement." He looked at Elgin, letting the words hang in the air before repeating them—"A timely settlement"—indicating the shift in policy. No collective bargaining agreement between the county and any of its nine unions was ever settled on time. In Elgin's fourteen years with the Department of Labor Relations, he had never seen it happen. No settlement meant no pay increase. For three months. Six months. Nineteen months. Money in the bank for the county. Late settlements were so ingrained in the bargaining culture that the unions, while always pressing for timely settlements, couldn't really arouse their membership over the issue for at least a year after any given contract expired. A shift with the cops would cause problems with all of the other units, every union leader crying for patterned bargaining, for "me too," creating a snowball effect, and a heavy cost increase for the county.

"I don't know," Elgin said, playing dumb, waiting to hear the rest, shaking his head and looking down at his hand wrapped around the glass of scotch in front of him. The Printer coughed. Klister stood and poured another drink. McCabe's breath whistled through his nose. Elgin said, "There's no advantage in this for us. We do this, we change the whole culture, and then—"

"Come on," Klister said. "What, you don't have ears?"

"Bobby," the Printer said, and Klister said, "I read through you, Elgin," and the Printer said, "Shut up, Buddy." Then he waited. "Robert," he said.

Elgin looked at him.

"Now listen to me," the Printer said. "Don's thinking about a run for the governor's office." Putting it out on the table, what everybody knew, making it official, in this room, anyway, handing the radioactive information to Elgin, giving him the chance now, tonight, to get on board or walk away. "And you, of all people, you know that labor peace is always important to the executive's office."

Elgin suppressed a smirk. They were creating a new mythology, a new reality, in which the county executive, McCabe, would be the friend of labor. After all the years of ill will, there was just no way in hell anyone would buy into it. It was laughable. "I don't think Pearson will go for the policy shift," Elgin said. "It will cause too many headaches with the other units, everybody crying for the same fast settlement, and cost us way too much down the road."

"Cut the shit," Klister said, slapping his hand on the table. "Who the fuck do you think Pearson works for?"

"Robert," McCabe said, and he turned on the paternal politician's smile, the warmth, the I-like-you, I-want-to-help-you, work-with-me-here bullshit. "Stan's played his role, and played it well. We want to signal a shift in tone here, a new direction."

Yeah, Stan Pearson had played his role, which was hatchet man asshole for McCabe. Squeeze the unions, humiliate the unions, despise the unions. The joke was that the county unions didn't have collective bargaining; they had collective begging.

"I'm not stupid, Robert," McCabe said. "I know how you handled the cops in the last round. And I know you're loyal to Pearson. That's admirable. I wouldn't want you around if you didn't have that quality, wouldn't want to elevate you. And it was very clear to me in that last round with the cops that you made the deal happen. That the labor leaders can work with you, will give you more than Pearson." He cleared his throat, took a drink, waited for Elgin to look at him. "Robert," he said. "I want you to handle this next round of negotiations with the cops. By yourself. For me. For the party. A clean slate."

"Bobby," the Printer said, "for you, it's a promotion. What the hell? Pearson'll stay on as director of Labor Relations. You'll be called deputy director. Sort of a grooming position for state office."

"A new title," McCabe said. "And much more direct responsibility."

"More money, a county car, blah, blah, blah," Klister said.

Elgin folded his hands over the table and looked directly down into his drink. The adrenaline was starting to run out to his fingers, the excitement, just what he didn't want.

"We need a three-year contract," McCabe said. "These are good times and the police work hard. Deserve to be rewarded. These guys put their lives on the line every day. For all of us."

More myth making, Elgin thought, the early line on how the deal would be spun to the public.

"We're thinking a four percent salary increase each year," McCabe said. "Hell, we could afford seven percent a year, but the press might not like that." He smiled, waited for Elgin to smile back.

"A little too obvious," Klister said. "And not that the crybabies deserve it."

"What'd they get in the last round?" McCabe said. "Three and a half percent a year?"

"Threes," Elgin said. "First year two and a half percent, then two years of threes. Plus we killed their overtime—a lot of money out of their pockets—and squeezed them on the medical, upped the co-pay, plus a twenty percent contribution on the premium. And prescription drugs are a problem now. That's our fastest-growing liability."

"Fuck it," Klister said. "We can swallow the prescription costs."

McCabe looked at Elgin, raised his eyebrows, meaning, Can we?

Elgin shrugged.

"Bobby," the Printer said. "Is Artie Lynch aware of the prescription problem?"

"Sure," Elgin said. "Of course." Artie, the president of the POAOC, the cops' union, was aware of everything.

"So, you give them that," the Printer said, "and you make sure Artie makes the rank and file understand what it's worth. Then the cash settlement can be three years of threes, which looks much better in a state run. Reasonable but not out of control."

"Okay," Elgin said, knowing that Artie Lynch and half the county were already aware of McCabe's hunger for the governor's mansion, and that after all the years of bad blood between McCabe and the cops, Artie would do whatever he could to hurt McCabe. Including walking away from an easy contract settlement. "But why does Artie go along?"

"Because it's a good deal," Klister said. "Because it benefits his people."

"Because of what he gets in his back pocket," the Printer said.

Elgin looked at the Printer, waiting, the twinkle in his eyes, the amusement, his whole face saying, *I love my fucking life.* The Printer nodded to McCabe, meaning, Tell him, and McCabe said, "A timely settlement with a nice salary increase."

"But that's not the main thing," the Printer said. "We've been over that," and McCabe said, "Okay, and the main thing would be that we give them agency shop."

Elgin nodded. Yeah, that was a main thing. Now he understood. Agency shop meant that every member of a bargaining unit—whether the employee chose to be a member of the *union* or not—had to pay the union as a bargaining agent. Union members paid dues. Every employee who chose not to join the union paid an agency fee, which was equal to dues. No matter what, the local got paid.

Elgin calculated the gains to Artie's coffers. As it stood, Artie represented roughly fourteen hundred cops at the table, though only nine hundred or so were actual dues-paying, card-carrying union members. By law, Artie represented the five hundred non-member cops, as well; they simply didn't pay dues as a result of their choice not to join the union. Agency shop meant those five hundred cops would now fund the local at the same rate as the dues payers. Agency shop meant about three hundred grand to Artie's organization. Annually.

"Lot of money for the local," Elgin said.

"Half a mil," Klister said, and Elgin said, "Minus about two hundred to the state organization."

"Right," the Printer said.

"Whatever," Klister said. "Three, five, it buys a lot of fucking trips down to Florida or Cancun, a lot of rented Jaguars, a lot of expensive pussy."

Elgin had never heard of Artie using dues money for junkets or any other gravy for the leadership.

"And if it comes out of the crybabies' pockets," Klister said, "I don't give a fuck. As long as they remember how to vote and how to get the vote out."

"And what does it look like," Elgin said, "if we're the first public sector employer in the state to roll over for agency shop? That's not going to help in a governor's race—especially coming from a Republican."

The Printer could hardly contain his joy, his eyes sparkling like they did when he played Santa Claus at Children's Village every Christmas. "We don't bargain it," he said. "They win it through arbitration. Ten, eleven months before the election. The cops up in Saginaw got it last month. It can be done."

"What? And you can guarantee the timing and the arbitrator's decision?" Elgin said, but even as he said it, he realized the situation, that the arbitration was to be fixed, and that Artie Lynch would have to be apprised of that and convinced to go along with it, a dirty deal with management. And this would be how McCabe would get to the POAM—the Police Officer's Association of Michigan, the POAOC's state umbrella, and the most powerful political organization in the state, outside of the parties—with an implied promise of agency shop for the state cops and other locals around the state, guaranteeing plenty of campaign contributions, but far more important, an early endorsement backed by a significant, disciplined voting bloc in nearly every election district, not to mention help in getting to the private sector unions, especially the UAW, which represented some cops and corrections officers and so had a relationship with the POAM.

"And what if Artie doesn't go along with it?" Elgin said.

"Boo hoo," Klister said. "What if Artie doesn't go along with it."

Elgin looked at the Printer, who looked at Klister.

"You remind him," Buddy said to Elgin, "not that he'll need it—about Fritz Keller and the CME."

"Fritz Keller," Elgin said.

"That's right, Bobby," Klister said. "You remember, don't you?"

Fritz Keller was in prison for fraud, embezzlement, racketeering, and tampering with the elections of his local, the five-thousand-member County Municipal Employees, which he'd presided over for twenty-three years. "Fritz Keller was dirty," Elgin said.

"Don't I know it," Klister said. "Don't we all know it. Didn't I always know it. Didn't I help the world know it."

McCabe examined his hands on the table. The Printer watched Klister, who lit a match and held it up to a cigarette, all the while fixing Elgin with his eyes, playing his intimidation game. Elgin held his gaze.

Klister shook out the match and dropped it into a dented aluminum ashtray. "Everybody's dirty, Bobby," he said. "Everybody's got something to hide, to be ashamed of, to protect."

Especially you, Elgin thought, and Klister, as if reading his mind, said, "But I did my time and my past is behind me."

Klister smiled at Elgin.

Elgin studied his forehead.

The Printer said, "Artie's a good guy—quality," and Klister said, "Artie's a piece of shit, just like all of them."

"Oh," the Printer said. "Excuse me." He ran his hand over his flat-top, over his jaw. "Did you hear what I just said?" His lips were drawn tight and he stared up from under his lowered brow at Klister, until Klister turned to face him. "Answer me. Did you hear what I just said?"

Klister nodded.

"Say it."

"Artie's a good guy," Klister said. "Quality."

The Printer turned to Elgin. "You can talk to him, Bobby," he said. "You can work with him, show him how it's a win-win."

Klister's pager went off. He squinted at the readout, stood and said, "I gotta go." He walked around the table, then stopped behind Elgin's chair, placed his hands on Elgin's shoulders. "This is when we find out what separates the men from the little girls, Bobby," he said.

"Come on, Buddy," McCabe said to Klister. "Knock it off."

Klister walked to the door, the imprint of his hands burning Elgin's shoulders. It wasn't a known fact that he'd ever killed anyone, but there were plenty of rumors. Before Fritz Keller went down, two of his officers were found dead in a Detroit whorehouse. Overdoses. And no way in hell were these guys junkies. Drunks, maybe. But not junkies. There were other stories as well, two poor Irish slobs who underbid on municipal carting contracts. Car accidents. A week apart.

Elgin took a drink.

"It's going to be a beautiful thing," the Printer said, lifting his glass. "Don here winds up in Lansing with union support. The unions get agency shop and more money to operate. You, Bobby, take a much larger role in the county and start cutting your teeth for handling the state organizations. Job growth. Self-realization. Everybody wins."

Except the public, Elgin thought. Or McCabe's opponent, who wouldn't likely have the ability McCabe had to buy votes. But the public always got just what it deserved, and the opponent would have his own dirty tricks, and the wheel would keep turning. Elgin would be elevated or diminished, depending on how you looked at it. McCabe's point man with the unions, public *and* private. A state office. And if it wasn't him it would be someone else. He wasn't a naive child.

"Just stay in line," Klister said to Elgin, "remember who feeds you," and McCabe said, "Buddy, we're all good friends here."

"All on the same team," the Printer said.

And they all looked at Elgin, waiting to see if the statement were true.

On the Saturday of Memorial Day weekend, Elgin woke to Laura's hand in his boxer shorts, her breasts pressed against his back. He stirred, pretending to still be asleep, or to be waking slowly, afraid to kill the moment. Since Carrie's birth, almost six years ago, sex had become another scheduled event, certainly never occurring when the kids were awake. Laura rolled him onto his back and straddled him. The song he sang when they were younger—much younger it seemed to him—came into his head for the first time in years, and as he opened his eyes, he whisper-sang it to her: "Nothing could be finer than to be in your vagina in the mor-or-or-ning."

Laura smiled, then put her face down close to his, her hair tickling his neck, and kept moving, Elgin letting her do all the work.

"Mommy?" Carrie called from outside their door.

"No, honey," Laura said. "Mommy's busy." But she'd sat up and stopped moving.

"Tommy's using my scissors," Carrie said.

"Supervise him," Elgin said, and he pulled Laura back down to him.

"It's dangerous," Carrie said.

Laura leaned herself against a stiff arm and held a finger up to Elgin, meaning stop moving. "Mommy and Daddy are talking," she said, but she didn't stop Elgin when he reached for her breasts. "Go help your brother. We'll be down in a minute."

"Mommy?" Carrie said.

"Now," Elgin said. "We'll be down in a minute."

When they heard her padding down the stairs, Laura said, "Don't talk to her like that," and Elgin said, "What?"

She looked away, her jaw set and brow wrinkled in concentration as they moved against each other.

In the car, on the way to Bear Lake and Laura's parents' house, where they were meeting her family for the weekend, Elgin told her what had been offered at the Printer's.

"So?" Laura said. "Don wants to be governor and wants to take you with him. I'd live in Lansing. And, God, a little more money now wouldn't hurt."

"No," Elgin said. "It's *how* they want to do it. It's dirty."

"Oh," Laura said.

In the backseat, Carrie said, "I'm a rude pirate."

Tommy said, "I'm a rude pirate, too," and Carrie said, "No, you're the polite pirate," and before Tommy could start to cry, Laura turned and said, "You can both be rude pirates," and Carrie said, "All right."

Laura settled back into her seat. "It's all seemed dirty to me," she said, "everything you've ever told me."

"That's not true," Elgin said. "Hardball negotiating, contract enforcement, interpretation, being better prepared in arbitrations, there's nothing dirty about it."

"Underpaying people when the county has the money, or making them beg for what they deserve, refusing to ever settle on time—it all strikes me as dirty."

"Well, it's not," Elgin said. "We have a duty to the taxpayer."

"Oh, please," Laura said. "Don't start with that bullshit."

Elgin smiled. She was right. "Maybe it's time for a new career," he said, testing the idea.

Laura looked out the window, adjusted her hair.

When her father had gotten him the job as a labor relations tech, it was going to be a one-year deal, but it turned into two, three, six, ten. The job had been what Laura wanted initially, a real, stable life, but he was good at it, and it was kind of a goof, a Deadhead sitting on the management side of the table. And they got used to the money, not much, but a lot to them, started flying out to San Francisco for the New Year's shows, staying at the Hyatt, and, of course, one by one, their friends got respectable jobs, and they got older, and he kept moving up until he was the number two guy, and the Dead had come to seem like a childhood infatuation, though, for a while, he and Laura still caught a few shows a year and were sad when Jerry died, but it was like being sad that you're not twenty-three anymore. And now it had been more than fourteen years on the management side, and they were asking him to commit a felony.

"I could still go to Cornell," he said.

"Oh, come on," Laura said. "They're creating a position for you. More money. Maybe a lot more down the road. A state office. Come on."

"I thought it was dirty."

"I thought you liked it."

In the backseat Carrie and Tommy made low-throated pirate noises, Carrie calling Tommy "cruel matey," which he liked, and "Bonebeard," which he didn't.

They were fifty miles from Grand Rapids, traffic slowing ahead for construction. Before they came to a standstill, Elgin said, "This is a felony, Laura, what they want me to do. This is fraud."

"Oh, please," Laura said. "So take it to Wolffson and be a hero."

Elgin grunted. Before he'd left that night, the Printer had told him—not as a threat, but as a warning—that Wolffson, the county prosecutor, was already on board and planning his own run for the attorney general's seat. "Yeah," Elgin said, "Wolffson." And Laura said, "I mean, for a guy who breaks balls for a living, you seem awfully sensitive all of a sudden."

"I am not Bonebeard!" Tommy shouted.

"Carrie, let him be a cruel matey," Laura said.

Elgin crawled with traffic toward the bottleneck.

"Of course it's illegal," her father said that afternoon on the deck of the lake house, "if it's the way you say it is," implying, it seemed, that Elgin had misunderstood, or was lying now. "But, the way you tell it, you're inferring conclusions, and, besides, that's not Don talking, it's the Printer, who's always had a lot of big schemes."

"Yeah," Elgin said, "but Don listens to him more than anyone. Come on. You know that." He regretted bringing this up with the old man; it seemed like an indiscretion, or, worse, a solidification of the reality, a tightening of the trap, as if admitting it made it real.

"If it's what you say it is, you can take it to Wolffson or the attorney general."

"And take the whistle-blower's reward of permanent unemployment," Elgin said, and the old man laughed.

"Well, yeah, there's that."

The screen door slid shut, and Elgin turned to see Donnie, Laura's sister's husband, walking a big glass of red wine toward them. "Am I interrupting?" he said.

"Naw," the old man said. "Come on and sit down."

"I made a garlic tarragon balsamic marinade for the chicken," Donnie said, "that I got from a chef at Shinto in San Francisco. I think y'all are going to love it."

"Sounds good," Elgin said.

"Robert's talking about going back to school," the old man said. "Cornell."

"Yeah, I don't know," Elgin said. "Probably just talk."

"Little job burnout there?" Donnie said.

"Nah," Elgin said. "Not really."

"I could probably help you get in," Donnie said. "We recruit pretty heavily there." Donnie had an MBA from Harvard, which he seemed to announce indirectly in every statement he made.

"That'd be mighty white," Elgin said. Though he'd grown up in Chicago, Donnie was from an old Charleston family with a proud slave-holding tradition, something Elgin liked to remind *him* of.

"What is that, an MPA program?" Donnie said.

"Industrial Labor Relations."

"What, so you work in HR?"

"You could do that," Elgin said. "Or maybe you'd become a professional organizer. Move down to Texas or Virginia or one of the other right-to-work states and fight for the oppressed masses."

"God forbid," the old man said.

Elgin had said it as a joke, but why should it be so ridiculous? Management held most of the cards, he knew that well enough; why not fight on the underdog's side?

"I was wondering when you'd get fed up with that public sector bullshit," Donnie said. "I don't know how you've done it this long, what they pay you. I mean, Jesus, look at the HR guys at GM or Chrysler, Unisys, guys in your own backyard, negotiating and administering contracts just like you do, and what are they making? Three, four times your salary?"

"It's not just about money," Elgin said.

"Oh, yeah, it's about the incompetent bureaucrats, the crooks and liars."

"And of course, GM isn't just jam-packed with incompetent bureaucrats."

"Not like government," Donnie said. "Nothing dirtier than that."

"I work in government," Elgin said, "to save pricks like you money on your garbage pick-up and police protection."

"Knock it off, Robert," the old man said.

"Sorry," Elgin said. You weren't supposed to fight in this family. No name-calling allowed.

Donnie looked out over the water, at the small sailboats gliding across the lake. He shook his head, took a drink of his expensive wine.

Corporate pig, Elgin thought. Donnie and his kind constantly bad-mouthing government when they relied so heavily upon it for their roads and sewers and labor laws and tax breaks and trade deals that fed their bloat. Elgin took a sip of his drink. He'd never been antibusiness in his life, even all those years as a Deadhead, had never been anticorporate. And, now, suddenly it seemed, he was.

"No, but you say it with 'Donnie,'" Elgin said to Carrie, "instead of 'Taffy.'"

"What are you guys talking about?" Laura said as she walked into the kids' room.

"Listen," Elgin said to Laura. "I'll go first," he said to Carrie: "Donnie was a Welshman," and Carrie said, "Donnie was a thief."

"Donnie came to my house and stole a leg of beef."

Laura was smiling. She couldn't stand the prick, either.

"I went to Donnie's house," Carrie said, "Donnie was not home."

"Donnie came to my house and stole a marrow bone."

Tommy ran in from the hallway in his pajamas, chased by Sasha, Donnie and Nicole's brat, screaming "Bunge," a swear word he'd developed when he turned two. "All right, all right," Elgin said. "Shh. We have to finish."

"Bunge," Sasha said.

"Bunge, bunge," Laura and Carrie said.

"Bunge!" Tommy screamed.

"Okay, come on," Elgin said, and Laura said, "Bunge, bunge, bunge," leading to more screaming bunges.

Elgin said, "I went to Donnie's house, Donnie was not in."

And Carrie picked it back up: "Donnie came to my house and stole a silver pin."

Laura was whipping Sasha and Tommy into a frenzy, but Elgin had to get to the crucial last line. "I went to Donnie's house, Donnie was in bed."

"I took up the marrow-bone," Carrie said, and then screamed, "and *flung* it at his head!"

"High five," Elgin said to Carrie, who slapped his hand.

"Come on, Sasha," Donnie said from the doorway, "it's time for bed."

"Hey, Donnie," Elgin said, surprised and embarrassed, wondering how much of the rhyme he had heard.

"Now, Sasha."

"She's sleeping in my bed," Carrie said.

"In my bed," Tommy said.

"It's all right, Donnie," Laura said. "They'll have fun."

"No, it isn't," Donnie said. "Come on, Sasha."

Sasha threw herself into Laura's lap on Tommy's bed, screaming, "Bunge!" which Tommy and Carrie echoed.

"We could move her later," Elgin said, getting up off Carrie's bed.

Donnie ignored him. "Sasha. Now!" he said, a command you'd give to a dog. And she walked toward him and out of the room.

"Good night, Sasha!" Carrie yelled.

"Good night, Sasha!" Tommy yelled.

"Good night, Sasha!" Elgin yelled.

Laura narrowed her eyes at him. "Come on, guys," she said. "It's time for bed."

After closing their door, Laura pulled him into the bathroom across the hall. "I can't believe you have to do this every single time we see them."

"Not at Christmas," Elgin said. "I was good at Christmas."

"Yeah, and Donnie wasn't there."

"What, so we use his name in a nursery rhyme; what's the big deal?"

"And you call him a prick out on the deck. My mother heard the whole thing from the kitchen."

"And just had to tell you."

"No, Robert," Laura said, "she didn't want to tell me, but she also doesn't want the weekend to blow up between you two. After you came downstairs, he said to my dad, 'I don't know why that guy hates me so much,' or something like that, and my mom said he was really hurt."

"Oh, I'm sure," Robert said. "And besides, you thought the Donnie-was-a-Welshman thing was funny, too."

"Why can't you just try?" she said. "This is my family. Can't you just make the effort for me? I mean, someday Carrie's going to bring home some asshole like Donnie, or worse, and you'd better believe that I won't let you run her away."

As if Elgin hadn't been preparing himself since her birth for all the horrible assholes Carrie would bring home.

"Okay?" she said. "Will you just try? Apologize or whatever?"

The bathroom was dark except for a halo around the weak night-light, casting Laura's face in strange geometric shadows, making her nose appear grotesque, enormous and misshapen.

"I'll try," he said, and he followed her out of the bathroom.

He was stirring another pitcher of martinis in the kitchen when the old man walked in from the deck and slapped his back a few times, a locker room bonding gesture. "You know, a state office wouldn't be such a bad thing," he said.

"You bring your glass in?" Elgin said.

The old man put it on the counter, watched Elgin pour.

"You've been in this game long enough to know about the gray areas."

"Yeah," Elgin said, dropping in two olives, "I know."

"Is this new position—deputy director—is that still civil service?"

"I'm not sure," Elgin said. "I think it's appointed."

"Well," the old man said, "you have to take some risk sometimes." He opened the screen door for Elgin, who walked out with the pitcher and a bowl of olives.

So, the old man, a former judge, a guy who was supposed to uphold the law, was encouraging Elgin to commit a felony. Jesus, everything and everybody was dirty, the whole world a fucking toilet. As if he hadn't known that for years. What was with this innocent babe in the woods bullshit? Donnie put his hand over his glass when Elgin approached to pour. "Glass of wine?" Elgin said.

"Nothing for me," Donnie said, looking away.

Prick.

Laura's mother, Joyce, waved him away as well. It looked like he and the old man would be getting bombed. Or maybe just him.

Elgin sat on the bench against the rail, his back to the lake. Nicole, Laura's sister, said, "And the thing of it is, these people have children as if they're acquiring a pet. I mean, *so* many people we know use day-care forty, fifty, sixty hours a week. It's like, if you're going to have somebody else raise your kid, why bother?"

He knew he shouldn't say anything, that he should not enter this conversation, that he should drink the entire pitcher of martinis, eat dinner, and go to bed; instead, he said, "So, you're saying that people who use daycare shouldn't have kids?"

Nicole turned to him. "Exactly," she said. "You have to work it out so that someone stays home. That might mean sacrifices."

As if Nicole knew a thing about sacrifices, with her Lincoln Navigator, house in Malibu, house in Montana. "But, what if neither party wants to stay home? What about career?"

"That's just it," Donnie said. "Someone's *got* to make the sacrifice."

"I agree with Nicole," Joyce said. "This is what's wrong with the family today."

"What about you, Donnie?" Elgin said. "Would you give up your career?"

"I didn't have to," Donnie said.

"But what if Nicole was a corporate lawyer or an executive in a company like yours, and she loved her job, and she knew that there was no way in hell she could take a few years off and come back into the game at the same level? Who would quit?"

Donnie shrugged.

"I wouldn't," Elgin said.

"Yes, you would," Laura said.

"No, I wouldn't," Elgin said. "What about you, Ed?" Elgin asked Laura's father.

"It was different for us," the old man said, "easier. We didn't have to make those kinds of decisions. But I don't think I could or would have done it, no."

"All's I'm saying," Nicole said, "is that most of these people do it for the money, so they can buy a boat, or go to Europe. People don't need these double incomes to survive."

"Not with Donnie's income, they don't," Elgin said.

"Well, I don't think that's the issue at all," Nicole said. "Just because we're blessed doesn't mean we don't make sacrifices."

Elgin could think of no response to this logic.

"Well, I did give something up," Laura said. "I did give up a career."

Elgin suppressed the urge to call her on the lie, if she even realized it was one; surely the story she told herself was different from his version, which was that she had eagerly quit her job as a fund-raiser for Planned Parenthood down in Ann Arbor when she became fed up and frightened by the escalating harassment and threats of the pro-life protestors. And in the six and a half years since she'd quit, she had never once expressed any interest in going back to work, had never once even mentioned it.

Laura was watching Elgin, who poured another martini. Hell, why not just drink directly from the pitcher, lift it and pour its entire contents down his throat.

"Well," Nicole said. "So did I. I put my career on hold, too."

The statement was so idiotic that no one said anything for a minute. Nicole had given up her stewardess *career,* a job she'd hated.

"Are you saying that I'm the only one who should make sacrifices?" Laura said to Elgin.

"Not at all," he said. "I'm saying that I was unwilling to give up my career. At least then. If you had been, too, we would have used daycare. That's all. And I don't think it's a crime."

"Not for the parents, maybe," Nicole said.

Joyce touched Laura's arm. "Help me with the salad," she said.

"Do you think daycare is the best option?" Laura asked him.

"No, I don't. I'm glad we don't have to use it."

"But if I was unwilling to quit—if we were both as selfish as you are—that would have been the only option?"

Joyce stood and said, "I'm going to make the salad. Check the coals, Ed."

"Laura," Elgin said, "we never even discussed it. You wanted to quit. You wanted to stay home with the babies."

"Yeah, well, I just think this sounds sick."

"Your father said the same thing," Elgin said. "Donnie wouldn't have quit, either."

"Don't put words in my mouth," Donnie said.

"Come on, Donnie," Elgin said, getting a little sloppy now, taking another drink anyway, and slowing down the words to try to get them out cleanly. "What do you work? Sixty, seventy hours a week? You gonna just stop that cold to take care of a baby all day? Come on."

"Yeah, I would."

"And you're gonna live on Nicole's stewardess income?"

"It's flight attendant," Nicole said. "And yes, we would."

The old man walked into the house. Without one of the parents present there seemed to be no audience for the argument. Two mallards flew low over the deck and landed in the middle of the lake. Elgin poured more gin in his glass. "I just don't think this is a very honest discussion," he said.

"Oh," Donnie said. "So now we're all liars."

Laura walked into the house without looking at Elgin.

"You're just lucky you have Laura," Nicole said. "I would never put up with this bullshit."

Elgin pictured Nicole on her knees, her ass up in the air as he fucked her, pulling her hair hard, tilting her head back, her throat exposed and vulnerable.

He was drunk and in the sewer but somehow smart enough to keep his mouth shut.

He woke to Tommy's finger in his eye, a pasty mouth, a headache blooming out to the edges of his skull. "Stop it," he said, pushing Tommy's hand from his face. "Come here," he said, pulling Tommy into bed with him.

"It's breakfast," Tommy said. He wriggled away and ran from the room.

The fragments of a dream replayed themselves in Elgin's mind: Groovy Larry fucking Laura on her hands and knees, grunting, who turned into Nicole fucked by Klister with a dog's face, who turned into Elgin fucking Nicole, except that, no, he was alone making pottery in Laura's old studio in Dexter, but then Groovy Larry was there, perched on a dentist's chair, saying, "Come on, man. One love. Try a little tenderness," Elgin's hands shaping a clay vulva reminiscent of the series of clay vulvas Laura had made in the year before Carrie was conceived. Fertility symbols. Vulvas on the wall. Holding flowers. A candy-dish vulva Elgin had mistaken for an ashtray, for which he was punished with silence from Laura for two days, the crushed butt lying in the purple vulva for over a week as evidence of his transgression.

Elgin shook his head, downed three aspirin, and jumped in the shower.

Dinner had been civil enough, though his sincerity may have been clearly false when he questioned Joyce about the problems in her church. There was a lot of safe discussion about movies and the scrapbook clubs all the women belonged to, Laura watching him there to see if he would insult anyone, which he most certainly did not do. Taxes didn't come up, sex didn't come up, money didn't come up, politics didn't come up, religion didn't really come up. And at the end of the night, lying in bed, he'd promised to get up with the kids, which he'd obviously failed to do.

Upstairs, the breakfast dishes had been cleared and the kids were coloring in the dining room. Laura and Joyce stood at the kitchen counter making sandwiches. Elgin poured a cup of coffee. Laura looked at him without glaring.

"Sorry I overslept," he said, sitting at the kitchen table, and picking up a piece of dried out banana bread. "I'll do the kids tomorrow."

Laura nodded.

Joyce said, "We've all been through job stress before, Robert. When Ed lost in '74 and had to go to the Department of Elections, it was the longest two years of our lives. Do you remember that, honey?"

"Sort of," Laura said. "I guess I remember Dad being crabby and then all those nights at the Printer's before the next run."

Was Elgin suffering 'job stress'? If it would let him off the hook, he'd take it. "Yeah," he said. "It is a weird time."

"It's always darkest just before the dawn," Joyce said, turning to him and smiling. "It sounds like there might be big opportunity ahead."

Elgin smiled back, nodded, thinking of the quote attributed to Mao, something about it always being darkest just before it became totally black, wondered how much Laura or the old man had told Joyce, how much she'd ever known about Ed's sewer. Wondered if Ed had cooked up this job stress bullshit.

"We're going down to Orchard Beach," Laura said, stuffing a plastic bag full of cut carrots. "Have a picnic."

"Great," Elgin said. "I'll get the kids ready."

There was no time or need to wonder just how or why he'd been pardoned, but he knew enough to be grateful, and to renounce his previous sins with good behavior. Which meant not bitching about a sand lunch, which meant taking the kids for a long walk down the beach so that Laura could sleep or read on the blanket. "You want to come with us?" he said to Donnie. "Bring Sasha along for a walk?"

"Sure," Donnie said.

Weren't they just the closest of brothers-in-law?

Carrie held Sasha's hand as they ran along the water line, Tommy struggling to keep up.

"Sorry about being a jerk last night," Elgin said. "A lot of shit's going down at work." How much mileage could he squeeze out of this nonsense? "Not that that's an excuse."

"It's all right," Donnie said. "I've been there myself. I mean, maybe not this bad."

"What do you mean?" Elgin said. "This bad."

"No," Donnie said. "Just that Ed said this morning that there's some heavy political shit going down, some ethical questions, maybe, a delicate time."

"Right," Elgin said. So the old man *had* bailed him out.

"And I'm sorry, too," Donnie said. "About the political comments."

"Forget it," Elgin said. "You were probably right."

How insanely mature they were being.

Up ahead the kids had stopped and were circled around something in the sand. "Dad!" Carrie screamed. "Dead fish!"

"Leave it alone," Donnie said. "It's dirty."

The kids squatted around it, not quite touching it. Elgin remembered as a kid all the dead alewives littering the beach down at Warren Dunes, not so many anymore.

"What's it doing?" Carrie said.

"Nothing," Elgin said. "It's dead."

Tiny black flies peppered the carcass.

"Is it going to heaven?" Carrie asked.

"I don't know," Elgin said. "Some people might believe that."

"I believe that," Carrie said, and Sasha said, "So do I."

On the Christmas after her second birthday, Carrie had approached Elgin and asked him who Cheezus was, a name she must have picked up from the Christmas carols. Elgin smiled and said something about Cheezus being a teacher, something about Christianity, and some people believing that Cheezus was the son of God and a kind of god himself, and Carrie had said, "I believe that." And a few months later in the car, driving home from a birthday party, juiced up on cake and apropos of nothing, Carrie had burst into tears, and finally blubbered, "I want to be real forever." She was crying so hard that Elgin had to pull over and crawl into the backseat with her. Laura was at a baby shower for a neighbor. Carrie kept saying that she wanted to be real, and when Elgin finally asked her if she was talking about dying, she nodded, and was wracked by another wave of sobs. "But that won't happen for a long time," Elgin said, "a long, long time." The mere thought of her dead or injured in any way scared the hell out of him. "But it will happen," she said, "and then what?" Elgin said he didn't know, and Carrie kept crying, and Elgin finally told her that some people happened to believe in a place called heaven where dead people lived forever, and Carrie stopped crying and said, "I believe that."

Tommy's face was down close to the dead fish. "Come on, guys," Elgin said. "Let's keep going."

"We have to bury it," Carrie said.

"Okay," Elgin said, and they dug a hole and scraped the fish in with part of a beer carton.

"Do fish die in heaven?" Carrie asked, patting the grave.

"I don't think so," Elgin said.

"Do people die in heaven?"

"No," Elgin said.

"What do they do?"

"Is there McDonald's in heaven?" Sasha asked.

"No," Elgin said.

"They're with God," Donnie said, and Carrie squinted up at him: "Why?"

"To be happy and safe," Donnie said.

"Are they happy to be dead?" Carrie said, and Elgin said, "Nobody knows," and Donnie said, "Maybe," and Tommy screamed, "Bunge!" and took off down the beach.

"Now, go," Elgin said, and the girls tore after Tommy.

When they got home, after the kids had been bathed and were playing in Sasha's room, Laura asked him if he wanted to take a shower, meaning with her. "Sure," Elgin said. All the forgiveness and unplanned sex seemed too good to be true. And was, because before they were finished there was a banging on the door, and when Laura left him turned toward the wall of the shower and opened the door, Elgin heard Nicole say, "We've got an issue here, Laura. You've got to come out now."

"What?" Laura said. "What is it?"

"Just get dressed."

"Is somebody hurt?" Laura said, dropping the towel, and pulling on her underwear.

"No," Nicole said, "but come on," and she closed the door.

Nicole was full of shit, constantly creating *issues* out of nothing.

"Let's go," Laura said.

If no one was hurt, this could wait five minutes, though he knew it wouldn't. Elgin turned off the water and gestured toward his hard-on.

"What am I supposed to do with this," he said, half grinning at her.

"Put it away," she said.

"They were sticking things in each other's vaginas," Nicole explained out in the hallway, "these little sticks from the Tinkertoy set Mom got them." Carrie was crying hysterically in the room across the hall. "I mean, this is not cool," Nicole said.

"Just wait a minute," Elgin said, wrapped in a towel and closing the bathroom door behind him. "Why is Carrie crying alone like that?"

"Donnie caught them in Sasha's room," Nicole said. "With these Tinkertoys."

"Okay," Elgin said, "but let's get her settled down."

"I'm trying to get the story," Laura said.

Carrie was facedown on her bed, crying and gasping and hyper-ventilating into her pillow. Elgin rubbed her back. She jerked away from him, rolled onto her side facing the wall, just wailing.

"Carrie," Elgin said, "honey." He tried to wrap her in his arms, but she thrashed and flailed, completely out of control.

"Baby, come here," Elgin said. "You've got to settle down." He got a tight enough hold on her that she finally gave up thrashing. "It's okay," he said. "Shhh."

She turned into his arms, but kept crying.

"Okay, okay," Elgin said, petting her hair.

When she tried to talk, Elgin couldn't understand her because of her jerky, labored breathing. "Wait, just wait," Elgin said. "Shh."

Laura came in and sat on the other side of the bed. Carrie reached for her and Laura pulled her into her lap. "I didn't hurt her!" Carrie wailed.

"Okay," Elgin said, rubbing her back.

"Of course you didn't," Laura said.

Carrie settled into her mother's hold, her thumb in her mouth, but still deep red and hyperventilating.

"Get dressed," Laura said to Elgin. "Get that wet towel off the bed. Find out what Tommy's doing."

Elgin walked towel-skirted across the hall and into the bathroom, where he gathered up his clothes, feeling useless, and then angry with Laura for walking in late to play the savior commander. Upstairs, Joyce was feeding Tommy dinner. There was no sign of Sasha or Nicole or Donnie. Walking back down the hallway toward Carrie's room, he heard Donnie say to Sasha through her partially opened door, "And you are not to be alone with her."

Prick.

"Our private parts are only for us," Laura said as Elgin entered Carrie's room. Laura stopped and looked at him, as if he were interrupting. He sat on the bed beside them, rubbed his hand up Carrie's back.

Carrie nodded against her mother.

"It's not something we share with other people," Laura said.

"But I didn't hurt her," Carrie said.

"But I want you to promise me," Laura said, "that you won't do that again."

"Okay," Elgin said, "let's not make this an inquisition." Why plant seeds now for later guilt and dissembling? At some point she would be touching other people's private places and you didn't want to create some kind of crazy hangup about it.

Laura glared at him over Carrie's head.

"We'll talk about it more tomorrow," Elgin said. "It's not a big deal."

Which is exactly what he said at cocktail hour out on the deck after the kids were in bed, when Nicole was explaining that this kind of early promiscuity was often the first sign of abuse.

"Promiscuity?" Elgin said. "Are you kidding me?"

Laura still wasn't talking to him, though she looked at him now as if awaiting some fresh horror.

"She's five years old," Elgin said.

"Almost six," Nicole said. "And Sasha's not even four. I just don't want that."

"Joyce," Elgin said to Laura's mother, "isn't this totally normal behavior? This is experimentation. This is what kids do, right?"

Joyce screwed up her face as if she were listening and thinking hard. The old man looked down at the deck boards.

"Studies show that this is often the first sign of abuse," Nicole said, and Donnie said, "Absolutely."

"What studies?" Elgin said. Nicole was forever quoting unnamed studies to support whatever idiotic point she wished to make.

"I think there *is* a lot of normal curiosity in kids," Joyce said. "But, objects . . ."

"Right," Elgin said. "We all did things like this."

Nobody said anything.

Nicole said to Laura, "I'm just saying that if there is a sign of abuse, you have to look into it."

"What is all this abuse talk?" Elgin said. "We don't *use* daycare. Remember?"

Nicole studied him. So did Donnie and Laura. And then he understood.

"We're leaving," Elgin said when Laura came down to retrieve him. "I'm not going to sit here and be accused of molesting my kids."

"Nobody accused you of anything," Laura said. "They're just concerned."

"They're *making* this into a problem," Elgin said, gathering dirty clothes from the floor, "making the kids feel like criminals." He latched his suitcase.

"We're not leaving tonight," Laura said, "so just forget it. And I'm concerned, too. Where did she learn about that?"

"Where does anybody learn about it? Christ, every kid in the world plays doctor at some point."

Laura opened the sliding glass door, which was beneath the deck upstairs, so that the sound of voices came into the room. Elgin walked by her and closed it.

"Somebody has to *teach* you," Laura said, sitting on the bed.

"You didn't do it?" Elgin said. "You didn't figure it out?"

"You learn about it from older kids. And I'm just wondering who."

"I don't buy that," Elgin said. "You've seen her examine herself before."

"Well," Laura said, "we can't have her doing that to other kids."

"We also can't monitor her twenty-four hours a day. And I don't want her to be freaked out about her sexuality."

Laura looked up at him. "She doesn't *have* sexuality, Robert," she said. "She's five years old."

"What?" Elgin said.

"You heard me."

"She doesn't *have* sexuality," Elgin said, and Laura said, "Don't repeat my words to make me sound like an idiot."

"I can't believe you actually think that," Elgin said. "That's completely delusional."

"Oh, really?" Laura said. "Protecting my child's innocence is delusional?"

"What are you talking about?" Elgin said, walking toward her and standing above her. "What they were doing *was* innocent. And, besides, that's not something you can protect."

"Of course you can," Laura said. "That's why we don't let her watch certain movies."

Elgin looked at the stucco swirls on the ceiling and felt himself breathe. Slowly. "What we really need to do here is talk to her about sex," he said, "tell her what it's all about." The swirls on the ceiling looked like clouds or waves. "But not in a way that makes her feel guilty or dirty."

"Do you think *I* would do that?" Laura said. "What are you saying? That I'm a prude or something?"

"No," Elgin said. "But you're the one who said she wasn't ready. Well, maybe now she is."

"Clearly," Laura said. She stood to walk out of the room, moving him aside.

"Laura," Elgin said.

She turned and looked at him, waiting, enduring him.

"This is not a big deal."

"I hope you're right," she said, and she walked out of the room.

Elgin looked at his suitcase on the bed. Of course they couldn't leave, but how could he go upstairs and sit with these people, some of whom seemed to believe that he was capable of hurting his daughter? Even Laura, if only for a second, had been appraising him. He sat on the bed, ran his hands over his skull. What had happened to them, anyway? And when? And how? There didn't seem to be a day that went by that there wasn't some kind of conflict, that he didn't have to monitor his behavior around her, what he said, what he did, to keep from pissing her off. Was it the same for her? Of course it was. One thing he'd learned from all the years of stalled negotiations and grievance handling was that *both* sides were always, but always, wrong.

On the wall across from him hung one of the clay vulvas, "Like a cowry shell," Laura had explained to her parents, who dutifully hung it on the wall to haunt Elgin's dreams years later. He took it off the wall and examined it. Was Laura a prude? Had she fucked Groovy Larry—the name Elgin privately referred to him by, and which Laura despised—during the vulva art stage? When he had reappeared in Ann Arbor from Seattle or San Francisco or God knew where, Groovy

Larry had evolved from a patchouli-drenched, feminist skirt chaser with a sensitive side and pork chop sideburns, into a fat, dirty, Honduran-pants-wearing, bald ponytailed clown of a hippy. Elgin had been in a suit for seven years and liked it just fine. Laura bumped into GL at the Falafel Hut one day after not seeing him since college, her former teacher, her lecherous mentor, her artistic and inspirational guru, but more than a teacher, a mentor, a guru: her *friend*.

At Laura's urging, Elgin met him a few weeks later at Del Rio for drinks on a Friday. He fingered the lapel of Elgin's suit coat. "Whoa," he said. "You don't even look uncomfortable, man."

"And you're still in tie dye and clown pants," Elgin said.

Groovy Larry smiled. "Oh, yeah," he said. "Absolutely. Got to keep it hanging free."

And you're as fat and bald as David Crosby, Elgin didn't say.

Laura showed up a few minutes later, hugging Elgin first, then GL.

"Larry's got studio space," she said to Elgin, beaming. "Did he tell you?"

"Sort of an artist in residence gig," Groovy Larry said. "Space at the university for free."

"And he said I can use it whenever I want." Laura smiled at Elgin, radiant, waiting for his approval.

"That's great," he said. She'd given up the pottery, or it had simply faded from her life several years before when they'd moved from the house in Dexter. They'd bought a place and there wasn't a barn out back waiting to be converted into a studio. It would be good for Laura, Elgin thought, to get back to the art—an escape from the fire-bombing threats and crucifix-toting protestors at Planned Parenthood.

And then it was Larry this and Larry that and the house became filled with vulvas as Laura concentrated upon her metamorphosis into a fertility goddess. Quit her job and prepared for motherhood.

Elgin looked at the blue-glazed vulva in his hand. Had she fucked Groovy Larry? He didn't know. It didn't seem likely. They were different then. Happy. Partners against the world. The vulvas had struck him as funny at the time, but as he thought about it now, the vulva-making Laura was much closer to the woman he had fallen in love with than the woman who organized PTA meetings, birthday parties, and play groups, and read only parenting books and magazines, devoting herself so singularly to her children that who she had been or could become was glazed over, annealed by her one-dimensional, all-encompassing transformation into *Mother,* leaving no room for anything else. And where did that leave Elgin?

Chairs scraped against the floor upstairs, meaning dinner was ready.

What a selfish bastard he was, what a child, to resent Laura for devoting herself to her children—to their children.

He put the vulva back on the wall, then walked into the room Carrie and Tommy were sharing, lay on the bed beside Carrie, who curled her body into his, her breath soft and sweet against his neck. He knew that he loved the kids as much as Laura did, as much as anyone could. And he would try. He would be the one to make the good faith effort to get back to where they got along and loved each other. As if that were possible. Who was being delusional now? But, Jesus, you couldn't be cynical or pessimistic about it, not if you were really going to try. The thing was, though, that Laura *did* seem delusional, that bizarre comment about Carrie's sexuality. They needed an arbitrator was what they needed. He ran his hand over Carrie's hair, and she stirred, opened her eyes and looked up at him for a minute, then closed them and put her thumb into her mouth. It was as if Laura didn't want the kid to grow up.

On the way home, and for the next few days, conscious change and effort—*trying*—governed his behavior around Laura and at home, but at work, something else was going on. He went about his duties as if no deal had ever been presented to him, his days blanketed by inertia, enervation. Then, on Friday, Alice, McCabe's secretary, called to say that his car was ready, and not the typical bland sedan, either, but a Jeep Grand Cherokee made down in Detroit. McCabe got on the phone. "Look out your window," he said.

"Wow," Elgin said. It was black, a hit man's ride.

"Susan's got the keys," McCabe said. "Hope you enjoy it. God knows you've earned it."

Not yet he hadn't, and he made himself work another two hours, pretending to consider his decision, pretending that accepting the car meant nothing, before walking out to Susan's desk to pick up the keys. Pearson stood in his office, arms folded. Elgin failed to notice him, until he said, "That sure beats the hell out of a Pontiac."

Elgin had just picked up the keys and already they seemed to be burning him. He was stuck for words, stuck for motion, frozen, caught. Pearson waved him in, gestured to a chair, closed the door behind them.

"Funny," he said, "I didn't get a car until I was director."

"It's kind of a surprise," Elgin said, stuck between lying to the man and telling the truth, either choice seeming impossible. "It's part of the promotion, I guess."

"Promotion?" Pearson said. "I wasn't informed."

Elgin could spill it all now, start the ball rolling toward exoneration and justice and unemployment. He could confide in the man who had been his boss for eight years, who had allowed him to negotiate several tough contracts, who had twice promoted him, who had let him make mistakes, incrementally doling out more and more responsibility, who had listened to him and trusted him practically as a peer, who had taught him most of what he knew. He could do that. But he didn't.

Behind his desk, Pearson pressed his hands together flat in the air like a child dutifully praying, one of his negotiating poses, and waited.

"I thought they told you," Elgin said. "Deputy director. A new position."

Pearson's hands were a teepee in front of his face. He pushed fingertips against fingertips, the index fingers shrouding his nose, and looked straight into Elgin's eyes, still waiting.

"Don said everybody would win on this."

Pearson held his right hand up as a stop sign.

"I don't think this is meant to hurt you, Stan."

Pearson nodded, stuck his lower lip out, looked up at the ceiling, another negotiating pose, this one signifying an attempt to process a lie, to reconcile conflicting information. Elgin realized that McCabe had done this on purpose, had delivered the car to the office as a message to Pearson as much as a bribe to him.

But it still didn't mean anything. Elgin had agreed to nothing, and

Pearson's silent condemnation was starting to piss him off. Besides, it wasn't as if Pearson wasn't capable of being a complete asshole. Elgin believed his own style of negotiating was far more effective. Get what you want without the bullying and bad feelings afterward, as evidenced by the last contract with the cops. Elgin had pretty much skinned them, but still maintained a good relationship with Artie Lynch, while Pearson was reviled.

Stan was nodding now, still looking at the ceiling, waiting for Elgin to look up there as well before speaking. But Elgin knew this game. He crossed his legs, looked out the window over Pearson's shoulder, and now *he* would wait. He thought about driving to lunch in the new ride, then about Susan's long strong legs under the short furry poodle skirt she was wearing today, her breasts and the way she smelled and how competent she was, and how she was practically young enough to be his daughter and how he had never cheated on Laura and how glad he was of that and how much he regretted it. And how tough it was for Susan, with a cop husband killed in the line of duty and a three-year-old daughter, forcing her to become one of those daycare moms Nicole had bitched about. And how Pearson wasn't nearly flexible enough with her schedule, another stupid hard-ass move that would probably drive away the most competent office manager they'd ever had. And how tired you could become of trying to please everyone, to make sure nobody's feelings were hurt. And maybe taking the kids down to Cedar Point, how much Carrie would love that, big enough now to go on some of the thrill rides, and Tommy, too, on the kiddy rides, how much pleasure their joy and excitement would bring to Laura and him, a kind of glue.

He noticed that Pearson had lowered his head from the ceiling-gazing pose and was likely looking at him again, but he continued to stare out the window, until Pearson said, "So what do you have to do?"

Elgin feigned waking, tearing himself away from the parking lot view and returning to the room they sat in. He returned Pearson's eye contact. "What's that?" he said.

"What's the quid pro quo?" Pearson said.

"It's a new position," Elgin said. "I assume more work, more responsibility. Maybe a way to reduce your load."

Pearson squinted, baring his teeth in a kind of grimace, another gesture Elgin had seen countless times.

"Stan," Elgin said, "I didn't go looking for this. And you know as well as I do that if I turn this down I'm shit out of luck. I have always been loyal to you." It was true. Christ, what did the guy expect, for Elgin to go down with him?

"I know," Pearson said. "I've only got a few years left anyway. It's just—" He shook his head, wrapped his hand around his chin, rubbing his cheek.

"It's just a shitty way to be informed," Elgin said. "Honest to God, I thought they told you." In fact, if he'd stopped to consider it for one second, he would have known they hadn't told him. There had been no change in behavior. No tension. No awkward attempts to solicit information. What kind of a lie was this? Was he trying to protect Pearson or himself?

Elgin looked at the man across from him, who suddenly seemed tired, beat. The wheels had stopped turning, and now Pearson seemed merely empty and sad, which opened up a hole in Elgin's gut. "I don't have to take it, Stan. Fuck it. I won't do it."

"No," Pearson said. "You're right. There's no choice."

"I should have told you. I thought you knew."

"It doesn't matter," Pearson said. "But you've got to be careful. They're going to want something. You know it and I know it. I hope you can come to me if you need help."

"Thanks," Elgin said. "I will." But even now he knew that the guilt—and the new authority, and the lie—would make asking for help impossible.

"Why don't you go to lunch," Pearson said. "And this afternoon tell me how we'll proceed." He was grinning a little. Jesus, the guy was already accepting it, already handing over power. One thing about Pearson was that he could cut right through the bullshit. And he was strong. Stronger than Elgin would ever be. Though, of course, they *had* approached Elgin. There had to be a reason for that. They had to consider him the better man for the bigger job down the road.

"I'm sorry, Stan," Elgin said. "I didn't go looking for this."

"I know you didn't," Pearson said, waving him off. "Go to lunch."

He couldn't get out of there fast enough. He felt Pearson's eyes on him as he walked through the parking lot, restraining his excitement about the car, not even checking it out, just opening the door, starting it up, and pulling away, as if he'd driven it a hundred times. He pulled into a gas station a mile down Woodward to inspect it.

And it was nice. More than nice. Four-wheel drive, power everything, disc player and cassette. He hadn't had a new car in five years, and that one, a Mazda, was for Laura and the kids. He drove a nine-year-old four-cylinder Chevy, a shitty car new, but he'd felt that he had to buy GM, since they employed so many people in the county. But this was something else. The smell, the feel of the seat, way up high like you were on the flight deck of an airplane. He got on 75 and headed north toward Flint, to open it up a little, see what it could do on the highway.

He turned on WDET and cranked the volume, which sounded better than his system at home, Howlin' Wolf belting out "Wang Dang Doodle," rolled down all the windows, rolled them back up and turned on the air, took it up to a hundred, and felt plenty more power in the engine beyond that. And Laura would love it, too. Maybe they'd start camping again. Not that he'd become one of those assholes with four-wheel drive who just tears everything up. And it did beat the hell out of Stan's Pontiac, there was no doubt about that.

Poor Stan. But, really, there wasn't a damn thing Elgin could have done about that. These things just happened. At least the guy was near the end of his career and wasn't being completely hung out to dry. Christ, they could have eliminated him entirely, fired him, sent him home with his pension. And now Elgin would finally have his chance to run things.

He drove for forty-five minutes, then returned to work, parking in the side lot so Stan couldn't see the Jeep from his office. They'd probably give him his own parking space now, too, with a sign and everything. Not that that meant anything.

Pearson's door was closed. "Is Stan busy?" Elgin asked Susan, who was eating yogurt at her desk.

"He's on the phone," she said. "But he said to go in when you got back."

When Elgin opened the door, Stan waved him in, pointing to the seat he'd been sitting in earlier. He looked okay. It was a shitty deal, but the guy was going to be all right.

"So," Pearson said when he'd finished the call, "what's on the agenda?" and Elgin told him about the approach to the deputies' contract, the desire for a timely settlement, Pearson grimacing, but listening, nodding, asking a few pointed questions, and understanding the political ramifications, just as Elgin had that night at the Printer's.

"So the question becomes how much you have to give them to go along and ultimately to get the POAM and UAW to help McCabe get elected governor."

"That's my guess," Elgin said. He didn't mention agency shop and the dirty arbitration.

"Have you contacted Artie Lynch yet?" Pearson asked.

"No," Elgin said. "Of course not. I didn't know how you'd want to go."

"McCabe came to you with this. It's a matter of how *you* want to go."

There was a knock on the door, and Susan poked her head in. "Sorry to interrupt," she said. "Robert, your wife's on the phone. Says it's an emergency."

"Take it in here if you want," Pearson said, sliding his phone across the desk.

"Laura?" he said into the phone, pissed off at the interruption, but when he heard her voice, its deep, raw, demented timbre, he was certain that someone was dead.

"Come home," she said in that low vibrating moan. "You've got to come home."

"What is it?" he said, fear gripping his chest. "What is it? Who?"

Pearson pushed away from his desk and walked out of the office.

"Carrie," Laura moaned, and then she started to cry, quietly, choking, coughing sobs, to keep the children from hearing, most likely. "It's Carrie."

"Is she alive?" His stomach turned over on itself.

"She's alive."

Thank God.

"She's hurt. She's hurt."

"Which hospital?"

There was no air in the room.

"No. She's home. She's here."

Her voice was otherworldly, a drone, an animal's last sounds.

"Is the ambulance coming? You've got to tell me which hospital."

His throat was closing. Not one of his kids. This couldn't happen to him.

"She's here. She's here."

Laura was clearly in shock, incapable of acting or thinking rationally.

"Laura, listen to me," he said. "You've got to call an ambulance. No, I'll call the ambulance, and then—"

"No, listen to *me*," she said, a frustrated child. "We have to figure it out together. Come. Home. Now."

"What is it?" he said. "What happened?"

She growled, and then he heard rustling, the phone moving away, then the splashing and coughing sounds of her vomiting into the toilet.

"Laura!" he said. "Laura!" Why wouldn't she tell him anything?

And then her voice was controlled and quiet, drained of animation. "She's been fucking raped," she whispered. "Okay?"

And the tears came to Elgin's eyes immediately, running down his face, as he tried to control his breathing, tried to keep from vomiting himself. "Okay," he said, talking to the child Laura had become, gathering strength from his role as parent. "And that's why we have to get her to the hospital."

"No!" she said. "It wasn't today. Two days ago. And before. Corey Newkirk."

Corey Newkirk? Who the fuck was Corey Newkirk?

"Angela's brother," Laura said.

The fucking neighbor kid. And Elgin would kill him. Gouge a screwdriver into his eye and scrape his fucking brains out.

His baby. His little girl.

"Okay," Elgin said, "okay. Keep it together. I'm coming home."

He wiped at his face, ran out the door, Pearson and Susan wearing worried, helpful sympathy faces. "Emergency," he said. "Nobody's dead."

"Go," they said.

And he went, flying home in the old Chevy, forgetting all about the new Jeep parked in the side lot, out of view.

FOUR

JUNE

L aura was on her knees in the kitchen with a brush and a bucket, scrubbing the floor, when Elgin walked in, the sickly sweet smell of baking brownies blanketing the kitchen, him, everything in the house. He touched her shoulder. The brush flew out of her hand, and she screamed.

"Shhh," he said. "It's okay." He lowered himself to the wet floor beside her, took her in his arms, and held her. She trembled against him. He was shaking as well. "Where is she?" he whispered.

"Upstairs," Laura said, pushing herself away from him. "In her room playing. Tommy's still napping." She crawled toward the brush, picked it up and resumed scrubbing. "We can't talk about it now," she said to the floor. "We have to wait until she's asleep. I've thought this through."

"What about the doctor," Elgin said, "the police? I mean, shouldn't we do something?"

"I have no idea, Robert," she said, still not looking at him. "I'm making brownies. Cleaning. You could mow the lawn. The appearance of normalcy."

She was out of her mind and pulling him with her. He crawled toward her, soaking his pants further. He put his hand over hers to stop her movement. But she wouldn't look up. "Come on," he said. "You have to tell me what's going on here."

"Why? So you can undo it?"

He ran his hand through her hair, looping a strand around her ear. "Baby," he whispered, "we have to be together on this."

Her face was blotchy and wan. "The brownies are done," she said to the oven.

"Okay," he said. "You take care of that. I'm going to go say hi to Carrie while you take them out of the oven, okay? And then we're going to figure it out." He held her shoulders. "Okay?" And when she nodded, he let her go.

Walking up the stairs, he was seized by the same controlled panic that had overcome him on the drive home, the fear of seeing his daughter transformed, but if this had happened days ago, and before that, how had he failed to notice the change, the signs of trauma and resulting damage? And he still didn't know a goddamn thing, still had no idea what had happened or how or why.

He could hear Carrie talking to her dolls in her room. He knocked on the door, then opened it, and stuck his head in, terrified of what he would find.

"Hi, Daddy," she said.

He was careful not to appear to study her. "Hey, baby," he said. "What are you doing?"

"These girls are sisters," she said, holding out two floppy dolls for his inspection. "This is Cassandra and this is Emily. They're going on vacation."

Tommy started crying across the hall. "Where are they going to go?" Elgin asked.

"Switzerland," Carrie said. "They're both Indians."

"Those don't sound like Indian names."

Carrie furrowed her brow. Tommy was cranking up to a wail. She seemed fine, normal. Maybe Laura was losing her mind. Maybe the whole thing was some kind of misunderstanding.

"You mean like Pocahontas?" Carrie said.

"Right," Elgin said. "Or in our language, names like Beargirl or Bright Flower."

Carrie looked at the dolls in her lap. "But their names are Cassandra and Emily."

"That's fine," Elgin said. "I'm going to get Tommy."

"Your clothes are wet," Carrie said as he walked out of the room.

"I know," Elgin said. "Isn't that silly?"

Lifting Tommy out of his crib, Elgin was overcome by a sense of gratitude and relief. Carrie was fine; everything was going to be okay. After calming Tommy and changing out of his wet clothes he took both kids downstairs and into the backyard. It was as if nothing had really happened. Not yet, at least. Maybe never.

"Don't open the gate," he said to Carrie. "I want you to play back here for a while." And then he went to find Laura.

She was in the downstairs bathroom and had been crying again. "Is the gate locked?" she asked, peering around the door she shielded herself with. "I don't want them back there alone."

"No, they're okay. They're safe."

"She can't see me like this. It'll make everything worse."

"We'll go upstairs. I can watch from the window."

She held on to the door.

"Come on," he said. He took her hand, led her upstairs and into their bedroom. She allowed him to embrace her. "It's going to be okay," he said. "We're going to work together. Sit down on the bed. I'll stand by the window. You're going to tell me what happened."

He eased her down and backed toward the window, steeling himself as if awaiting biopsy results. "What do you know?" he said. "What did you find out?"

"Okay," she said. She closed her eyes, clenching her entire face, opened them, and clenched up again.

Elgin waited. In the backyard the kids ran around the cherry tree he'd planted before Carrie was born.

"I got a book out of the library," she said. "You know, a sex ed book for kids. I thought, after Bear Lake, it was time to go over some of that." She looked at him now for the first time since he'd been home, and her hands shook as she gestured and held them against her face, but she was back. "And so," she said, and her voice was shaking, too, "I told her about how babies are made and showed her these drawings and photos, you know, of sperm and ova, and, you know, about how when people love each other very much"—She wiped the tears methodically with her shaking hands, one eye at a time, and Elgin could feel it, too, but she kept going, all of it spilling out—"like Mommy and Daddy, and how Daddy puts his penis inside of Mommy when they love each other so much and how Daddy's sperm goes into Mommy and fertilizes the egg and it's the beginning of a new baby and how special that is, and I was so glad we were talking about this, and she was asking questions and none of it was weird or strained, and she wanted to know if it hurt, to make a baby, and no, I said, it felt good, that it was something mommies and daddies who loved each other so much liked to do, and that it's one way we show each other how much we love each other, and that it can be playful and silly and fun, and she said—" Laura swallowed and kept wiping at the tears that wouldn't stop, her hands doing a delicate, tremulous dance around her face, Elgin feeling six huge lines of coke in his blood without the euphoria, thinking, Come on, come on, come on. "And she said, 'Well, do you ever put Daddy's penis in your mouth?' And I didn't know where that was coming from, I mean this book was entirely clinical, but for kids, and our discussion had all been so open and honest, but here now was a line I didn't know how to cross, and so I was just kind of stunned and said something like, 'Why would you ask that?' and she said, 'Well, I've done that before with someone,' and it was like this horrible weight pressing on my chest, forcing all the air out, and all the pain of the restraint, of just trying to figure out what she was talking about without freaking her out, and I said something like, 'Well, honey, what are you talking about?' And I'd hidden it all, and she wasn't afraid, and she said, 'Corey and me play a game, but I'm not supposed to tell,' and she sort of snuggled into my arms, like she was feeling so close that she could reveal this secret, and she said, 'It's a kissing game and a touching game.'"

Outside, Carrie was at the gate, lifting and lowering the latch. Elgin opened the window. "Keep it closed, Carrie!" he shouted down, and she latched it. "Go on," he said to Laura.

"So I said, 'And you touch each other in your private places?' and she said, 'Yes,' and I said, 'And you kiss each other in those places?' and she said, 'Yes,' and I said, 'Remember at Bear Lake what I said about our private places being only for us?' and she nodded against me, and I said, 'And when mommies and daddies love each other so much and want to make a baby, that's different than children touching like that, and Corey's so much older than you are,' and I could feel her shutting down, withdrawing from me even as she seemed to burrow deeper into my lap."

"And what about the rape?" Elgin said. Let the fucking guillotine fall already.

"What are you talking about?" Laura said.

"The rape," Elgin said. "When did he rape her?"

"All those times," Laura said. "I don't—"

"Did you ask her about penetration?" Elgin said.

"Yes!" she said. "That didn't ever happen. You're not trying to downplay this," she said. "You're not suggesting this isn't bad enough, that this isn't fucking rape?"

"No, I'm not," Elgin said. "I'm just trying to figure it out." But part of him was relieved even as he was nauseated by what had occurred, and by his relief. "And none of it was forced?" Elgin said.

"She's five years old!"

"I know," Elgin said. "I'm just saying—she didn't seem profoundly traumatized, right?"

Carrie and Tommy began to scream in the backyard. Elgin wheeled around, but they were only playing.

When he turned back to Laura, her face had shifted to anger and contempt. "If you think this isn't rape, if you think this isn't traumatizing, damaging, I don't know who you are."

"That's not what I'm saying."

"What are you saying? That it could have been worse?"

He approached the bed. She held her hands out, stiff armed.

"No," he said. "I'm trying to think of what I'm going to say to the cops. Wondering how we drag her through *that*. Because what I really don't understand is just what we're supposed to do now. I'm not downplaying anything." He sat beside her on the bed, put his arm around her, and though she resisted, pulled her toward him. "We have to be together on this," he said, a repetitive prayer he'd been issuing all afternoon.

But it seemed that Laura was gone again.

=

He knew that he should want to kill Corey, to torture him mercilessly, and part of him did, the screwdriver in the eye fantasy graphically playing out in his mind over and over—so that he could actually feel, in the palm of his hand, the eyeball puncture from way out on the plastic handle of the screwdriver, and then gouging the blade through the eye socket, he probed deeper and felt the somewhat resistant but ultimately gelatinous substance of the brain, the words, "scraping away" playing through his mind to the music of Jethro Tull's "Skating Away" as he held the kid down by his hair, nearly pulling his scalp off—but the fantasy seemed to get weaker and less graphic with each repetition as if his hatred were dissipating, which felt like a horrible failing. And as they went through the motions of the normal family routine, dinner, baths, both he and Laura ridiculously cheery, his mind raced, struggling to form some kind of coherent plan of action, uncovering all of the pitfalls of anything he might do. Bring in the police and subject Carrie to interrogation and physical examination, possibly drowning her in guilt, fucking her up later. Or, would she be more fucked up if you did nothing, if you discounted what had happened, so that, when she was fifteen, sixteen, seventeen she would begin to despise her parents for failing to act on her behalf when she had been so clearly taken advantage of, all right, *abused. Victimized.* But she certainly didn't feel like a victim at this point, at least she didn't seem to, and would all the police business, the possibility of court, for Christ's sake, would that teach her to be a victim, or, again, would failure to act plant the seeds for later agony? He went around and around it as he went about the routine—and would it reach the papers?—until the children were finally tucked in and he and Laura were alone with themselves. He sat her at the kitchen table, poured them drinks.

"It's just what kids do," Laura said. "Isn't that what you said at Bear Lake?"

"Laura. Don't."

"No big deal."

He took a drink, closed his eyes. "You were right. I was wrong. Okay? Let's move forward." The refrigerator clicked on. "I'm going to call the police," he said, testing the statement, not sure if it was true or not.

"Oh, great. Officer Bob and the drug dog."

"Not the South Lyon police," he said. "The sheriff's office. The county cops."

"I want that kid in jail," she said. "The parents. Whoever. Somebody's going to suffer," she said. "I'd like to cut his fucking dick off with a rusty knife."

She seemed to be directing her hatred at him, with the hard glare, and he said, "I'm just concerned about subjecting Carrie to everything."

"Right," Laura said, sighing, "I know." She reached for his hand. "I know what you're saying. I do. But I also know that we can't let him get away with this. We can't just let that fucker walk." She held his eyes with her own. "We have to do this for Carrie. For later."

He called Susan at home, told her something horrible had happened but that he couldn't talk about it, asked her to go into the office, only a mile from her house, yes, now—Could her mother watch the baby?—and get Artie Lynch's home phone number, call him with it immediately. And thank you, thank you, I'm so sorry to ask.

When he hung up the phone, Laura was crying again at the table, sobbing, her fists to her face. Robert pulled his chair close and wrapped his arms around her. "She's just a little girl," she said. Over and over. But this was better than the hatred or the earlier emptiness or the contempt. At least they seemed to be united.

Twenty minutes later Susan called with Artie's number.

"We're going to get good treatment," he said to Laura. "We're going to get the best cops." He hoped it was true, hoped that whoever handled the case wouldn't realize that Elgin was the man who had beaten the cops so badly in the last round of negotiations. But Pearson was the prick, in Artie's eyes at least. At least, that's what Elgin hoped.

He dialed Artie and got the machine. "Artie," he said. "Something's happened here. Something, uh, horrible has happened. This is Robert Elgin. I need to talk to you as soon as—"

And Artie picked up. "Robert," he said. "What is it? What's going on?"

"I . . ." Elgin hadn't really considered what he would say, but it became obvious that he would not be able to hide this horrible personal tragedy from Artie, not if he wanted his help. "Artie," he said, "my daughter. Something's happened to my daughter." And even now he wondered how this confession, this revelation of suffering and victimization—of weakness—would affect the bargaining dynamics in the next round, would affect the dirty deal he was to approach Artie with, and he hated himself for even considering such meaningless possible eventualities, Laura sniffling at the table, watching him, seeing that he could do something to make the situation better, finally something connected to his job that she could be grateful for, and he said, "Artie, my daughter—she's only five years old."

Laura nodded, urging him on.

"And she's been hurt, uh, abused—um, sexually, I mean—by a neighbor kid, who's older. Okay?"

Artie let out a long sympathy sigh. "Okay," he said. "Shit."

"I can't go to the town cops," Elgin said. "I don't know what I'm supposed to do, but I have to have somebody good, somebody who's not going to fuck her up."

"No, no," Artie said. "Right. Of course. The locals would come through us anyway. Listen. Okay. Shit. Okay. I'm going to call the head of sex crimes. He's not in my unit anymore because he's a command officer, but he used to be a member of my executive board, and he's a good guy. Okay? He's going to pick his best cop, who *will* be one of mine, and he'll also call you and tell you what's going to happen. And then—"

"Artie," Elgin said. "I don't know if this is the best thing. To go through the cops."

"No, it is," Artie said. "You'll regret it if you don't. It's the only way."

Elgin felt the burden of responsibility for making the wrong decision lifting, felt an outpouring of gratitude for Artie's sympathy, and willingness and ability to help.

"I'm sorry about your daughter," Artie said. "But you're going to have good people who know what they're doing. Okay? So don't worry. Just hold it together. It'll start rolling right away."

"Thanks," Elgin said, and he hung up the phone.

Laura looked at him, waiting to be informed.

"It's all going to start happening now," he said.

He didn't know if he slept, all the half-dreams of shootings and stabbings and other violence weaving themselves into the strands of his half-conscious worry as he twisted in the sheets. At four he walked downstairs and poured a drink, then emptied it into the sink and made a pot of coffee, wishing he still smoked. Laura was either asleep or pretending to be asleep.

Lieutenant Hearn had called fifteen minutes after he got off the phone with Artie and had given him instructions for the morning, Laura listening in on the living room extension. They were to meet at the Child Advocacy Center in Novi, where Carrie would first be interviewed by a cop and then examined by a SANE nurse, which meant sexual assault nurse examiner. The case officer would be Officer Jervac, Lou Jervac, and Laura said, "Wait a minute, I thought it would be a woman."

"No," Hearn said. "Artie asked for my best cop."

"I think a woman makes a lot more sense."

"Lou's very good with children," Hearn said. "You gotta trust me on this."

"Well, why can't we do it at home, here, where Carrie feels most comfortable?"

"We want a neutral site," Hearn said. "And listen to me: don't rehash the story with her. You're going to hurt her, brand the incident on her, and we want to make sure we get the statement in her words, not yours and not rehearsed."

As if all this cop shit wasn't going to 'brand the incident' on her. "Well, what if she brings it up?" Elgin said, knowing she wouldn't, and the cop said, "If she brings it up, let her talk about it, support her, listen, but don't push her."

"And what about the kid?" Laura said. "The criminal. Are you going to pick him up tonight?"

"No," Hearn said. "We have to get her statement first."

"What, so he's just going to be running around on the loose?"

"We'll interview him tomorrow. Afterward."

"Interview him?"

"I know how difficult this must be," Hearn said, and Elgin thought, no, you don't.

"I want that kid in jail," Laura said.

"I understand, Mrs. Elgin, but we have to get her statement. Have you had any contact with the family, with the Newkirks, regarding this?"

"No," Elgin said. What could he say to them, what could he do, except kill them all?

"Good," Hearn said. "Don't contact them. We want them to be unprepared when we arrive, catch the kid off balance. In the morning, tell your daughter that you're going to see some people about what happened, but, again, don't rehash the story."

"What does this nurse examiner do?" Elgin said, imagining Carrie being poked and prodded and terrified and humiliated.

"She has a sexual offense evidence kit." Rape kit, the cops called it, Elgin knew. "It depends on what we learn in the interview. You said it was a couple of days ago, so I should tell you that the odds of obtaining evidence are slim."

"Which means what?" Laura said.

Which means there isn't going to be any evidence, Elgin thought, and the cop said, "We'll just have to see what we learn in the morning."

Elgin poured a cup of coffee and walked out onto the back patio in his underwear. A few hundred feet to the east, on the other side of McKechrin's place, was Corey Newkirk's house. They were bland, boring people with a daughter, Angela, Carrie's age, and a child molester son. The father—Hank? Frank?—sold something. High-risk insurance for boats and campers and snowmobiles or something like that. They'd moved in two years ago. The wife was a miserable knockout, morose and mildly bitchy. Terribly unhappy, according to Laura. The type who peaked in high school, and was now fallen from homecoming queen status to wife of Hank the insurance salesman.

A mockingbird called, a hideous, strangled cat's cry, the first bird of the morning, and one across the field answered. If these people were so fucked up, what was his kid doing at their house? And were they so fucked up? Or were they normally fucked up? Had he and Laura been fools for ever letting Carrie into the house of an adolescent boy? Had they been negligent? Elgin hadn't even seen the kid since last summer's barbecue, except once or twice when he noticed him dragging garbage cans to or from the curb, and maybe a few times mowing the lawn. And at the barbecue he'd seemed typical. Bored, pimply, remote. Neither noticeably bright nor dull. And Angela seemed like a normal five-year-old girl. It seemed that there was a whole hidden world of torture and agony your children could be subjected to. What about McKechrin, the mailman, teachers, Uncle fucking Donnie? Who else was out there waiting to fuck with your kids?

They would have to move, of course, that much was clear. How could Elgin drive past that house every day, see it from his backyard? How could Carrie? So the fuckers were going to run him out of his own house. And how was he supposed to notify people as to the event, his mother especially, who would find a way to blame him for the *defilement* of her only granddaughter. And all the cops and the prosecutor's people, all the people he knew and worked with, people he struggled and fought with. And his little girl with Corey Newkirk's cock in her mouth. He swallowed against the bile rising, the puke reflex. This would be how he would cultivate the hatred, keep it alive and redeem himself as a father and failed protector. Just store that image and bring it up whenever he felt himself softening. He held his face in his hands.

When he finally looked up, the sky was lighting pink to the east. It was Saturday. Day one. But still pancake and bacon day. He'd do that with Carrie, as usual, and then he'd drive her to her interrogation.

The Children's Advocacy Center was located in a strip mall off 96, owned, Elgin noticed, by Deputy County Executive Roan's development corporation. They'd dropped Tommy off with Claire Bratwaithe, Laura's closest friend, and, on the drive, told Carrie that they were taking her to talk to some people about what had happened with Corey.

"Nothing happened," she said.

Laura sat in back with her, petting her hair. "It's okay," Laura said. "You're just going to tell them what you told me."

Elgin saw the tears start to roll down Carrie's cheeks and had no idea if they were the result of pain from the event or the possible fear and guilt being imposed upon her now, or both. Or who the fuck knew? Laura held her and made soothing mothering noises. Elgin felt like a chauffeur.

They parked in front, and as they approached the entrance to the center, Jervac pushed open the door for them. He must have been six-five, two-fifty, with a buzz cut and a good suit, maybe forty years old. "Hey. You must be Carrie," he said.

Carrie shrank against Laura's leg.

Elgin stuck out his hand, introduced himself and Laura.

Jervac smiled, nodded, ushered them into a reception area, gestured toward a couch. No one else was there.

"Hey, Carrie," he said. He took off his jacket and threw it over a chair. "My name's Lou." He sat on the floor, his legs extended under a large square coffee table in front of the couch. "Come on and sit on the floor," he said, holding out a miniature silver deputy's star toward her. "I want to deputize you."

Carrie seemed torn between the safety of her mother's hold and the trinket. Laura eased her toward Jervac, who handed her the plastic star. "Put that on your dress," he said. "Right over your heart. That's a beautiful dress you're wearing. My daughter used to love dresses like that, with flowers on them."

"Why doesn't she now?" Carrie said, pinning the star on her dress.

"Maybe she still does," Jervac said, "but now she's older. That's all." Jervac's big meaty face beamed. "Hey, Carrie," he said. "I'm a police officer. A deputy sheriff."

"Do you have a gun?" Carrie said.

Hearn had been right. This guy was good. It was rare for Carrie to be so open with a stranger, to actually engage in conversation.

"I do," Jervac said, "but I don't really need it. The bad guys take one look at me and surrender."

"They do?"

"Naw, I'm just kidding. But, listen, do you know why you're here today?"

Carrie looked down at the table. Jervak took off his loafers, watching her, waiting. Carrie nodded.

"Cool," Jervac said. "Good. I made some juice earlier this morning. It's strawberry apple. My daughter, her name's Sandy, she likes that kind. Do you like that kind?"

"Yes," Carrie said, pulling her eyes from the table, watching him again.

Elgin silently thanked Hearn, Jervac, Artie, all the cops in the world.

"I thought we'd have a little juice, maybe a couple of doughnuts. You know that all cops love doughnuts, right?"

"They do?" Carrie said.

"Yes, they do," Jervac said. "And if you're my deputy, I sure hope you like doughnuts."

"I like chocolate doughnuts," Carrie said.

"You do? I like those, too. I also like the kind that have chocolate *and* sprinkles."

"That's *my* favorite kind," Carrie said.

Laura took Elgin's hand, squeezed.

"Excellent," Jervac said. "So, I thought we'd have some doughnuts and juice, and, you know, just talk for a little while."

Carrie looked down at the table, then back to Jervac and nodded.

"There's two different rooms," Jervac said, putting his shoes back on. "I could show them to you and you could decide where you'd most like to have a snack." He stood, and moved away from the table toward a door, as if he didn't want his massive bulk looming over Carrie. "Come on," he said, opening the door. "I'll show you."

Carrie looked at her mother. Elgin stood. "Let's go see," he said. Laura nodded at Carrie, who stood and waited, looking toward Jervac, then back toward her mother, before finally walking to the door. Jervac ushered Laura through as well, then said to Elgin, "After she chooses, you two will wait out here."

"We're not going to be there?" Elgin said.

"No," Jervac said, and he walked ahead. "This is the living room," he said, walking across a room that had clearly never been lived in, though it had a couch, another big coffee table, two bookshelves, no windows, a dining room table with four chairs, and two recliners. "And this," he said, opening a door on the far wall, "is the playroom."

Carrie stood at the threshold looking in.

"Go ahead," Jervac said. Elgin took Carrie's hand and led her into a carpeted room with low shelves piled with toys, buckets of crayons and paper, a dollhouse, and a low kids' table with two chairs. The wallpaper featured dancing clowns.

Carrie stood in front of the dollhouse, clearly coveting it.

"Um, I think the living room," she said.

"Okay," Jervac said. "I'll get our doughnuts and juice, while you choose where you'd like to sit."

When Jervac returned with a tray of juice and doughnuts, he said, "And your mom and dad will be waiting right outside that door."

And the panic came up on Carrie's face.

"It's okay, honey," Elgin said.

Laura said, "We can be here if you'd prefer it."

Carrie nodded.

Jervac poured juice into two coffee mugs. "Actually," he said. "I only have four doughnuts, and I think Carrie and I will each require two." He placed a mug on the coffee table in front of Carrie. "And also, this way you can talk to Lieutenant Hearn." He pushed the plate of doughnuts across the table toward Carrie. Laura hadn't budged. Elgin took her hand. She pulled against him. He pulled back. "We'll be right on the other side of that door," Elgin said to Carrie. Laura hesitated, then allowed herself to be pulled. "It's okay, baby," she said. "We'll see you in a little bit."

Hearn was seated on the couch, but stood and introduced himself when they walked back into the waiting area. "They almost always choose the living room," he said. "Like it's more formal or something."

"Why can't we be there?" Laura said.

"Can I get you some coffee?" Hearn said. "And then we'll talk about it?"

"Sure," Elgin said.

"I think we should be with her," Laura said after Hearn had left the room.

"Let's sit down and wait," Elgin said.

Hearn returned and passed out Styrofoam cups from a tray that also held milk and sugar and sugar substitutes and red plastic stir sticks. He looked more like an accountant than a cop, in his cheap wrinkled suit, knit tie, and big bush of wiry black hair going gray. "I'm sorry about your daughter," he said, pouring three packs of sugar into his cup.

"I think she'd be more comfortable if we were there," Laura said. "She tends to withdraw around strangers."

Hearn stirred his coffee. "I understand," he said. "But remember that she saw or felt your reaction when she first revealed what happened. She might feel responsible, that she hurt you. And then we'd get nothing from her." He looked at Laura. "This is the best way," he said. "I hope you can trust us."

He took a long drink of coffee, expert with the pauses, irritating Elgin, making Elgin feel as if *he* were being examined or interrogated.

"See," Hearn said, "a lot of times, if a parent's in the room, she'll interrupt and try to shape the story: 'That's not the way you told me,' she'll say. The mother's words are no good for us. The victim—the child—must say that it happened."

"Okay, fine," Elgin said. "So what happens next."

"Once we get a signed and notarized statement, and have her examined for evidence, we'll interview the perpetrator, as I told you last night."

Evidence, Elgin thought. His stomach turned over again. Sometimes he felt like an actor or a player in some kind of *procedure*, with words like "evidence" protecting him. But then, his mind would revolt, sending a signal to his stomach. Hearn's *evidence*, if they were lucky enough to get it—*lucky* for Christ's sake—would be traces of Corey Newkirk's semen.

"But isn't her statement enough to arrest him with?" Laura asked.

"It might be," Hearn said. "But what we want to get from the perp is a statement that incriminates him. We want him to hang himself. See, if we just arrest him, then his lawyer will control how he answers in the interview. We don't want that."

Laura looked at the door leading to the "living room," where all the sordid details were being teased out of Carrie. "So you take him in there?" she asked, nodding toward the door.

"No, we do it at his house."

"Oh, and will *his* parents be there?"

Laura was pissing Elgin off, coming on way too strong with the only people they could turn to.

"Yes, they will," Hearn said. "They have to be because he's a minor."

"And that's when he's going to confess to you? That's when he's going to hang himself?"

Hearn turned to Laura. "The thing about this kind of crime," he said, "is that there's a great weight of shame that goes along with it."

He took another long drink of coffee. "Any other crime, burglary, car theft, knocking off the liquor store, even murder, the perp goes to a bar and starts telling stories. Starts bragging about it. Nobody ever brags about sex crimes. What we'll offer him, depending on how it goes, is the opportunity to confess; we'll offer help, if you see what I mean."

"Okay," Elgin said. "I think we get the picture."

"Well, I'm not so sure I get the picture," Laura said. "This kid lives two doors down from us. When is he going to be removed?"

Hearn shook his head. "We'll just have to wait and see what we learn."

"He'll end up in Children's Village," Elgin said, referring to the juvenile detention center in Pontiac. "At most."

"Children's Village?" Laura said. "How darling. You mean he's not going to go to jail?"

"Laura, he's just a kid. All right?"

"Mrs. Elgin," Hearn said, leaning toward her. "I don't have enough information right now to be able to predict what will happen. I don't have confirmation of the perp's age, and I don't yet know what actually occurred. That's what Officer Jervac is trying to confirm. We just have to try to be patient, go through the steps and learn what we can. It's possible that what occurred is what's called a designated felony. That's what will determine whether family court or criminal court will handle the case. If we even get a case."

Laura had started to cry, silently. Elgin looked up from his coffee when he noticed movement, her hands around her face, wiping at her seemingly inexhaustible supply of tears. "And you're defending *him?*" she said to Elgin. "*Just a kid?*"

"No," Elgin said. "Honey." He slid closer to her on the couch, put an arm around her shoulder. He was getting goddamn sick and tired of being the only adult in this crisis.

"Mrs. Elgin," Hearn said. "I might be out of line, but I want to give you some perhaps unwanted advice. Both of you: don't get into the blame game. I see this all the time. You're going through hell, I know you are, and you have to find a reason for it, someone to blame. But that's just going to make everything worse for everybody."

Laura took the handkerchief Elgin offered her.

"And you don't want Carrie to see you like this."

Laura nodded, wiped her eyes and sniffled. "You're right," she said.

There didn't seem to be anything else to say, and the relative silence, the hum of the air conditioner, the sounds of movement behind the door through which Hearn had disappeared for the coffee had a hollowing effect on Elgin. Since learning of what had happened to Carrie only yesterday, less than twenty-four hours ago, Elgin must have shit twelve times. And the quiet now, the fact that there was nothing else to say brought on the urge again.

Hearn directed him to the bathroom and remained seated in the armchair next to Laura. Elgin walked through the side door, past the open door of the examining room, the table covered with a strip of white paper, and into the bathroom. It would be nice, he thought, to stay here forever, locked in a little cubicle, with food handed through a slot in the door. The toilet paper showed mostly blood, all this shitting and wiping. When he came out, he heard Jervac say to somebody, "Oral sodomy. But you're not going to get anything. Last incident was Tuesday."

Jervac was talking to the SANE nurse in the examining room. Elgin didn't recognize her at first, the words "oral sodomy" still echoing in his ears. He had wanted to thank Jervac, to show him that they weren't the typical, fucked-up crime family. And then he recognized her and she him, he guessed. She was from the county hospital, the local president of their Michigan Nurses' Association chapter, a complete bitch who had sat at the table with the MNA negotiator from Lansing in the last round of negotiations.

Jervac turned to Elgin. "Hey," he said. "I'll be out in a minute. Carrie was great. She's doing real well."

Bitch gave him the same blank stare she'd worn through the negotiations, through the strike vote and the eleventh-hour negotiating that had just barely avoided a strike. The local had wanted staffing ratios and had no idea how close they'd come to getting them, finally settling for a departmental review of possible ratios and three years of two and a halves. A shitty settlement for them. But Pearson had told them that the minute they walked he'd be bringing in replacements from a staffing agency in North Carolina. Which would have cost the county a fucking fortune, but the nurses had stupidly bought it. If they'd held out for another hour, they would have gotten threes. If they'd struck, they might have gotten fours. Possibly even the ratios, given the national shortage of nurses.

"Hello, Mr. Elgin," she said to him now.

No way could he have her touch his daughter. No fucking way.

"Hello," Elgin said. "How are you?"

"Oh, I'm all right," she said, and Jervac said, "Mr. Elgin, this is Connie Skyler."

Elgin reached his hand toward her, which she took and shook. "We've met," she said, a big fake smile plastered on her face. "I'm so sorry about your little girl," she said, and she was no longer smiling and there didn't seem to be anything fake about her. What Elgin saw in her eyes was a generosity of warmth and sympathy that ignited in him a horrifying mix of emotion—of gratitude and weakness and shame and loathing.

"Does this thing have to happen?" he said to Jervac. "I heard you say there'd be no evidence. That it was too late."

"It does," Jervac said.

And then Skyler actually took his hand in both of hers, all that sympathy in her face seeming to try to absorb whatever pain she thought he held, and she said, "You can be right here with her. It'll only take a second, and she won't have to get undressed or anything like that. We'll make it real quick and easy. Okay?"

"Okay," Elgin said, stunned, numb. It didn't seem possible that minutes before, she had been capable of radiating any sort of bitchiness or phoniness whatsoever. Instead, it seemed quite possible that *he* was capable of misreading anything and everything. And, God, how long had this been going on? He turned from them, walked back toward the reception area. Just when had his judgment failed? "Thank you," he called out. "Thanks a lot." And how the hell was he to determine just what and how much would have to be undone?

Carrie was quiet on the ride home, a little flushed and anxious, fidgety. Laura sat with her in the back again, and before they picked up

Tommy, she said, "You know that you didn't do anything wrong, right?"

Carrie nodded.

"Not a thing."

"It was *him*," Carrie said.

"That's right," Laura said.

Elgin wondered if Carrie would now be taught to hate the kid, if the hatred would be carefully cultivated by Laura and the cops and whomever else, and if that was the right thing or if it would be better if she just forgot all about it. He didn't know if that was possible or not. Or if that would be good or bad. He didn't know anything.

Tommy was in the yard at Claire's house running through the sprinkler with her little boy when they pulled into the driveway. He ran to the car, screaming, "Yo, bunge, nana ho," his face beaming with joy. Laura talked to Claire, no doubt feeding the gossip machine, while Elgin dried Tommy and wrestled him into a fresh diaper. Carrie sat in the car, dressing a doll.

Jervac had said that he'd be calling later on that night, after the interview with Corey, so it was almost like a reprieve, a good number of hours before they would learn anything or could do anything. After the examination by Skyler, just a swab in the mouth, which Elgin decided not to watch, Laura had been so anxious to get out of there that she didn't even think to ask for a copy of Carrie's statement, which Hearn had told Elgin they would not be allowed to have. And so it was a relief that a fight over that had been avoided by Laura's urgency to leave. Hearn did say that Jervac would go over both Carrie's and "the perp's" statements when he called that night. That there would be plenty of information to chew on.

But not right now.

While Tommy napped, Carrie helped Elgin mow the lawn, then finger-painted with Laura at the kitchen table. Elgin asked her if she wanted to make cookies, which, of course, she did. The brownies yesterday, the cookies today, tomorrow would be cake. Laura didn't bring up Corey's name again or the morning interrogation, for which Elgin was grateful, but even during this reprieve, there was an underlying sense that he was just waiting for the hammer to fall and crush them all.

On the way out to dinner, Elgin saw a brown Crown Vic parked in front of the Newkirks' house. He touched Laura's leg, nodded toward the unmarked cop car.

"I see it," Laura said. "I only wish I could be there."

"Be where?" Carrie said, and Laura said, "At the beach."

"We saw a dead fish at the beach," Carrie said, "and buried it."

"Bearydit," Tommy said.

"Can we go to Mickey-D's?" Carrie said, and Elgin said, "Sure," thinking, we can go wherever you want, whenever you want. Because it's your special day, week, month, year, life. And he wondered how much damage they'd do by indulging her every whim. Or if they would even do that, or if he would ever again be able to help doing that. But, God, he just had to stop analyzing everything.

"Are you going to get a shy meal?" he asked Carrie.

"I'm going to get an excited meal," she said.

"I'm gonna get a mad meal," Tommy said.

"I'm going to get a tired meal," Elgin said. It was a family joke, started unwittingly by Carrie when she was almost three, before Tommy was born. They'd been driving to Chicago on the July Fourth weekend to see Elgin's sister and her boys, the traffic an absolute nightmare, backed up from Chicago, through Indiana, all the way to the Michigan line it seemed, Elgin fuming at all the assholes on the road. Laura sat in the backseat to occupy Carrie and they were playing a counting game, and Carrie was so excited to have her mother in back with her, that at every third or fourth turn, she would shriek the number, and Elgin would say, "We don't scream in the car," and, "Hey, really, stop screaming." But she was so excited that she couldn't seem to help herself, even after Laura had said, "Really, we can't startle Daddy while he's driving," and she did quiet down for a few minutes, but then shrieked, "Nineteen!" nearly jolting Elgin out of his seat. Without thinking, he reached back and squeezed her wrist, hard, too hard, and said, through clenched teeth, "No screaming in the car! And I mean it!"

The horrible part was that Carrie didn't make another sound. She cried silently in the backseat, as she rubbed her wrist where Elgin had hurt her, Laura refusing to talk to him, but just quietly soothing Carrie.

And five minutes later, nearly choking on guilt, Elgin had said, "There's a McDonald's up here. Should we stop?"

"Whatever," Laura said.

"Yeah, let's," he said, and before he pulled off the interstate, he said to Carrie through the mirror, "Are you going to get a happy meal?"

And Carrie, all snotty from the tears, said, "I'll try." She looked down, then back up at him again in the mirror. "Are you going to get an angry meal?" she asked him.

Elgin smiled, the guilt nearly strangling him. "No," he said, and he apologized to her—"that was wrong of Daddy"—and told her he'd try to get a happy meal as well.

"It's okay, Daddy," she said to his apology, and he wondered how she could possibly forgive him, certain he didn't deserve it.

Now, in the car, it seemed possible that you could do all manner of unforgivable things to your children. How could he have been so angry with her as to physically hurt her? What else had he done or would he do to hurt her?

Stop, he thought, pulling into the parking lot. Stop, stop, stop.

"We're here!" Carrie shrieked. "We're finally here!"

After the Happy Meals and the ritualistic opening of the crappy toys, which Carrie informed Tommy had been made by slave children in China, something Elgin had once said as a joke—and, God, she never forgot a thing—Carrie asked if they could go to the McDonald's "Playland" outside, which consisted of a scummy ballpit and a network of human habitrails, like the kind used in gerbil cages, with plastic bubble windows at various platforms along the network from which the kids could look down at their parents, show their faces, reveal that they were still alive in there. Elgin and Laura sat on a bench and watched the kids play. Tommy hurled himself into the pit, waded through the colorful plastic balls. Carrie followed.

Elgin put his arm around Laura's shoulder. The hazy sky was lighting pink to the west. She leaned into him, the humidity bringing out sweat wherever they touched.

"Come on, Little Man!" Carrie called to Tommy, using the name Laura and Elgin often called him. He was buried in the balls, thrashing around in them. "Let's go up the tunnels!" She took his hand, helped pull him up to the platform above the ballpit, at the entrance to the first tube of the habitrail.

"You're going to be my deputy," she said, and she took off the star that Jervac had given her earlier that morning and pinned it to his shirt. Tommy studied the badge. "Go!" he shouted, and he scrambled up the tube after Carrie. And it was clear to Elgin in the full humidity, his wife nestled into him, both of them sweating in the crappy Playland of McDonald's next to the highway, careful not to talk, not to spoil it, Carrie waving now from one of the bubble windows fifteen feet above them, and then Tommy's face appearing in the bubble, both of them waving frantically, the sound of their muffled laughter floating down in the summer air, it was clear that his children were going to be all right, that all of them were, that, somehow, they were going to come out the other end of this thing intact, that, somehow, everything was going to be just fine.

FIVE

SEPTEMBER/OCTOBER

After Portland, Elgin found a hotel in Murray Hill with weekly rates and suites with kitchens. He studied the city, walking in places he knew he shouldn't walk, Atlantic Avenue in Bed Sty, through East New York, the Grand Concourse in the Bronx, all the way to the top of Manhattan through Harlem and Washington Heights, proving, perhaps, that he was in fact dead, since nobody even tried to mug him, let alone kill him. He did get plenty of looks, though, most of them curious—like, what's this white fucker in a suit doing here?—and a few, the ones he wanted, threatening, menacing, bringing on a rush of fear. And all the looks proved, of course, that he was not invisible, that he was alive. Some days, it seemed, more so than others. And it wasn't as if he walked at night. It wasn't as if he were honest in any way. Except that he knew he wasn't.

There was no point any longer in not smoking. The money, still more than four hundred grand, certainly wouldn't last forever, and it seemed unlikely that he would ever be employed again, except as unskilled labor, since he had no skills to sell. His health, or setting an example for his children, had become irrelevant. Still, at his current rate of spending, around eighteen hundred a week, he would last for years.

He'd never met people easily, never struck up conversations with strangers in grocery stores or restaurants. One day as he turned the corner onto Lexington Avenue in midtown, he saw an older man, maybe sixty, punch another older man in the face on the sidewalk not twenty feet from where he'd stopped to light a cigarette. The struck man's glasses flew off as he fell to the sidewalk, and the man who'd hit him got into a Mercedes and peeled away. "Did you see that?" Elgin said to a Latino kid unloading a delivery van, who had watched the confrontation.

"What happened was this," the kid said. "Dude in the Mercedes honks at the glasses dude who's walking drag ass across the middle of the block. Glasses flips him off, right? Mercedes jams it into a quick double park, jumps out his car, and tags the motherfucker." The Latino kid was grinning.

Elgin could think of no response, but was struck that this was the first interaction he'd initiated in weeks that didn't involve a transaction. Two people, a man and a woman, helped the man up, brushing him off, handing him his glasses. Elgin felt no impulse to assist. But he did admire the confrontation somehow. How many deserving people had he failed to punch in his life?

"See you," Elgin said, and the kid said, "Take care."

In the Disney film, *Snow White,* Carrie's favorite line had been when Snow meets Grumpy, saying, "How do you do?" and Grumpy sneers, "How do you do *what?*" Elgin applied it now to the Latino kid's words: Take care of *what?* There didn't seem to be anything to take care of at the moment.

And so, during the day, he walked. He got a library card to fill up the evenings. When his appetite started to return, he cooked and listened to the radio and ate. He lost weight from all the walking, started doing push-ups and sit-ups in his room, perhaps preparing to punch somebody. He tried not to think too much, though at times he was overcome with grief, an aching for his lost children. But he couldn't think in terms of right or wrong, because he was no longer capable of telling the difference, except in the broadest terms, like, that it was wrong to kill people. Usually. That is, if they didn't deserve it. And determining that would get you to the tricky part.

Suicide seemed redundant. And though he frequently considered stepping into traffic, or dropping from the subway platform in front of a hurtling express train, could actually feel the pull of commitment to the act, he was either too weak to commit or was merely indulging in adolescent suicide fantasies. So he walked, he ate, he smoked. He rode the Long Island Railroad out to Montauk and back. At restaurants, he left 100 percent tips, sometimes more.

On the train ride up from Miami, after he'd withdrawn the dirty money from the bank in Barbados—the money that Klister and McCabe had skimmed from the County Employees' Health, Welfare, and Benefit fund—he'd experienced a rush of euphoria, a sense of freedom and fearlessness. He'd done it, ripped the bastards off, escaped the shitty Holiday Inn he'd been sentenced to, and was finally free of his irrelevance regarding Carrie's therapy, Corey's incarceration, and everything else. As much as anything, the money was a form of payback, or, better still, proof that they couldn't manipulate him so easily, proof that he could still be an actor in his own life.

Now, he wondered what he had ever done in his life that had meaning, if there was anything one could do that had meaning, beyond having children, which seemed like nothing more than the fulfillment of biological destiny. He remembered anticipation, for a particular day at work, for sex, for a new bike, for the births of his children, for Christmas to finally arrive, for a week to end, for the potential viciousness of negotiations, for a vacation to begin, for getting out of the house, for returning home. In the palm of his hand he remembered the feel of his children's skin, smooth, rubbery cheeks, Tommy's forehead during fever, like a radiator, the pull of the brush through Carrie's hair after a bath, the phantom pain of cracked knuckles as he imagined punching Corey's face into a sticky pulp. As best he could, though, he tried not to remember. On the streets, the people surrounding him, engaged in their daily business, seemed ignorant of the misery of their lives, entirely focused on getting to the gym, getting home from work. Everyone had appointments to keep. They were meeting lovers, taking the children to piano lessons, clamoring to get into theaters. And they were talking to each other, flipping each other off, fucking, fighting. Even the beggars had jobs to do. Only Elgin, it seemed, was silent, disengaged.

Then, at the beginning of October, he met Carla. Hired Carla. Rented Carla. In his previous life he would have been incapable of such a transaction, not because he found it morally wrong, but because he thought it would dehumanize him somehow—just the sheer embarrassment of the transaction would reduce him to something less than he was. Maybe he'd been a romantic. Maybe he'd had an inflated opinion of himself. Now, though, it seemed entirely appropriate. His loneliness drove him out of his room, but he couldn't bring himself to speak to anyone. The only person he deserved to talk to—could even risk talking to—it seemed, was a rental. But she couldn't be a streetwalker, couldn't be a common whore. She would have to be clever enough to create the illusion of desire for him, to create the illusion that there was anything in him worth desiring. And it had nothing to do with sex. That was over. Since his escape, his disappearance from his life, sexual thoughts or urges had disappeared as well. His libido had died with his former self, it seemed.

He filled two days researching the escort services, a gift in and of itself, inquiring about prices and the education levels of the *girls*, viewing photos and bios, sort of what he thought a purchase of livestock might be like, examining teeth and pedigrees. And he settled on Carla. Laid down the money and arranged the meeting. And, sure, he was nervous, didn't really know if he could go through with it or not, but what happened—what he'd never expected or dreamed he was capable of any longer—was that he liked her. For Christ's sake, he found himself wanting to know her opinion on the current erosion of civil liberties, allowed himself to believe that she might even like *him*, might want to know his opinions. And it might have been a romantic gesture, or he might have just been trying to burn through the money, but, before their second meeting—lunch for Christ's sake—he bought her a ridiculously expensive piece of jewelry, found himself nervous before what he was able to pretend was a date. For their third meeting, another lunch, he bought her a watch. Christ, how hungry he had been for human contact. Or at least for a major distraction, and he didn't want to fuck it up, even though she reminded him frequently enough that she was only a rental. But she was so good at her job that he was actually able to imagine what it would be like to interact with people on some level that wasn't merely financial. She listened to him. They had conversations. And he wasn't so delusional as to believe that this was anything more than some kind of expensive therapy, or a way to fill time. But he didn't care. The illusion was enough. More than enough, really. It was all he had.

≡

Teddy calls Friday, after I'd left explicit instructions not to disturb me for weekend appointments, that I was out of commission, on the rag, bloated, etcetera, Teddy a little deficient in math, or biology, or both, as I was also on the rag two weekends ago, but he says, "You're not going to believe what tipless is willing to pay," and I know right away he means Mister-Sensitive-Damaged-Moneybags, and I'm sort of intrigued, and start to salivate a little with greed, and I say, "Yeah. Go on."

"Get this," Teddy says. "Dinner tomorrow, eight to eleven. Overnight rate. You wonder this guy's dick even works. I mean, I know you said you were off call and everything, but Jesus."

"No," I say. "You're right," and he gives me the place, Café des Artistes, a romantic dinner for two. Goodness. What a lucky girl I am. My cut for three hours of eating, drinking, and consoling will be twenty-five hundred bucks. Sometimes the Lord's work *is* rewarding.

But, then, getting ready, I catch a little flutter in my stomach. And I'm like, whoa: I realize it's been there all day. I stop cold as I'm plucking my eyebrows, like, wait a minute here, this rush of excitement a little too close to the kind of pathetic pre-date nervousness that the amateurs experience, a little too close to some kind of teenage excitement before meeting Bobby Parsons at the soda shop after the big game. Since early this morning, even while reading *Absalom, Absalom!,* I've been considering and rejecting different outfits, finally settling on a conservative wool dress. And now, looking at myself in the mirror, taking far too much time on my fucking eyebrows, I'm like, You've got to be kidding me. As if I don't know what the fucker's up to. The necklace. The watch. The chastity. The earnest pain.

Café des Artistes, my perfectly sculpted ass.

I throw the country club dress on the floor and pull on a low-cut, up-to-my-ass little black dress with sequins. Garnish with real whore's gartered stockings and stilettos, and, voilà, I am ready to go.

Call me a bad girl, Daddy. Pweeeeeeeease.

I show up thirty minutes late. He's at the bar in the back room, stands when he sees me and actually beams. "Hey," he says, looking me up and down, the dress doing its job, "great to see you."

I give him a quick business smile. "Vodka on the rocks," I say to the bartender, taking the seat Elgin pulls out for me. "Sorry I'm late," I say. "I had to finish another appointment."

"Oh," he says. "That's okay. Our reservation's not until nine."

"And I don't want one of these shitty tables back by the bar," I tell him. "I want to be in the main room, with the nymphs and shit."

"No problem," Elgin says.

"It will be a problem," I say, "if you don't talk to the maître d'. Go give him a fifty."

"I gave him a hundred."

Touché. The joint is packed with loud rich people, mostly couples, some—the ones stuck at the bar tables—most likely in from Long Island or Jersey to celebrate momentous occasions. Elgin orders another scotch. "How's school?" he says.

"Stimulating," I say. "Real stimulating. What about you?" I say. "How's, uh, whatever it is you do?"

"I don't do anything," he says. "Remember?"

"Oh, yeah, right," I say. "How's that?"

He shrugs. "Here," he says, "I got you something," and I think, oh, God, not another fucking gift. How pathetic can this man be? He hands me a book, unwrapped, a first edition of *The Sound and the Fury,* which must be worth quite a bit, since only about three were printed in the first run, and I feel completely taken advantage of, somehow, like this guy has no right to even be able to guess what I might or might not care about, not that I care about this, though it's not a bad guess. I flip through the pages. "First edition," I say. "I've never understood why people are willing to pay more for these. I mean, the words are the same, right?" I lay the book on the bar.

The fucker's smiling like he's just shit the golden egg. I swivel toward him and hook my heels on the rung of his stool. "I got you something too, Daddy," I say in my breathless voice. I lean toward him, giving him a good look down my dress, then reach my hand between his legs and grab his package. "I'm horny as a sailor," I say.

He doesn't move except under my hand. "My last client left me in the lurch," I say, "if you know what I mean."

"Well," he says, taking my wrist and moving my hand away, "I could take you into the bathroom and bend you over the sink."

"Charming," I say, turning toward my drink.

"What's with your little act tonight?"

"Act?" I say. "I know what *I* am. Remember?"

He pushes himself from the bar and walks away without a word. And I'm like, Oh, no, buddy, you don't walk away from me, but, then again, no way am I going to make a scene. I'm not going to show a care in the world. In fact, on a Saturday night at an expensive restaurant in the center of the universe, I'm going to drink my drink and read. A few minutes pass, and my breathing starts to return to normal. Maybe he's not coming back. I notice the flutter in my stomach, a nervous sort of spasm like I felt before every appointment in my first month on the job, before I learned to use the fuck-me-Daddy voice. It's not as if I care that some client walks away from me in a restaurant, though; I'll get paid no matter what. I count backwards from a hundred. When I reach zero, I'll walk.

And then he's back, a hand on my shoulder. "Sorry about that," he says. "You're right."

"Of course I'm right," I say to my drink. "I'm always right." He doesn't sit, doesn't talk, doesn't move his hand from my shoulder. When I finally turn, his head is a little bowed so that his eyes sort of look up into his eyelids, giving me the half pissed, half disappointed, I'm cool and can wait for you to grow up piercing stare.

"Oh, come on," I say. "Sit down, already. Let's have a good time." Whatever that's supposed to mean—just stop bugging me, I guess.

"You know what's funny?" he says, sitting, then draining his watery drink and gesturing to the bartender for another round. Lord knows I'm ready for one. "My mother collected things." He crunches a few ice slivers, holds his empty glass under his chin. Down the bar behind him, a man tells a woman a story so heartbreaking that she touches his face, leaves her hand on his cheek. "And I knew it when I bought that book," he says, "that there was something stupid about it."

The drinks arrive. "Oh, I don't know," I say. "Some people are wild about that kind of thing."

"Yeah, she collected spoons, and bells, and these little glass dogs, really stupid shit that just cluttered up the house. A couple times, when I was really pissed, I'd take one of the dogs out into the woods and smash it with a hammer. Nothing gave me more satisfaction than pulverizing a green glass schnauzer into dust." He holds up his glass, as if to toast.

"To destruction," I say, touching his glass with mine.

"Right," he says.

"Were you often pissed as a child?" I say, thinking, this guy seems to live in his childhood—probably has some sort of Mommy complex.

"No," he says. "Were you?"

"Not really," I say. "But for one stretch, my father was a collector, too—of unemployment checks." I take a drink. He looks at me like, yeah, go on, and I take another gulp of vodka, and for some reason, I do go on. "See, GM bounced him from plant to plant as they were shutting down what seemed to be the entire city of Flint, and finally, when his seniority ran out, he was given the option to either move to a plant out of state, or go on unemployment." This couldn't possibly be me talking. "The poor, dumb bastard took unemployment." I take another big drink of vodka. "And we ate generic canned peaches and wiped our asses with generic toilet paper, though, of course," I say, "you wouldn't know about that."

"What do you mean?" he says.

"I mean being a child of privilege and all. Not that we had it bad. I mean, we were solid, bland middle class. And, eventually he was back on the line, anyway."

"Privilege?" he says.

"Trust fund," I say, "right?"

"You misread that one," he says. "I grew up the same middle class."

"How darling," I say, thinking, mis*read*? Not likely. What, so he earned the money? Or, no, the identity business. Some kind of crime. How frightfully romantic. The gangster and the whore. And right then, I feel something give in my stomach, like I'm coming entirely fucking unglued from the inside out, like I'm going to fucking *cry* or something.

"Hey," he says, touching my hand. "What's up? What's the matter?"

"No, nothing," I say. "I didn't get much sleep last night." And I see myself in his mind's eye on my back under some fat rich john in an expensive hotel room, and I say, "I was reading this novel. I was up all night, reading," starting to actually hate myself a little for justifying anything I may or may not do to anybody.

"Yeah," he says, "I get insomnia, too."

"No, this wasn't insomnia," I say. "This was reading. This was not being able to put a book down," and he nods, nonchalant, like, *whatever*, and I say, "I just need to splash some water on my face."

Fucker helps me with my chair as I push away from the bar, bringing steel up from my legs with every step I take away from him, and I am so fucking pissed, feeling every ounce of power in my legs, so fucking pissed, and I know that I just need to sit down for a minute by myself to get strong and realigned. But if I was like so many of the others, trotting off for a quick snort, I swear to God a blast of coke right now would kill me.

=

After another drink, they were finally seated, Carla drawing the attention of every man and woman in the dining room as they were escorted in, all of her long legs visible under the dress and practically falling out of the top, but getting away with it, too, somehow not coming off as cheap. Not that Elgin gave a shit. She told him a little about growing up in Flint, they were getting drunk, and she said, "I just could not wait to get out of there. Once I went to Ann Arbor, I knew I'd never go back."

Elgin had been through Flint many times, a decrepit, dying dump of a town in Genesee County, one county north of Oakland. He told her as much, and she laughed. "Oh, yeah, when I was growing up it was turning into a real shithole. The weird thing is that my parents and all of my grandparents grew up there, so it was like they were stuck, couldn't get out, like their escape muscles had atrophied. Like GM had made them into UAW junkies."

"Yeah," Elgin said. "And what were you escaping from?"

She dropped her fork—a ridiculously dramatic gesture—so that it clanked against her plate loud enough for several people to take the opportunity to look at them—at her—again. "Oh, please," she said. "Don't start with that bullshit. Don't try to figure out what makes me who I am. Okay? And I won't do it to you."

He watched her saw at her steak. He liked that she ate, that she didn't treat eating as some distasteful or mildly repulsive fueling exercise, as so many women seemed to do. Not that she ate like a hog or anything.

"Stop looking at me," she said, "mooning over me like I'm your precious daughter."

"I'm not that old," he said. "My daughter's in first grade. And the way you're dressed, it seems that you must want to be looked at."

"Yeah, well," she said. "Ninety-eight-year-old men can have daughters in first grade. Believe me. And the way I dress is none of your fucking business."

When the plates were cleared and the waiter asked about coffee and dessert, Carla looked at her watch, and said, "Our little session's running late."

"You want a cab?" Elgin said.

The waiter shifted his weight from side to side. Carla smiled, looked down at the table, then back into Elgin's eyes. God, he felt like a fifteen-year-old kid, giddy and idiotic and trying to hide whatever it was he felt. "No," she said, "let's have dessert."

Later, walking down Central Park West, he felt part of a clichéd romantic movie, Carla wearing his jacket over her shoulders in the cool fall air as they strolled, Elgin acutely aware of the bubble of space around his body, nearly flinching when they brushed up against each other, wanting to take her hand or put his arm around her, this beautiful, funny, intelligent woman he rented, but not daring to touch her. The silence between them was comfortable and then unbearable, and Elgin said, "Let's take a trip," not having considered the idea until this moment. "Let's get out of town, go on vacation."

Carla laughed. "School," she said, "remember? I can't miss class."

"Right," Elgin said. "Of course. What about a weekend?"

"I don't know," Carla said. "There's a traveling rate. You could talk to Teddy, but, really, I don't know. I've never done that."

Teddy. He didn't fit the stereotype of a pimp, if in fact he was one.

He seemed more like an office manager. A liaison. Shit, a madam. Still, Elgin felt that he would like to kill Teddy, beat him to death with a frying pan or a cane, a screwdriver in the eye. In front of Carla, preferably. Defending her.

They'd reached the bottom of the park and were walking east on Fifty-ninth toward Fifth, the romantic horse-drawn carriages lined up at Grand Army Plaza or clip-clopping into the park. "These stupid things," Elgin said. "Could you imagine riding around in one of those?"

"It's late," she said. "I have to go." She handed him the jacket, which smelled like her. He resisted the urge to plunge his face into the fabric and inhale.

"Really," she said. "I have to get going. Church in the morning. You know. Early worship." She smiled.

He had to turn away. He hailed a cab, then held the door for her, but she didn't get in. She stood by the open door, waiting, looking at him as if studying him, as if she could see something in him, or maybe nothing in him—no, as if she'd never looked at him before, or never shown herself to him before—and it was terrifying.

"Where do you live?" he said, his voice small and desperate in his ears. "We could share this one."

"No," she said. "I have to go," and before Elgin could even pay the cabbie, she'd folded herself into the backseat and was gone.

He watched the taillights move down Fifth as he walked south toward his place.

His place. It was a hotel, for Christ's sake. He didn't have a place. And, now, with her gone, it was obvious that she had been waiting for him to kiss her. Of course she had. Any fool could have seen it. Or, maybe not. Maybe she'd been considering an apology for leaving the stupid book he'd gotten her at the restaurant. He decided to stop for a nightcap. He walked into Mason's, an old man's serious drinking bar. No, she had been waiting for a kiss. She liked him. He liked her. He'd arrange a weekend rental with fuckhead Teddy, go up to Boston, down to Charleston, somewhere.

He smoked a couple of cigarettes, ordered another drink. Who cared that he had to pay for her time? That would probably pass, too. But he'd never bother her to get out of the business. Never treat her as a possession. At some point she'd probably *want* to get out anyway. He'd support her. Whatever she wanted to do would be fine. Maybe he *could* find a way to get a real job. Maybe that was just what he needed.

For the first time since the train from Miami, he felt a jolt of happiness, the thrill of being alive, a sense of hope for something down the line, something to live for, to anticipate, and then he realized what an idiot he was, lost in a fantasy of building a new life, and with Carla no less, as if he deserved her. As if he deserved anything. And her name was Stacey, anyway, not Carla. But he couldn't think of her as Stacey; he wanted her to be Carla. He didn't know why. He was drunk. He ordered another drink. He wondered if he'd ever get caught. He wondered if there was a warrant out for his arrest. It seemed unlikely. The money was dirty, skimmed by Klister and McCabe from the Benefit Fund, stolen a second time by Elgin. But, of course, that meant that other people were likely looking for him, people that Klister had hired, people far more dangerous than the cops. But who gave a fuck? He had no right to care if he got caught. Tortured. Mutilated. And his kids at home asleep, maybe Carrie crying out right this minute—he looked at his watch; it was 12:48—maybe right this minute calling out from a nightmare, or screaming that Corey was under the window or in the closet. Did she call his name anymore? He was drunk. He had no right to care. He was a liar. He couldn't stop thinking about Carla, couldn't stop a part of himself from feeling good, wondering if he had a chance with her, thinking that maybe he did, maybe he didn't. He ordered another drink. He couldn't call Carla again. He had to put a stop to this. His job was to suffer forever. Fucking idiot. He was a liar. He had no right to feel this way. He couldn't stop sticking his face into the shoulder of his jacket and smelling Carla.

≡

Tuesday's seminar I have one of those moments where I'm like, What the fuck am I doing here? The only people on campus who seem real to me are the custodians and grounds crews. Every day that passes in my third semester here, I'm less sure of what it is I think I'm doing.

What could be more pointless or idiotic than a doctorate in English? I mean, the discussions are sometimes engaging, this one chick, Raisa, always seeming to find real weird, but defensible readings in the works, but, really, there's something decadent about the entire endeavor. I should be training seeing-eye dogs, or out bombing buildings, protesting the World Bank or the IMF or electricity deregulation or any of the other filthy enterprises that support the pigs who pay me. Instead, I'm learning what, how to read? No, learning how to read in a way that completely limits a text. Even that word, *text*, has crept into my vocabulary like a poison. And all the earnest students. Oh, my God. Sitting in a seminar room arguing over the author's creation of his fictional world, you'd think that half the actual world wasn't starving to death. Not that *I* really give a fuck, but these people would argue that they do. And Nabaum seems to think that he has privileged access to all of Faulkner's intentions, that he alone can discern the meaning of all those words.

He's droning on, half the students actually taking notes, and I'm looking at my perfectly manicured fingernails, wondering if there's something immoral about all of this. I mean, I'm a realist. At Michigan, I was a good student, a *serious* student, but, once that neared an end, I was like, now what? I'd think about my profs up there prattling on about great literature, grading a few papers, and I thought, man, that sure beats working for a living. My father could never get his hands clean, the skin over his knuckles perpetually broken. And these guys got paid to read. Though, of course, they had to go through the torture of publishing, of writing about their monstrously insightful readings. But if the only hurdle's the circle jerk of academic publishing, you'd be stupid not to go for the easy life. That's what I thought, anyway. Plus, I had some kind of naive, burning belief in something—literature or art, I don't know what. Now, though, all of these people are making me a little sick, the students, the profs, the undergraduates, just everybody.

And how am I ever going to get a job in academia if I refuse to teach? Though, on the other hand, that seems to be the point of a job in academia. Not to teach, that is. Still, you have to do it sometimes, especially when you're just starting. Last year, I was a TA, had a section

of freshman comp each semester, for which I received a tuition waiver
and a stipend equal to about six months rent. I don't know when I
started to hate it, sometime during the second semester, I guess. My
students were either rich or poor, which is to say that I didn't recognize myself in any of them. Egocentric, I know, but their papers were
just so trite and idiotic that I found myself paralyzed before them, like,
what, I'm supposed to respond seriously to another fucking car accident essay in which the writer wishes to share another valuable lesson
about looking both ways before crossing the street, or draws the same
tired conclusion about how precious every day is and how we must
treasure each and every moment? I mean, I'm sure it was all my fault
and everything. I tried to help them find interesting things to write
about, lighting fires and shoplifting and running away to join the cir-
cus and the moment they realized they despised their parents and sexual politics in high school, but it seemed that all I got were dead pets
and dead grandmothers and valuable lessons. Then, even with the
almost immediate burnout, I thought, Oh, this is just comp, this is just
the grind. Once I graduate and land a killer tenure track job, I'll tran-
scend that immediately and teach important graduate seminars.

At least I knew enough to quit the TA bullshit. Plus, I'd become a
little fed up with the impoverished graduate student routine. It's as if I
were twenty years younger last fall. Winter break, I even went out with
one of my profs, Harold Stanley, from the Depraved American Mind, a
course I actually enjoyed, though I was capable of enjoying all manner
of bullshit then, but five minutes into the date, I was like, this guy is a
complete idiot. He couldn't stop lecturing, didn't know how to turn it
off. We went out for drinks at the Safari Room—so hip—and he was
droning on about Henry Miller and Anaïs Nin, as if I couldn't see
exactly where he was going with *that,* no room whatsoever for my
opinions or human discussion, no ability in him to abandon his phony
mentor role as he strained to get into my pants, as if the various theories he was weaving into his current book were an aphrodisiac, for
Christ's sake. After about an hour of that, my every attempt to change
the subject rebuffed by him, the line from that Sebadoh song started
looping through my mind: *"Black chalk living room couch professor/
when will you be through with me/ i'd like to know."*

And after that date, I was twenty years older as well. Which now puts me around sixty-five, I guess: retirement age. Somehow, though, even at the end of last year, I still believed that school was the right thing for me, that I would find a life in the academy. I look at Nabaum, grilling a student on some interpretation I missed, asking questions he knows the answers to. Fucking fraud. They all are. Everyone in this room.

I notice a vein rising up a little on my right hand, another reminder. I know I can't squeeze more than three or four years out of the business, and even that seems suddenly unbearable. You can't think about all the dates and fucks, though, all the repulsion to be held at bay; you have to behave like an alcoholic, which is to say one fuck at a time. But, Jesus, two years, three years, four years, then what?

But it's just a bad day is all it is. I feel like a bored, spoiled child. It's like I'm starving to death, but can't think of one single thing I want to eat. I have no idea how people get ruined but they all seem to be. And, fuck, I do not want to be one of them.

=

Sunday, he didn't get out of bed. He awoke with an erection, the first time in months, it seemed, and after pissing and refusing to take aspirin, he lay in the sheets from ten to three and tried not to move, pretending he was paralyzed. All of the drunken good feeling of the previous evening had evaporated during his sleep. What was he doing in this fucking hotel, in this fucking city? He'd always hated Sundays, had always felt weakest and most vulnerable on Sundays. Maybe it would be worth going to prison or being killed if he could just see his children one more time. If he could just touch them. But, really, five minutes wouldn't be enough. He wanted them forever.

And Laura alone to do all the work of raising them. It didn't seem possible that this was his life, that he would be capable of this kind of despicable behavior. He must have known all along, in the back of his mind, that Laura's parents would take care of his family financially. What a prick he was. What a complete asshole. What a pathetic weakling. Even with the money, she'd have to work full time, just because she wouldn't want to feel like a charity case. So who would take care of the children? And no way would she go back to Planned Parenthood, not after the kids. She had become a closet pro-lifer, another point of friction between them, more shedding of herself. If he could get to Laura, if he could talk to her, tell her what had happened, maybe they could work out an arrangement. But what *had* happened?

He had to at least get them some money, though Laura wouldn't likely accept an arrangement in which he sent cash from a location she couldn't disclose. She would disclose it. She probably wanted him in prison. Or dead. No, probably not dead. She certainly wasn't as horrible as he was, even if she did wish him dead. And, really, nothing she *could* do would make her as horrible as he was, except hurting the children—consciously, physically hurting the children—which she was incapable of. But would she deny him access to them? Would she prevent him from seeing them? He wondered if he should have taken them, a little kidnapping, if that would have been better. But for whom? As if he'd even be capable of raising them right.

He would never see Carla again, that much was clear, though he felt a gnawing hunger for her even as he dismissed her. He wished he were Catholic. He needed to confess. He was such a liar. If he really didn't care about his own well-being, he would call Laura from the phone on the bedside table, right there, and start trying to make amends. But he needed a plan. For the rest of his life he'd need a fucking plan. He wasn't ready yet. He picked up the phone, pretending, and put it back down. This was certainly progress. This would be enough for today. No matter which course he took, it seemed that he would be killing himself. So the thing to do maybe, at least for now, was nothing, not that there was any nobility in a survival instinct. No, there wouldn't be any nobility. But he would have to get them money. God, at least that. And, really, he didn't know if he could live without seeing his children again. He didn't believe it would be better for them if he were dead. But, as it was, as far as they were concerned—really, as far as anyone was concerned—he might as well be dead, though, in fact, it felt as if he were just waking up, as if he were finally reclaiming himself from the prick who had been inhabiting his body, and finding that, golly gee, a great big fucking mess had been made in his absence, so much of a mess that, come to think of it, it might just be better to go on and check back out. At least for today. God, it was Sunday. Thinking about all the shit he was in, facing it a little, that had to be a sign of some kind of forward progress, a sign of some kind of something, an indication there was a part of him that wasn't merely horrible. Didn't it?

$$\equiv$$

Tuesday night the shit hits the fan in colossal fucking chunks. Teddy's got a sick call, Mandy, and wants to know if I'll do a fill-in for a regular—real mellow, the guy's a tugger, which means I play with myself and watch him masturbate—and Mandy doesn't mind, in fact would be grateful, because the guy—Irving—is a major tipper, and she wants to show him that she can always take care of him. And I'm in one of those moods where I'm like, yeah, let me see just how weak and pathetic this guy can be. Oh, and by the way, asshole, I don't know what Mandy allows, but no way in hell are you going to come on me. The call's for nine o'clock at a brownstone in the West Village, on Bleecker between Perry and Charles. On the cab ride over, I have another moment like this morning's, where I think, what the hell am I doing here? There's got to be something to do in this world. But, for the life of me, I have no idea what it might be.

I pay the cabbie and realize I've been in one of these brownstones before, on Perry. Side by side, around four corners, they occupy an entire block, enclosing a giant courtyard in the middle, with planters and lawn furniture and a fountain, safe play for the darlings, some kind of socialist collective from the '20s or something, when everyone groovy was a communist. I check my address and walk up three steps to a purple door and ring the bell. When he answers, it's one of those displacement moments when you see someone out of context and can't recognize who the hell they are, like your brain trips over itself trying to process conflicting information.

He is clearly having the same kind of moment. He's wearing a sort of quilted Chinese smoking jacket over tweedy wool pants, his hair slicked back with Vitalis or some equally repellent slickener, accentuating the eggplant shape of his old man's skull, and I'm not quite sure who the hell he is, just that I know him and that this is bad. "Oh," he says. "Uh, Stephanie, right?" And I'm like, Oh, fuck, you've got to be kidding me, and Nabaum says, "What are you doing here? Can't this wait until Thursday? How did you get my address? Is something wrong?"

Standing on his stoop, waiting for God knows what—my faulty vision to clear, maybe, or the entire block to vaporize—I am speechless. And then I pull the storm door all the way open, brush past him, and walk into his foyer, but I know I'm really walking away from something, a lot of things, but it's like maybe this is just what the executioner ordered, or maybe it's not, but the adrenaline running out to my fingers and toes tells me that I'm going to light a major fire here. I take off my coat and hand it to him. "Close the door," I say.

"Really," he says, "I don't know how you got my address, but this isn't the time—"

"Close the door, and take off your pants," I tell him. "This is the time." Let it all burn, the whole fucking world can go up in flames for all I care.

He still doesn't get it, or pretends not to get it. I pull my dress over my head and throw it and my purse across the arm of an overstuffed chair in the living room or parlor, right off the foyer, and stand before him in my underwear. "I'm here to watch you jerk off," I tell him. "Close the door."

And he does, then hangs my coat on a tree in the corner. But he doesn't turn to face me, just sort of cowers before the closed door.

"Turn around," I say.

This is either the best or worst moment of my life.

"Look at me," I say.

"You won't tell?" he says looking into my eyes.

I slide the straps of my bra down my shoulders, exposing my breasts. "Get over here," I say. He walks toward me, head bowed, but sneaking glances. "We usually have a glass of wine first," he says. "Mandy—"

"I'm not Mandy," I say, leading him into the parlor, "and we're not having a glass of wine. Get on your knees." I've never gone in for the domination shit, but right now it's just instinct, payback, a last hurrah or something, like trying to find the absolute bottom. I stick my crotch in his face, and Grandpa starts to lick over the material, which is as close as he'll get, the dry paper skin of his face brushing against my thighs. His smoking jacket has fallen open, and I look down the decay of his torso as he fumbles with his pants and begins to work himself erect, tugging. "Is it good, Mommy?" he says, looking up, his eyes darting between my face and breasts.

"Shut up," I say. "Get on your back, and keep jerking off."

He lies down, and I stand over him, step out of my underwear, and observe the towering genius desperately working away at himself as he drinks in my flesh.

"Can you bend down a little," he says, grunts, his face red and the sweat popping on his forehead, "so your pretty titties hang down over me."

"Sure," I say, because I know what's coming next. I bend a little, swing my breasts three feet over his face, as he grunts and jerks, and right as he comes, a pathetic little dribble that sends a repulsive shudder through the features of his slobbering face, I let loose a stream of pee all over his midsection.

"No," he says, scrambling away, "not like that. The rug," he says, which is where I leave my puddle.

"*Just* like that," I say.

He sits on the floor while I finish, his back propped against some kind of lacquered sea chest, Chinese smoking jacket open, pants and underwear around his ankles, confused, befuddled, possibly horrified, looking only at the stain darkening his precious fucking rug. I reload my bra, throw my underwear in my purse, and slide my dress over my head. "I always thought you were gay," I say. "Everyone does." I grab my coat in the hall, fixing the image of him on the floor in my mind, the last time I will see that motherfucker, to hell with the tip, and slam the door behind me.

For about five seconds out on the street, walking toward Sixth, I feel like I own the place, the entire city—where everyone thinks they are so fucking smart or talented or tough—belongs to me, drops of pee still drying on my legs where I splashed when Gaybaum rolled away. I let cabs pass and walk among the students and fags on Bleecker as I replay the broken, horrified face of Nabaum, and then after a measly four minutes of triumph, I'm like, This is not even funny. And then it's a shame moment, a deep shame moment, when you actually speak out loud, and I say, "Get the fuck out of here," and then, twenty feet later, "Go."

I pick up the pace, trying to draw power from my legs, but, really, I feel like a clock unwinding, like a gravy that's been simmered down to burnt, black goop. I think of the hours I've spent on my knees, on my back, with dicks in my mouth, playing schoolgirl or Mommy, a client's—all right, a john's—clammy corpulent flesh up against my own, and the buckets of come, Dumpsters of come, and there aren't any more plans. No backup. Just the money to spend. And not enough of that. "Run away," the shame voice says. A guy walking toward me looks me up and down, and says, "Did you say something?" I keep moving. I don't want to do this. But I'm going to. The real shame is in losing to loneliness, like you're no longer capable of living only with yourself, or worse, realizing or deciding that being strong isn't enough. But I've already surrendered. And realizing that, surrendering to surrender, I even start to worry that he won't be there.

≡

The sound of the phone ringing was so foreign to his ears that his entire body jerked in alarm. They'd found him. Someone had found him. Klister was here to kill him. The second ring pushed him into motion, and by the third he had his pants on and was scanning the room for his shoes, hoping that the fire stairs exited somewhere other than the lobby, through a basement or something, where he'd find another set of stairs that would lead to an unmarked exit at street level. In a movie, he'd be sliding a round into the chamber of his automatic about now, parting the yellowed lace curtains or looking around the edge of a stained paper shade, waiting for the shoot-out. How stupid his life was. Fuck it. He picked up the phone, steeling himself.

"Hey," she said, "what are you doing? Can I come up?"

A narcotic relief flooded every cell in his body. "Sure," he said, "nine-seventeen." And then it was more than relief. Now, she was coming to him. To hell with the suffering. He'd have plenty of time for that later; he'd devote the rest of his life to it.

He piled the dinner dishes in the sink in the kitchenette, wiped down the counter, and then she was knocking.

He looked at himself in the mirror by the door, couldn't tell if he looked okay, or, really what that would even look like. She was only a few feet away, on the other side of a steel door. He opened it. She was smiling, but it was like a real smile, like a joy smile, like she was really happy to see him.

"Hey," he said, ushering her in. "What are you doing here? I'm surprised to see you."

"Is it too late?" she said, taking off her coat and throwing it over a chair.

"No," he said, exerting an effort not to look at her ass, hating himself a little for wanting to look, and for not looking. "Not at all. Can I get you something to drink? Coffee, wine?"

"Yeah, wine," she said. "Wine would be good."

She followed him into the kitchenette, sat at the table while he opened a bottle.

For a second, he thought she might be there to shoot him, even flinched a little, anticipating a round in the back, then shook it off. "So what are you doing here?" he said, putting a glass in front of her. "You want to sit in the kitchen?"

"Sure," she said. "No, I was just walking by your building. Oh, God," she said. "Hey, can I have a cigarette?"

He brought an ashtray from the living room and put it on the table between them, shook out a cigarette and handed her the lighter, then lit one for himself. "I'm just surprised," he said.

"Yeah, me too," she said. "Or, I don't know. I just got a wild hair or something."

She was nervous, sitting at his table, drinking his wine, smoking his cigarettes, her eyes all over the room.

"It scared the shit out of me when the phone rang," he said. "It never has here."

"Yeah," she said. "You're on the run, huh?" She smiled, and then the smile turned into a grimace. "I'm sorry," she said. "Forget it. That's none of my business."

"No," he said. "It's okay," but he wasn't ready to go on, didn't know how to continue. He jammed his cigarette out in the ashtray and shook out another one. She slid her hand across the table palm up. He shook out another cigarette for her.

"No," she said. "Give me your hand."

He put his hand on top of hers. Her palm was warm and dry. She wrapped her fingers around the side of his hand, pushed the crook of her thumb deeper into his, tightening the fit. He had never felt so grateful for anything in his life. She was looking down at their hands. He closed his eyes. When he opened them she was looking at him. "Did you hurt somebody?" she said, all eyes. "Did you kill somebody? Rape somebody?"

He shook his head, not trusting his voice. She put her other hand on top of his.

"I hurt people," he said, "yes." His throat felt too tight to talk. He pushed against it, and then couldn't stop. "But not like you think. Not like a crime. Not that kind of crime. Not physically."

"Okay," she said. "It's okay. Forget it. It's none of my business, anyway."

"No," he said. "I'll tell you some time." He pushed his hand against hers, answering her pressure. "It can be your business."

Her eyes started moving again, darting around the room, floor, table, wall, ceiling.

"Let's do have a cigarette," she said, but she left one hand in his. She picked up the cigarettes from the table, handed him one. "You know," she said to the wall over his shoulder, to the floor, "I prepared all kinds of lies on my way over." She laughed a little, looked at him, looked at their hands. He waited. Ten seconds passed.

"I just want to get out of here," she finally said. She lit her cigarette, handed him the lighter, then pulled her hand away from him. It was a loss and a relief. She looped her hair over her ear, a kind of tic. "I just want to get out of here," she said again, studying the floor.

"All right," he said.

"I mean the city," she said.

"I know what you mean," he said.

She wouldn't look up from the floor. Her forehead was wrinkled, and it seemed that she was exerting an enormous effort to contain herself, to keep from crying, to keep from falling to pieces.

He stood and walked around the table, put his hands on her shoulders. He felt like a robot, and she flinched at first, but then settled back against his touch. His hands started to move a little, just pressure, testing, and then he was caressing her, the first woman he had touched other than his wife since college, rubbing one hand through and then under her hair and up and down the delicate skin of her neck. She bowed her head, rotated it as he massaged her neck.

He cleared his throat. "What about school?"

"No," she said. "It's over."

"All right," he said. Her skin was warm, as soft as anything he had ever touched.

"It has to be all right."

"It is," he said. Anything would be.

"Do you want to know one of the lies?" she said, craning her neck to look at him, then turning back to the table.

"Not really."

"I was going to tell you that I'd gone independent. That I'd negotiate the out-of-town rate with you directly."

He ran the backs of his hands along the sides of her throat, then slid one down the front of her dress, rubbing her chest above her breasts, all this warm skin feeding the hunger he thought had died, then farther down with both hands.

"Stop," she said.

"I've got plenty of money," he said. "That won't be—"

She pulled his hands out of her dress and held on to his wrists as she twisted around in her chair. "Fuck you," she said. She stood, pushing his wrists away.

"What?" he said. "I didn't mean—I just meant that you don't have to worry about money, that money's not an issue."

She bowed her head, so that she had to look up at him through lowered eyelids, which she batted as she grinned. "You gonna take care of me, Daddy? Huh?" She ran the tip of her tongue around her lips. "Baby needs a daddy. Baby needs some of Daddy's big cock. And some pretty new shoes."

He turned from her, walked out to the living room. When he looked back, she was on the kitchen table facing him, her dress pulled up around her hips. "Come on," she said. "Here it is."

He sat on the couch. "That's not what I meant," he said.

"I try to tell you one true thing," she said, "and you reduce me to a cunt and torso with legs and a head attached."

"No," he said. "I'm sorry. I care about you."

"No, you don't. You don't even know me."

"And you don't know me, but you're here."

"But, then, again, I *am* a whore. You know that much."

"No, you're not."

"Yes, I am," she said. "Look at me."

She smirked, tossed her hair from side to side, her dress still up and her legs still open.

"Is that what you want?" he said. "You want me to treat you like shit."

"Yeah," she said. "I want you to slap me around. That's the only way I can get off anymore."

He ran his fingertips over his closed eyelids. He didn't deserve it anyway. Of course he didn't deserve it. He deserved to starve. And now he'd fucked up even the chance to ever talk to her again. He heard her feet hit the floor, her steps into the living room, and when he opened his eyes she was putting her coat on.

He watched her. When she turned her head to look at him, he said, "Don't go."

"Why not?"

"Because," he said.

She studied him, waiting.

"I don't know the right answer," he said. "Just because."

She still waited.

"We'll finish the wine," he said. "Order some food. Open another bottle if we feel like it."

Her face was blank as she looked at him.

"Because you like me," he said. "Because you came here. Because we're going to take a trip, get out of the city. Remember?"

She looked at the floor, then back to him.

"Because you want to know my story," he said. "Because you told me one true thing."

"Yeah," she said. "And what was that?"

"Take off your coat," he said.

"What was it?"

"About a lie."

She took off her coat, dropped it onto the back of the chair. "And you like *me*," she said, "even though you don't know me."

"I know you."

"No, you don't." She walked to the couch, stood before him and lifted the hem of her dress above her knee.

"I told you," he said. "I'm not going to treat you that way."

"Well," she said, "this is about one true thing." She put her left foot up on the couch beside him, still holding her dress over her knee. "I want you to put your face up against my leg," she said.

He shook his head, looked away.

"This has nothing to do with sex," she said. "Believe me. Or maybe it does, but not like you think. I just want you to get to know me. I want you to put your face against my leg and take a nice deep breath. Come on. This is one true thing, and then we can drink wine and order Chinese."

He moved his face against her leg.

"Smell it?" she said.

He inhaled, smelled piss, nodded, moved his head back.

She dropped the hem of her dress. "Still hungry?" she said.

"Why? Are you going to piss on me?"

"No, that was an earlier appointment. One of my professors," she said, walking to the kitchen and returning with the wineglasses, "though I didn't know it beforehand."

"Jesus," he said, taking the glass she offered.

"Yeah, it was pretty fucked up, but probably a long time coming."

"What, and he wanted to be pissed on?"

"No," she said, "that was for me, to mark the end of my academic career." She placed the ashtray and the cigarettes on the coffee table between them, then sat across from him, her legs thrown over one arm of the chair, and her head tilted back against the other, so that she faced the big picture window, showing him her profile in the dim light. He took a drink of wine, then sprawled on the couch facing the same window.

"You want to know more?" she said.

"It doesn't bother me," he said.

"It doesn't bother me, either," she said. "And I have my own money. What are you running from?" she said.

He pulled a cigarette from the pack, rolled it between his palms. Everything, he thought. He put the cigarette on the table, took a drink of wine. She waited, didn't look at him, seemed to be good at waiting. He lit the cigarette. "Things were fucked up," he said. "I'd pretty much lost my family, was living in a hotel for a couple of weeks."

"Why?" she said. "What did you do to them?"

"No, it wasn't like that. My marriage went bad, disintegrated—a lot of stuff happened—but that's not what I'm talking about."

"Throw me one of those," she said.

He tossed her the cigarettes.

And then he told her about the money, how he'd uncovered the scam in the Benefit Fund, how Klister and McCabe were using kick-backs from an insurance company and some care providers to skim the fund and move the money to an offshore account, how he'd flown down to Barbados to retrieve a portion of it, how he walked away with four hundred and fifty grand. How he walked out of his own life. He didn't tell her about Carrie, about Corey, about oral sodomy and ther-apy and prosecutors and cops. He told her about money. He told her how, fifteen years before, Klister had beaten a man nearly to death with a shovel for fucking his wife.

"Men are such assholes that way," she said.

"Yeah," he said. He closed his eyes.

"And what about your kids?" she said.

He put his hands over his face. The last time he'd seen them was at lunch on that Saturday before he'd run, before the second and last ses-sion of marriage counseling. He picked them up from what had previ-ously been his house, and drove them down to Ann Arbor to eat out on the lawn of the Diag.

"When are you going to come home?" Carrie asked.

"Here," he said. "You want some cole slaw?"

She shook her head. "When?"

"Remember when we talked?" he said. "It's just for a little while."

"Because of the trial?" Carrie said.

Tommy rolled on the grass toward a homeless-looking guy pounding bongos.

"No," Elgin said. "You know how you sometimes like alone time in your room?"

She held her sandwich in front of her face, not eating it, not moving.

Tommy stood and handled the homeless guy's dreadlocks. The guy was smiling, seemed harmless.

"See," Elgin said, "Mommy and I just need a little alone time."

"How long?" Carrie asked.

"Tommy!" Elgin called. "Come over here."

"Tomorrow?" Carrie said.

"I don't know," Elgin said, but he did know, and he knew that it was wrong to lie to her, but he didn't know how to say "never."

"Not so long," he said. "Tommy!" he called, standing to retrieve him. "Come on, now."

He took them out for ice cream and drove them home. He didn't try to talk to Laura. There was no point. He went back to his hotel and sat in his room, watching the day fade, knowing they were gone from him, that somehow, somehow, he'd lost them, but not knowing how or why exactly. Just that somehow, he'd become entirely irrelevant to them, to himself—

"Hey," Carla said.

He jerked his head, opened his eyes. She knelt on the floor beside the couch. She ran a hand over his hair. "It's okay," she said. "Come on, why don't you go to bed."

He lifted himself upright on the couch. "I just lost them," he said. "Okay? Like a set of keys. There's not a matter of degrees there. You don't partially lose your keys: they're either lost or they're not lost. I don't know why. I mean, I sort of do, but mainly they're just lost. I'm not saying that's good, but—"

"Okay," she said, offering her hands, "that's okay."

He took her hands and she pulled him up from the couch, put her arms around him, her face against his neck, the smell of her hair, the feel of it against his face. He held her against him, the drowning man, all this radiant warmth, ran his hands over her back, pulled her toward him tighter still, holding her, holding on, and she said, "Okay, okay," until he let her go.

He told her to take the bedroom; he'd take the couch.

"No," she said. "I should get going."

"Come on," he said. "What, you don't trust me?" Stay! he wanted to scream. You have to stay!

"Why should I trust you?"

"I don't know."

"I don't trust anyone."

"Neither do I," he said.

He kissed her at the door and she let herself be kissed and then she was kissing him back, and he put his arms around her again, pulling her toward him, and he was drowning in the touch, thoughtless, not breathing, breathing her breath, conscienceless, the warmth of her body as she held on to him, as she answered him, and nothing but touch and the warmth of her mouth, the skin of her neck, her hands, and everything underneath radiating this warmth, feeding and encouraging the hunger until she finally pulled away.

"I should go," she said, and he said, "Stay."

"But I should go," she said.

He walked her to the elevator, kissed her again.

"Okay," she said.

"I'll call you tomorrow," he said.

"We'll see," she said.

After she was gone, he sat on the couch, resisting the urge to take out the picture of the kids, resisting the urge to punish himself, and failing, clawing after guilt and self-loathing. Kissing another woman, wanting to hold on to her and fuck her and have her for himself, while Laura changed diapers and wiped up vomit and loved and took care of the children they had brought into this miserable fucked-up world. And he had chosen to be dead to them. And then to hold Carla against him, to feel the warmth and feed that hunger. He was either dead or he wasn't dead; he couldn't have it both ways.

"Daddy's in heaven," Laura would tell them, or, maybe, "Daddy won't be able to attend your recital, baseball game, parade, birthday party, breakfast, lunch, dinner, because Daddy's in hell."

If he had killed Corey, he would have lost them, but maybe not forever. If he had fought harder against Laura he would have lost them. And Laura he'd lost long ago, though he hadn't known it.

And if he'd stayed? Would he be more dead if he'd stayed?

Heaven or hell, he was gone.

He thought of the Dylan song "It's Alright, Ma," and wondered how long he'd been busy dying—all of his life? No, it couldn't be— and wondered if there was any way to reverse the trend, to get busy being born. He doubted it. He picked up the piece of paper with Carla's phone number on it, tasted her mouth on his lips. She was home by now, probably, asleep or not asleep, but there seemed to be little question as to whether or not she was alive. And Carrie asleep in her bed. And Tommy, maybe not in the crib anymore. And Corey in a cell in Children's Village. And all the kids whose parents had died, all asleep, all over the world sleeping. And Elgin in Carla's chair, holding her phone number, holding his chin in his hand, looking out the window of his box, waiting for morning, waiting for Carla, the warmth of her skin, her mouth, hoping and hating himself for the hope, and hoping anyway.

SIX

JUNE

Hearn and Jervac sat on the couch in the living room, while Laura organized coffee. "And you can't say anything until I get in there," she called from the kitchen. The kids were in bed asleep. Elgin offered the cops a drink, which they declined. "She gave us a lot," Jervac said. "She's real bright."

"Not until I get in there," Laura called out.

Earlier, when they'd returned from McDonald's and played Jervac's message on the machine—that he had good news and wanted to stop by—Carrie said, "Is Lou coming over? Because he could put Anika to bed if he wants."

"It's already late, sweetie," Elgin said. "You'll be asleep," and he ushered her upstairs and filled the bathtub.

"They got him," Laura said out in the hallway, after putting Tommy down. The color was high on her cheeks, her eyes clear and cold. Carrie talked to her dolls in the tub. "I just know they got him."

Sometime the previous evening, four or five hundred hours ago, Laura had appeared unable to hold her head up, her face wet and ragged and imprinted with the horror of death. Now she appeared fresh and vibrant, ready to host a cocktail party. Elgin was exhausted.

After calling Jervac, who told him nothing, except that he'd be over within the hour, Elgin read Carrie chapter two of *Black Beauty,* in which Beauty and several other young colts witness a hunt. The dogs kill the rabbit, but two horses go down, and a rider dies of a broken neck. One of the horses comes up lame. There's a gunshot, and then "the black horse moved no more."

"Why?" Carrie said. She lifted her head from Elgin's chest and looked at him, squinting, disgusted.

"Because he's dead."

"Why'd they have to kill him?"

Elgin propped the pillows up higher on Carrie's backboard. "His leg was broken," he said, "remember?"

Laura came in and lay beside them, hugging Carrie between her and Elgin.

"They killed him just because his leg was broken," Carrie said to Laura.

"That's what they did then, honey," Laura said. "They couldn't fix a broken leg."

"Because it was the olden days?" Carrie said, and Laura said, "Yes."

"Then I hate the olden days," Carrie said.

"And I don't like that kind of language," Laura said.

Who gave a shit about the language, Elgin thought, but they were both quiet, and he finished the chapter, with young Gordon being buried in the churchyard: "'twas all for one little hare."

"'Twas," Laura said.

"'Twas?" Carrie said.

"'Twas," Laura said.

"It's been a long day," Elgin said to Carrie, putting the book aside, and kissing the top of her head.

Laura gave her one last hug. "And you were very brave," she said.

And thank God it's over, Elgin thought.

He was surprised to see Hearn standing beside Jervac when he opened the door. Even though it was still full humidity and close to ninety degrees, Jervac had his jacket on and his tie knotted tight against his throat. Hearn's short-sleeve shirt was sweated through at the armpits. "Did you get him?" Laura asked, before Elgin had even closed the door, and Hearn said, "He's being detained."

"Excellent," Laura said. "I'll get the coffee."

Elgin ushered the cops into the living room, gestured toward the couch, where the two men sat. Hearn looked at the floor, at his feet. Jervac studied the walls.

"So what'd he do, confess?" Laura asked, distributing the coffee. She sat in the rocking chair across from Elgin.

"No," Hearn said. "He's been arrested on the strength of your daughter's statement."

"Carrie was very good today," Jervac said. "Very clear about time and the sequence of events. What she gave us is typical of this kind of crime, how a victim is groomed by a perp, how there's an escalation of deviant sexual behavior."

"Deviant?" Elgin said.

"It's all deviant at this age," Hearn said.

"What's not typical," Jervac said, "especially for a child this age, was the clarity of her statement and the specificity. I want to start by telling you what I learned today, which conforms to what you told Lieutenant Hearn on the phone last night, Mrs. Elgin. Carrie alleges that there were three separate and distinct incidents of criminal sexual conduct in the first degree—a felony—and that—"

"Meaning what?" Elgin said.

"A felony?"

"No," Elgin said. "Sexual criminal conduct, whatever you said."

And Jervac said, "Criminal sexual conduct in the first degree. Meaning penetration occurred."

"Penetration?"

Hearn nodded at Elgin. "Right," he said. "Oral sodomy. Just like what you thought."

His daughter, not even six, and they calmly said, "Oral sodomy."

"As if that matters," Laura said, glaring at Elgin. "Let him talk."

Oral sodomy; blow job; cock sucking.

Jervac mechanically discussed multiple events of fondling, misdemeanor counts, the perp's grooming of Carrie, the escalation, "and she said that it began just *before* you went to Disney World in the winter," he said. "When did that occur?"

"March," Laura said. "I can get you the dates."

Sodomy World; Fondle Mountain; Pedophiles of the Caribbean.

"Okay," Jervac said. "This specificity in the sequence of events is what the prosecutor's office likes so much, and again, this is what's so unusual in a child this age."

"And that's why you arrested him?" Laura asked.

"Right," Jervac said.

"But he denied it?"

"Right."

"Which is not unusual," Hearn said.

"I thought they liked to confess," Elgin said.

"There's still a lot of time for that," Hearn said.

They stayed for two hours, trying to nail down specific dates on which the various incidents might have occurred, which was, of course, impossible, asking questions about what Carrie might have been wearing on those unknown dates, wondering about "physical evidence," which they referred to as incriminating stains, asking about Carrie's behavior at school. Sometime in the middle of it Elgin poured a scotch, which the others declined. The smell of blood was in the room, the wolves gearing up for a kill. He found himself drifting in and out of the conversation, watching Laura ask and answer questions. She seemed happier than he'd seen her in years.

"Monday?" she said. "Carrie has an appointment at two o'clock with her therapist."

Therapist? *Her* therapist? "What therapist?" Elgin said. "What appointment?"

"Pat Connoly," Laura said. "I forgot to tell you. I set it up this afternoon."

"Who's Pat Connoly?"

"She's very good," Laura said. "Moved all kinds of appointments to fit us in."

"Anyway," Hearn said, "I'm sure the prosecutor's office will work around it. There'll be an arraignment for the suspect on Monday morning, when the judge will decide whether or not to keep him detained."

"You mean he could get out?" Laura said. "Where is he, anyway?"

"He's up at Children's Village," Hearn said, "but don't let the name fool you. He's in a lockdown."

"But now you're saying he can get out."

"This is why the prosecutor's office is going to want to move so fast. A lot will happen in the next week. They can tell you better than we can. They'll be calling you tomorrow."

Tomorrow? Tomorrow was Sunday. Couldn't they get a day off?

"And I know you know this, but don't have any contact with the family. We told them the same. There's absolutely no point in talking to them now." Hearn stood and then Jervac stood. "Is there anything else we can tell you or help you with?"

"No," Elgin said, pulling himself out of his seat. Just get out of here, he thought.

"Not right now," Laura said.

"Thank you," they said together.

After walking the cops out, Elgin found Laura in the kitchen. "Thank God they got him," Laura said, putting the last cup in the dishwasher. "I'm exhausted," she said. "I'm going to bed." She didn't seem exhausted. She pecked his cheek. "Are you coming up?" she asked.

"In a little while," he said.

"Thank God they got him," she said. "Thank God that's over."

Elgin poured another drink. He was bone tired. It hadn't really even begun. It seemed likely that the cure would kill them all.

Sunday morning, sometime during the phone call with Karen Shemerman, the assistant prosecutor from the Child Sexual Assault Section, Elgin remembered the Jeep—*his* Jeep—parked at the office. They'd go get it and take a ride up to Frankenmuth and have a famous chicken dinner and visit Santa's workshop. Of course it would be idiotic, but the kids would love it. Everybody would enjoy the ride. He wondered where the keys were, what he'd done with them. He hadn't seen them since the initial drive.

"Right," Karen said, "and at the conclusion of the interview, a multidiscovery team of professionals will discuss whether there's significant evidence to prosecute the offender, or if further investigation is warranted."

"Wait, what?" Elgin said.

"After the interview at Care House," Laura said.

"What interview?" Elgin said. "What's Care House?" and Laura said, "Are you paying no attention?"

"It's okay," Karen said, and she went over it again, how Carrie would be interviewed on Monday morning by Karen, with Liz—the prosecutor's social worker victim advocate—present, how there would be a one-way mirror in the room at Care House, behind which would be a video camera and the multidiscovery team, whatever the fuck that was, and Robert and Laura, as well, watching their daughter's words of victimization scraped out by the dull spoon of justice. And then a decision would be made as to whether or not they would prosecute.

"And then it's over," Elgin said. "Then she can go back to being a kid."

There were three or four seconds of silence. Laura sighed. Karen said, "I'm afraid not, Mr. Elgin. There will be an emergency arraignment tomorrow morning to determine if the suspect should continue to be held until the probable cause hearing later in the week. Based on what you've told me, where he lives and the threat he poses, we'll argue to keep him detained."

"What threat?" Elgin said.

"That will be determined at the arraignment," Karen said. "If there's a history, if there's the possibility of other children involved, if a preliminary investigation and therapeutic evaluation by Children's Protective Services reveals evidence that he himself is the victim of abuse. But, from your point of view, the proximity is the main issue."

From the window in the den, Elgin could see the Newkirk house on the other side of McKechrin's place, maybe four hundred feet away. There was no sign of life. He was not afraid of Corey getting his hands on Carrie again, at least not in the next few days. It wasn't as if he was going to advocate for the little fuck, but he could certainly protect his daughter from a pimply, skinny twelve-year-old. Not that he had in the past.

"And the real tricky part," Karen said, "will be the probable cause hearing on Thursday or Friday. If he's still denying, and we'll know that tomorrow, Carrie will have to testify."

"For what?" Elgin said. He pictured her on the stand being torn to shreds by some vicious prick of an attorney, trying to make her into a liar, forcing her to go over and over the sordid details, ingraining them as the most significant and memorable events of her life.

"To determine if he should continue to be detained until trial!" Laura said.

"Oh," Elgin said. "And what if we decline to press charges. What if there is no trial."

"That will never happen," Laura said.

"Even if it did," Karen said, "in many ways it's no longer your decision. If we decide to prosecute, it's in the name of the people and in consideration of *their* welfare."

"Oh," Elgin said. "So my daughter's welfare is now your prerogative."

"Robert, come off it," Laura said.

So it was already out of their hands and Artie had been entirely wrong.

"You should know, Mr. Elgin, that in most cases, the victim is empowered by prosecution. The victim feels a sense of justice and vindication. Most therapists recognize a therapeutic value in the process, and we have an excellent team. We're not going to use your daughter. Liz is a very strong advocate, and I'm not interested in seeing your daughter hurt any more than she already has been."

He wondered how much therapeutic value Karen herself derived from all of this, but there was no point fighting; he certainly did not want to antagonize the people who would be making decisions about how Carrie was to be treated in court.

"And we can recommend therapists, as well," Karen said.

"That's been taken care of," Laura said.

It seemed to Elgin that everything was being taken care of, whether he liked it or not. After the phone call, he took Carrie for a ride to pick up the new Jeep. He didn't tell Laura where they were going, just that it was a surprise. Frankenmuth and the famous chicken dinner seemed out of the question now, but he had to get away and be alone with Carrie. See how she was. Conduct his own evaluation.

And she seemed fine, if a little aloof. But, hell, maybe it was him that was aloof. It didn't seem right to talk to her about what was coming up with the assistant prosecutor, not until he talked to Laura and they could decide together how to approach that, but he brought it up anyway. After they picked up the Cherokee, which Carrie was not very interested in, and were headed home on 96, Elgin said, "Officer Jervac said you did a real good job yesterday." The car felt stolen.

"Yeah," Carrie said. "He took a picture of my hands on the copy machine and hung them on the wall. There were other kids' hands there, too."

"That's neat," Elgin said. "You know, tomorrow, some other people want to talk to you about it, a lady named Karen and a lady named Liz."

Carrie shrugged. "And Mom said Corey went away."

"Right," Elgin said. "These people, Karen and Liz, they're going to decide if they should, if they should—do you know what court is?"

"No," Carrie said. She was fiddling with the electric window, rolling it up and down.

"Come on," Elgin said. "Leave that alone."

She put her hands in her lap and looked at the road out the windshield.

"Remember that big jail, that big prison, in Jackson?" It was like a medieval castle, with enormous stone walls and observation posts rising up off each corner, the castle's towers, and plenty of modern razor wire over the chain-link fence surrounding the exercise yard.

Carrie didn't say anything, her hands fidgeting in her lap.

Elgin looked at her. "Remember?"

She nodded, looked down, then back up at him, then out her window.

"What's the matter?"

She had been fascinated and horrified by the prison, talking about it for days after they drove by it last year. Elgin remembered her waking from a nightmare about it, and having to explain that she would not have to live there, that it was for bad people, and he realized now what a mistake it had been bringing it up. She'd drawn pictures of it: where the bad people lived.

"Is Corey there?" she said.

"No," he said.

"Am I going to have to go there?"

"No!" he said. "Absolutely not."

"Oh," she said.

"Here," he said, "give me your hand."

He took her hand, and said, "What happens in court is that a guy, a judge is what he's called, like Granddaddy was, he decides if somebody did something wrong, if they have to be punished." She studied the floor, a grimace on her face, but he plowed on. "For grown-ups, for grown-ups who hurt other people or steal from them, sometimes that means they have to go to jail."

"Is that where Corey is?"

"No!" Elgin said again. "He's in a place for children that has doctors and people who want to help him."

"With his mom and dad?"

"I don't know," Elgin said. "I don't think so. But I think they visit him."

"Is he going to be there forever?"

"No," Elgin said. He should not have brought this up. "In court, though, the judge will decide if he should be away for a while, away from people that he could maybe hurt."

"Like who?"

"Well," Elgin said, "like you, I guess."

"He's going to hurt me?"

"No," Elgin said. "But what he did was wrong, and the judge will decide how he should be punished. And people will want to talk to you about it, to figure out just what happened."

"I already told."

"I know you did, baby. And you might have to tell a few more times, just so everyone understands. Do you think you could do that?"

"I don't know," Carrie said, choking out the words as she started to cry. "I don't want to go to jail!"

Elgin pulled over onto the shoulder. "Come here, baby," he said, pulling her onto his lap. She leaned against the horn and it blared, and he pulled her tighter against him. "You're not going to go to jail," he said. "I promise. You're not going anywhere."

"You're hurting me!" she said.

"It's okay," he said. "These people aren't scary or mean and they want to help you, and they want to find out what the right thing to do is."

"I don't want help!" she said.

"Shh," Elgin said. "It's really not a big deal. I like these people and I think you will, too." His capacity for lying was limitless—anything to calm her. He held her against him for what seemed like a long time.

Finally, she sniffled a little, wiped at her face. "Will Lou be there?"

"Yes," he said. He'd have to make sure of that. He continued to hold her, petting her hair as she went all the way limp in his arms. "Do you think we should go to Brown's?" he said. "Get a little lunch. Maybe an ice cream?"

"Yes," she said. "I think maybe we should get a little lunch and then have a little ice cream for dessert. Maybe the clown kind."

"Yes," Elgin said. "Definitely the clown kind."

A late model Cadillac was in the driveway when they returned home, Elgin failing to identify it for a few seconds, wondering if the assistant prosecutor had decided to come over to the house, or if it was Jervac's, until Carrie shrieked, "Gramma and Granddaddy are here," and even then he couldn't quite believe it, but, yes, certainly, it was Laura's parents' car, and just what the hell were they doing here, all the way on the other side of the state? Ed met him at the door, Carrie already in his arms. Joyce and Laura were in the kitchen with Tommy, more sweets baking in the oven. Elgin went upstairs and called Pearson at home, told him he wouldn't be in tomorrow, told him as little as possible about what had happened. "Jesus," Pearson said, "take as much time as you need." He took a shower, clipped his toenails, clipped his fingernails, shaved, brushed his teeth, and ran out of personal hygiene activities.

"Whose Jeep is that?" Laura asked him, when he finally went downstairs.

"Ours," he said. "The county's. Ours to use."

"Carrie said you went out to lunch, that you told her about tomorrow."

They stood by the washer and dryer in the mudroom by the back door. "Yes," he said. "I didn't intend to."

"Well, you could have called. I'd made lunch."

"Oh," he said. "And you could have told me your parents were coming."

"Why? Is there a problem with that?"

"No," he said. "I just didn't know."

"I thought we'd be happy to have them for the next few days. For Tommy. I think we'll be gone a lot, and I'd rather have family for this."

"No," he said. "You're right."

The day dragged on. He wished there was an emergency at work to call him away. It was like a wake, putting in time, waiting to leave, being polite to the in-laws. He and Ed took Tommy down to the playground at the elementary school. Ed asked about work. "It's fine," Elgin said. "It's going well."

"I've thought a lot about that arbitration you were talking about with the cops," Ed said. "It's really not much more than structured bargaining."

"No," Elgin said. "You're right." What had he been so uptight about? To think that a few weeks before he had considered this minor political deal some kind of enormous ethical dilemma struck him now as absurd. Negotiations were never what they appeared to be on the surface. A casual viewer would never see how deals were made behind closed doors, which, regardless of sunshine laws, were where they always occurred. And in this case, all parties would know exactly what was being bargained and how. Only the public wouldn't know. And they never knew anyway. The deputies, and ultimately the state police, would get agency shop in exchange for supporting McCabe. It just was not a big deal. He'd been acting like a child.

After dinner and a bath, he read Carrie chapter 3 of *Black Beauty*, regarding Beauty's breaking in, Carrie snuggled into the crook of his shoulder, smelling of soap and shampoo, and every other line of the book seemed weighted with significance in light of the last few days, as Beauty explains how a broken-in horse "must never start at what he sees, nor speak to other horses, nor bite, nor kick, nor have any will of his own; but always do his master's will, even though he may be very tired or hungry; but the worst of all is, when his harness is once on, he may neither jump for joy nor lie down for weariness." Elgin recalled his sense of loss during Carrie's first days in kindergarten the previous fall, when she, along with the rest of the children, seemed to be similarly broken in, standing in lines, harnessed with rules about when they could speak and how they could play and what they could draw. Then, at the end of the chapter, Beauty's mother warns about "bad, cruel men who never ought to have a horse or dog to call their own," and Elgin waited for Carrie to mention Corey, and was grateful when she did not.

Laura kneeled by Carrie's bed and gave her a kiss. "We're all so proud of you for being such a big, brave girl," she said. "Gramma and Granddaddy and me and Daddy. And tomorrow I know you'll be just as brave. And I think you're really going to like Karen and Liz."

"And Daddy said Lou was going to be there, too."

Laura kissed Carrie's brow, squinting at Elgin over her head.

"Yeah," he said. "I have to double check on that."

And when he called, and when Jervac actually answered his cell phone, and said that he'd planned to be there, it felt like a significant victory. Daddy could deliver after all.

Downstairs they dealt a few hands of bridge, but mostly talked about prosecutors and court and Children's Village and therapy and arraignments and probable cause hearings and Children's Protective Services and victim advocates and permanent scars and supportive families and acting-out behaviors and other symptoms of abuse and vindication and rehabilitation and catharsis and justice and the twisted predators getting younger by the minute. And Elgin could not wait to get back to work.

Jervac wore polka-dotted suspenders over a white starched shirt, a pink tie and no jacket, and he sat right behind Carrie, beside Liz during the interview. Whenever Carrie seemed unsure, she'd turn to Jervac, who would nod, or say, "You want to take a break?" or, "Just tell Karen like you told me." Karen Shemerman wore a black prosecutor's uniform, an expensive, well-cut suit with a skirt to the knee and big boxy shoulders and big silver buttons on the jacket. Carrie didn't trust her. Neither did Elgin. He sat beside Laura in the observation room, behind the mirror, with the video camera and Hearn and a few other people from the prosecutor's office. After introducing herself, Karen asked if Carrie knew why she was there.

"To tell you what happened?" Carrie said.

"Okay," Karen said. "Right. Do you know what my job is?"

"To ask me what happened?" Carrie said.

"Right," Karen said, laughing, like, ain't that adorable?

Carrie looked at the floor.

Already, Karen seemed to be playing to the camera. "I'm an assistant prosecutor," she said. "Do you know what that is?"

She was handling it all wrong, setting it up like a quiz, placing Carrie in a struggle to find the right answer. She obviously didn't have kids.

"It's a judge?" Carrie said.

"No," Karen said. "But my job is to help you tell the judge what happened, and to help the judge make a decision about it." She knelt in front of Carrie's chair, close to her, another mistake, crowding her. Carrie turned to Jervac. He smiled, nodded. Karen said, "Can you tell me what happened?"

Carrie was sliding down deeper into her seat. She looked at the mirror, right at Elgin it seemed. This was all wrong. This was fucking crazy. It wasn't fair that they should be observing this without Carrie's knowledge, without her consent. Five seconds passed. Carrie wriggled in her chair. Karen looked at Lou, who said, "It's okay, Carrie. Just tell Karen like you told me," and Elgin wondered if Jervac was irritated as well, if he felt that he was a better investigator. Why wasn't Karen creating any context for her questions?

"Carrie," Karen said. "Have you ever been touched in a way that made you feel funny or bad or uncomfortable?"

Carrie shrugged, rolling her shoulders and neck, wriggling her upper body as she slid deeper into her chair, so that her back was now flat against the seat.

"Sit up," Elgin said, and Laura shushed him.

Carrie's voice was tiny when she finally repeated Laura's words: "We don't touch people in their private areas."

"Okay," Karen said. "We can come back to this later, if you want. Maybe now we could play a game. Do you like games, Carrie?"

Carrie gave an obligatory nod: *I'm a child; you want me to like games; so, yes, I like games; is that the right answer?*

Karen sat in a chair across from Carrie and held a large floppy doll in her lap, and, for the first time, did the right thing. She started brushing the doll's hair as she talked, giving Carrie something to focus on, engaging in an activity that Carrie herself would enjoy. "What I want you to do," Karen said, "is to point to the body part that I name. So, if I say 'hair,' you point here to this doll's hair. Okay?" Carrie nodded and became noticeably more relaxed as Karen moved through the body parts and Carrie correctly identified each one. "Excellent," Karen said. "Okay, now I want you to say it, instead of pointing. "What do you call the part of your body that you walk on?"

"Foot," Carrie said. "Or leg."

"Good. What part of your body eats food?"

"Mouth," Carrie said, and now she seemed to be settling in, actually enjoying it. Maybe Karen wasn't so bad after all.

After ten or fifteen questions, Karen said, "And what part of your body goes to the bathroom?"

"Bottom," Carrie said.

"And what about pee?" Karen said, and Carrie said, "Vagina," and Karen said, "What about where a boy goes pee?" and Carrie said, "Penis."

"Okay," Karen said. "What part do you hear with?"

After a few more correct answers from Carrie, Karen said, "Can you tell me if lunch comes before dinner, or after dinner?"

"Before," Carrie said.

"That's right," Karen said. "You sure have answered a lot of questions for me. Now, I wonder if we could go back and talk about what you talked about with Detective Jervac."

"Lou," Carrie said, still in rapid-fire answer mode.

"Right," Karen said. "Lou. You told him that something happened. That there was some touching in private places. Did someone touch you that way?"

Elgin glanced at Laura, who was intensely focused on Carrie. He didn't want to hear this, and hated himself a little for his weakness or aversion, but who the hell *would* want to hear it?

"No," Carrie said. She turned to Lou, who raised his eyebrows. "Yes," she said, facing Karen. "But it was a game."

"What kind of a game. How did the game work?"

"Is Corey in jail?"

"He's in a place where he can't hurt anybody," Karen said.

"Did he hurt somebody?" Carrie asked.

"Did he hurt you?"

"No," Carrie said. "It was just a game."

"Can you tell me about it?"

Carrie looked at Lou one more time before launching into a narrative of the events, each detail making Elgin more uncomfortable, as if his bones were suddenly the wrong size, expanding and crushing down into his guts and pushing out against his skin, which seemed two sizes too small. They showed each other things down on the couch behind a locked door in the playroom while Angela watched television in the family room. There was candy and paper dolls, and they kissed and touched tongues and he tickled her a lot and played a licking game and she showed him her bottom and he showed her his bottom and they hugged and played house and Corey was the daddy and Carrie was the mommy and they used Angela's doll, Cathy, as the baby, and, when Karen asked if Carrie had ever seen Corey's penis, she said yes, his ding-dong, and was that what he called it? yes, and what did it look like? It looked like a big finger, but it was also their pet and it could change sizes and it was hot and red and there were little diamond balls underneath in a purse that you could feel and later they got to like walking around in the playroom without any clothes on and after the baby was in bed they would hug and kiss and Corey licked her in a tickly way around her vagina and he liked to rub his ding-dong against her and it felt hot and they would look at it and play with it and then later another time after they had lollipops a couple of times then they made that a lollipop too and she licked it a few times like a tickle game and sucked on it and they rubbed each other, and you could squeeze it and feel a heartbeat, and no they promised not to tell because it was a secret and Angela would want to play, and no, of course he didn't stick it in her, and his mother was out shopping or upstairs watching television, and it didn't happen every time, and it was like a sword, too and, no, stuff didn't come out of it, not at first, but then a few times it did, like a paste, and then he wiped it away with a tissue and it jumped a little, and she thought it was pee, but he made it come out rubbing it, and it shot out, and no, she didn't know what it tasted like, because she didn't taste it, but sometimes a little sticky stuff would come out when she licked it and it tasted kind of like ocean water, but she didn't like that, and he would rub her too and kiss her and the baby was asleep and nobody else knew and she didn't get hurt, and she didn't get hurt, and Corey didn't hurt her, and she didn't know it was bad, not really, she didn't know how bad it was, it didn't seem bad, she didn't know it was bad, she didn't know they would have to go to jail.

But, no, no, that would not happen, Karen told her, because she had done nothing wrong, and telling the truth was the right thing to do, and "Hey, boy, you did a great job," Jervac said, when Karen indicated that they had covered enough for the day, and Liz said, "Really great," and Carrie beamed at Jervac.

"Fucking asshole," Laura said between clenched teeth. "That motherfucking little prick."

Elgin put his arm around her and she stiffened.

"I think your mommy and daddy will want to come in now," Karen said to the mirror.

"Come on," Elgin said. Laura's face was pale and blotchy. He put his arm to her back to guide her toward the door, and she wriggled away from him. "Don't touch me," she said. "Do not touch me."

Carrie looked like she had a fever when they entered the interview room, her cheeks flushed deep pink, and her eyes a little bleary. She sat beside Jervac, outlining her hands with a crayon on a piece of paper at the little table. "Hey, Carrie!" Elgin said.

"Just a minute, Dad," she said.

"Carrie, can you finish up with Detective Jervac for a few minutes while I talk to your mom and dad?"

Carrie nodded, hardly looked away from Jervac. Karen led them out of the room and told them that at the arraignment that morning the judge had ruled to keep Corey detained, that he had pleaded not guilty, and that the probable cause hearing was set for Thursday, at which time charges would likely be filed and it would be determined if Corey would remain at Children's Village until trial. "I know how hard that must have been to watch," she said, putting her hand on Laura's forearm and leaving it there. "But, I'll tell you, she's a tough little girl." Laura sniffled. "I'm going to need to see her every day this week, to continue the investigation, to establish a sequence of events, to go over testimony for the hearing, to show her the hearing room, and the room she'll be in on the closed circuit. I'm going to want her to get comfortable with Liz and the entire process, prepare her for the suspect's attorney."

Elgin nodded. Toward the end of Carrie's testimony, after all the waves of revulsion and horror and anger, after the murderous rage he'd felt for the kid and then the mother and then the kid and then the mother and then everyone in the world, he'd begun to feel numb, deadened to any more response. And afterward, in the interview room, Carrie was fine, almost invigorated it seemed.

"I can tell you," Karen said, "that though our investigation has only begun, it seems likely that we'll be able to bring charges on Thursday. That's good news."

"Wait," Laura said. "He hasn't been charged yet?"

Had she been paying no attention?

"No," Karen said. "That's what happens on Thursday, remember? And we've got a lot of work to do in the meantime. You said you had Pat Connoly lined up?"

Laura looked at her watch. "Yeah," she said. "In fact, we're going to be late."

"Okay," Karen said. "That's good. I've worked with her before. You might tell her that we're going to want her testimony on Thursday. And I'll be calling her either tonight or tomorrow."

"Wait," Laura said, rummaging through her purse. "Should I write this down?"

"Forget about it," Karen said. "She knows. She's been through this before."

"So am I supposed to tell her something?" Laura said. "Am I supposed to write something down?"

"No," Elgin said. He'd forgotten about the therapist, could hardly believe that Carrie and all of them had more torture lined up. He wondered how many other professionals in the sexual abuse industry they would have to encounter.

"Don't worry about it," Karen said, touching Laura's arm again. "Or, if you'd like, just tell her I'll call."

"Are we done?" Elgin said. He wasn't feeling so numb anymore. In fact the shits were coming on again.

"We're done," Karen said. "And listen. I think we have a good little witness there. A real good little witness," and Elgin thought, You fucking bitch.

That night after putting Carrie to bed, after enduring Laura's new therapist-sanctioned terror tactics, he got out of the house and walked. On the far western edge of the eastern time zone it stayed light until almost ten o'clock, and now the sky was pink and orange and dark blue, and a few kids were still out on bikes, and a couple of teenagers walking hand in hand and swallows picking insects out of the air and the sounds of crickets and frogs and you would not know that the missiles had already been launched, and why would you want to know? He walked and he walked and he kept walking. Maybe Pat Connoly was a genius; maybe she knew exactly what she was doing. Who was he to judge? If it were up to him, he'd pack the kids into the new Jeep and head up to Mackinac or the Upper Peninsula, get the hell out of town for a few days or weeks or months. There was no time to figure anything out. They'd get a cabin, and after putting the kids to bed, they'd sit out on the porch and have a drink and play cards. People did that kind of thing.

A big moon was rising and Venus was visible as well. He walked south on a number of dirt roads that still had farms along them and white trash shacks, and a couple of bobbing oil pumps in backyards and wetlands and a few new subdivisions, the back way to Ann Arbor.

They'd stopped for fast food after the Care House interview and ate on the way to Pat Connoly's practice in Farmington Hills. Carrie seemed spent, slouched in the backseat, while Elgin and Laura sat silently in front. "You did such a good job," Laura had said five hundred times, and each time Elgin said, "Karen told us you were great," protecting the lie that they hadn't witnessed anything. And then there was nothing else to say.

Joyce was waiting in the parking lot, and sat with Carrie, while Pat did an initial interview with Laura and Elgin. They told her what they knew, told her about the upcoming probable cause hearing and then it was Carrie's turn. "I don't want to," she said. "I'm tired."

"I know you are, baby," Laura said, squatting down to hug her and talk close to her face. "But Pat's going to help you. She's going to help us all."

"I don't want to," Carrie said.

Pat appeared at the entrance to her office, beaming, holding two dolls. "Come on, sweetie," she said. "We'll make it quick and easy," and Carrie reluctantly disappeared inside.

Laura told Joyce about Carrie's interview with Karen and cried a little, while her mother comforted her. Elgin felt like an outsider. Eventually, Carrie came out, a little flushed, Pat following her, telling her what a big, brave girl she was, everyone constantly telling her what a great job she had done, what a brave girl she was, how wonderful were all her accounts of victimization.

They left Carrie with Joyce in the waiting room, and sat in chairs in Pat's office around a table covered with paper and crayons and the two dolls, which Elgin now noticed had genitals. "Well," Pat said. "She's not feeling it yet. Which is absolutely normal."

"She's burnt," Elgin said. "She spent a lot of time on it this morning." He was holding on to the word "normal."

"Right," Pat said. She wore a bright yellow sundress and white sandals with daisies on them, and while Elgin guessed she was fifty, or fifty-five, she seemed younger. The words "well preserved" came to mind.

"What," Laura said, "so she didn't tell you?"

"No," Pat said, "she told me a little bit of what you said had occurred. And, of course, I wasn't going to push her. But she's really not feeling this."

Elgin nodded. What the fuck did that mean?

Pat asked questions about Carrie's recent behavior, looking, she said, for anything atypical, looking for "acting-out" behavior or sexual behavior or anything unusual. "She's had a long day," she said. "A long couple of days. And it's going to be a long week. I'm going to need to see her again before Thursday, hopefully when she's fresh."

They set a time on Wednesday, and Pat seemed ready to usher them out, when Laura said, "So what do we do? I mean, how does she seem?" It was exactly what Elgin wanted to know.

"She *seems* fine," Pat said, settling back in her seat, "and that's what concerns me. Often in these kinds of cases, with kids this young, a lot can get buried, and come back later, often years later, to hurt the child. What you need to know is that regardless of how she *seems*, Carrie is a victim."

And Elgin thought, Oh, no, here we go, feeling his body stiffen as if to physically resist her.

"She's going to need a lot of support—"

As if he and Laura were just going to ignore her.

"And it's going to take a long time."

Of course it is. It's your paycheck. And then he thought, Stop. There was no reason to be so defensive, no reason to believe that this woman didn't have Carrie's interests at heart. Just a feeling, the resistance, but he had been so wrong about so many other things, really almost everything surrounding this, that he knew he had to force himself to surrender to people who maybe did know what the hell they were talking about.

"The healing process is going to be complicated by the depth of trauma here," Pat said. "To create a survivor—"

And Elgin felt himself cringe.

"—we've got to establish that victimization occurred; in other words, the victim has got to understand that she is in fact a victim. Otherwise, she'll never be a survivor. Also, if she doesn't know that she's a victim, you'll always have to be aware of who she's with, what she does, to protect her from further victimization."

"But we do that anyway," Elgin said. It sounded like whining to his ears, a denial: It's not really our fault.

"Of course," Pat said.

"And what depth of trauma?" he said, and Laura said, "Robert!" and Pat said, "Well, you've already outlined several acting-out behaviors, the sexualized play with her cousin, the secrecy and lying, her failure to really break the silence with me."

"But you said it was all normal," Elgin whined.

"Yes," Pat said. "It's normal to repress feelings of victimization. And what we're going to have to do now is help her to understand that she *is* a victim, and that it's not her fault, and that she will survive."

"Absolutely," Laura said.

"And the more she's able to express herself, the sooner it will be behind her."

"So, can we talk about it?" Laura asked.

"Absolutely."

"The cops said not to," Elgin said. "They talked about branding."

"Well," Pat said, and she smiled, her eyes crinkling up, inviting Elgin and Laura into a conspiracy, "in my experience, the police don't always know best in these matters."

"Okay," Laura said, "so we should talk about it with her."

"Sure," Pat said.

"Or should we just listen?" Elgin said. "Let her talk when she wants to talk."

"I think," Pat said, "that you should help her get this behind her.

And that means talking about it. I'll certainly be talking about it with her, but you can, too. Do bring it up. I'm not saying you should threaten or accuse her or make her feel bad, but help her get it out. Be careful to make her understand, though, that she won't be hurting you in the process."

"That's what we'll do," Laura said, and that's what she did before bed, asking Carrie if she wanted to talk, asking questions about what had occurred, relying on the illegal information they had obtained while secretly watching Carrie spill her guts to Karen. But Carrie didn't want to talk. "We have to, baby," Laura said, "we've got to get it out," and rather than disagree, or make a scene, Elgin walked out the door and into the night.

It was eleven o'clock when he turned around and headed back. The whole approach seemed wrong to him, but he had no support for his argument with Laura, who liked and trusted Pat and agreed with her approach as instinctively as he disagreed. Not that there was anything to dislike or distrust in the woman. It was just a feeling he had. What was the benefit in taking on the mantle of victimhood if the events had never made her feel victimized, if she'd willingly participated in them, hell, if she'd enjoyed them? This was how fucked up he had become. She was only five years old. She'd been used as a sexual toy by a much older kid, a sexually mature kid, and Elgin was trying to deny that she had been hurt by it. Of course there was damage. Of course she was hurt. But how much, and what cure? And why did she have to slog through it over and over again with strangers? And why couldn't he and Laura even talk about any of it without accusations, without blaming the other for the depth and degree of the immeasurable, invisible damage?

There weren't any answers. He walked and walked and walked.

Wednesday he went to work and was treated gently by Susan and Pearson, which was probably normal, but he couldn't bear to be in their compassionate presence. He went through a stack of grievances, denying all but one. To his horror, McCabe stopped by unexpectedly and took him out to lunch at the Sportsman's Club on Telegraph, and to make matters worse, Klister and the Printer were at the restaurant when they arrived. It was going to be unbearable. He would be trapped, talking strategy, or, worse, talking about his personal life. Klister and the Printer argued about the Tigers and White Sox. After the drinks arrived, McCabe held up his glass to toast, and said, "One thing I've learned after twenty-five years in politics is the difference between the game and what really matters, the difference between the political and the personal. I've made plenty of enemies in this game, but I've also made my closest friends, another family really. So," he said, holding his glass a little higher, "to what really matters in life: to friends and family," and they all touched glasses.

Later, over the smoked whitefish appetizers, Klister put his arm on Elgin's shoulder, pulling him close, and said, "I talked to Wolffson this morning. The prosecutor's office is all over this thing. Any problems you go straight to him. Any problems there you call me."

The Printer nodded at Elgin across the table. He nodded back. He had no idea how they all knew—Pearson? Lynch?—and didn't particularly care. No business whatsoever was discussed. Instead, McCabe talked about the death of his oldest daughter, eighteen years before, when she was seven, and how it had nearly destroyed his marriage. He got all choked up—who the fuck wouldn't, talking about his dead kid?—had to wipe at his face a couple of times. Then Klister, of all people, revealed what everyone in the county already knew, that his first wife had cheated on him, that fifteen years ago he'd caught her in a car, in *his* car, fucking a neighbor, that he had no idea how he hadn't killed the motherfucker, how he found out that the little whore had been cheating on him all over the place, how McCabe and the Printer had helped him through it, the jail term, the political rehabilitation.

"Yeah," the Printer said. "Sometimes, the bad times are when you find out who can help you. Not that that's any consolation."

And, finally, Elgin started to spill, talking about the kid, the cops, the fucking therapist, his daughter fucking molested by some scrawny twelve-year-old, rape was what it was, oral fucking sodomy, he corrected himself, so they wouldn't confuse it with the other kind. It seemed that he talked for a long time, through lunch and another drink.

"Anything you need, man," Klister said, and McCabe said, "Whatever we can do."

And back in his office he was surprised by how good he felt, how much of a relief it had been to finally talk about some of this shit with people who understood all the complications surrounding such admissions of weakness and pain. And he was grateful.

The previous evening, when Mrs. Kunkel, Carrie's kindergarten teacher, had called, asking Elgin how Carrie was doing, how she was getting along, Elgin was furious to discover that Laura had told her what had occurred, that Laura seemed to be leaking this business all over town. They had another quiet, jaw-clenching little whisper fight in their bedroom, while Laura's parents waited downstairs. "It's her last week of school," Laura said, "and Mrs. Kunkel loves her. Of course I'm going to tell her. The only way I could get Carrie through this was to promise that she could see Mrs. Kunkel next week. They're going out to lunch, okay? What is the big deal, with the one adult, who knows her better than anybody but us, knowing what she's going through? Maybe you think you don't need any help, but Carrie does and she's going to get it, whether it embarrasses you or not."

Now he wondered what he had been so upset about. Carrie loved her teacher and was devastated at missing the last week of school. So if Mrs. Kunkel could take her out to lunch, give her some special attention, that could only be good. Maybe even Pat was right. Maybe you did have to get shit behind you. God, just having spilled at lunch had reinvigorated Elgin, had shored him up to get through the next couple of days.

He stopped at the grocery store on the way home from work to pick up some steaks for dinner. He'd let Laura know that he'd been wrong, that he understood now, that he'd been holding it all in, that his vision had been distorted, contaminated, as a result. As a form of apology, he'd cook tonight. The last supper, he couldn't stop himself from thinking. The hearing was the following morning.

At the butcher's counter he ordered four fat ribeyes, and as he was waiting, he saw Corey's father examining a family pack of boneless chicken breasts at the cooler to his left. He looked away, examined the bastard out of the corner of his eye. Newkirk was slouched over the freezer as he handled the packages of meat, picking one up, discarding it, picking up another one. When Elgin turned to get a better look, Newkirk was looking right at him. The fucker nodded, then dropped the meat and approached. Elgin hadn't been in a fight since freshman year of high school, but his body remembered how to prepare, adrenaline pushing out through his extremities, his balls moving in, heart and lungs picking up the pace. "Meat Slaying," the *Free Press* would call it.

But Newkirk didn't seem to have the same reaction. He was shuffling toward Elgin, his head bowed. "Hello," he said through a deep sigh, shaking his head. "What a mess we have." His face was chalky, deep greenish circles under his blood-streaked eyes.

Elgin grunted.

"How's your daughter?"

"Shitty," Elgin said. He adopted a negotiating pose, staring at the motherfucker with contempt, so that Newkirk bowed his head and talked mostly to the floor, glancing up now and then to gauge response or threat. "Yeah," he said. "And Corey's up in Children's Village. I don't know what happened. Don't know if we'll ever know."

"Really?" Elgin said. "I have a pretty good idea of what happened."

The butcher dropped Elgin's package of meat on the counter. "You want anything?" he said to Newkirk, who shook his head. The butcher walked away.

"The cops and the prosecutor seem to think they have a pretty good idea, as well."

"Yeah," Newkirk said. "I guess we'll find out tomorrow. It's not for me to decide. Corey said he didn't do anything—"

Elgin grunted again, could feel the muscles in his face pulling up a sneer. "Yeah, and so Carrie just made it up, huh?"

"No," Newkirk said. His golf shirt had a tear along the seam of the shoulder. "It's killing his mother," Newkirk said to the floor. "That's not your problem."

"Nope."

"Me and Angela as well, I guess." He looked at Elgin. "Whatever happened, I'm sorry."

Elgin nodded. The man was pathetic. "It'd probably be better on him if he just confessed," Elgin said.

Newkirk shook his head. "He says he didn't do it."

"Did you ever think that maybe he was lying?"

Newkirk looked him in the eye. "Did you?" he said. "Your daughter, I mean?"

"Fuck off," Elgin said.

"Yeah," Newkirk said, shaking his head. "One day everything just falls to pieces."

"Uh-huh," Elgin said, picking up his meat.

"I hope your little girl's all right," Newkirk said. "I don't think Corey will be. Not if they keep him locked up in there with all the gang kids."

Elgin was halfway down the cereal aisle.

"I know it's not your problem," Newkirk called after him, and Elgin kept walking, wishing the limp bastard had expressed anything but his pathetic, devastating loss and sorrow, wishing he could have pounded his skull against the meat counter until the glass splattered with brains and blood.

The nerve of that fucking guy, to come off hurt and sad, to believe his child-raping son without anger against the child responsible for what he had to believe was a wrongful incarceration.

"I'm sure something happened," Newkirk said.

Elgin turned and the motherfucker was right there, the rows of cereal lined up behind him. The adrenaline was pumping again. He could feel his heart in his chest.

"Whatever it was, I just keep wondering, is this the remedy? Is this the solution?"

"Get away from me," Elgin said. "The cops told you to stay the fuck away from me."

"It wouldn't happen again, whatever it was. If anything ever did. I'd see to that."

Elgin moved a step closer to Newkirk, who was looking at the floor again. His fingers wanted to make fists, bones wanted to crunch bones. "Something happened," he said close to Newkirk's bloodless face.

"I said that," Newkirk said to the floor.

"Shut up," Elgin said, a little spit landing on Newkirk's cheek.

"You've got all the cards, I know—"

"Shut up!"

"My kid's life's going to be ruined—"

"And he fucking ruined my kid's." Elgin turned away before he hit the man, and walked.

"I just can't help thinking there's got to be a better way."

Elgin turned one last time and hurled the package of meat toward

Newkirk's head. Newkirk ducked, and the meat crashed against a row of cereal boxes, a dozen or so flying off the shelves and scattering on the floor around him in his pathetic crouched pose.

Elgin walked out of the store, the adrenaline still pumping, priming him for action, violence, murder. He peeled out of the parking lot and drove the Jeep hard, to hell with the meat. Laura would already have plans for dinner anyway.

That night and the next day at the hearing, Carrie performed her role perfectly, demonstrating a very real fear of Corey and what he might do to her, showing the bloody wounds of her victimization. After dinner, during the newly ritualized "talk time," Carrie kept asking if Corey could get out, if he would come and get her. "No," Elgin said, "he's locked up," and Laura said, "which is why it's so important that we keep him that way."

"Why all the fear suddenly?" Elgin asked, and Laura said, "Well, who wouldn't be afraid? *That's* normal," and Carrie said there was a seven-year-old girl up in Saginaw who had been cut into pieces with a butcher knife by a fifteen-year-old boy who had raped her.

"Wait a minute," Elgin said. "What are you talking about?"

"It's true," Laura said. "It was in the paper."

"When?"

"Two or three years ago. Pat showed us."

"*She* didn't survive," Carrie said. "I *want* to survive."

"Of course you do," Laura said.

Elgin remembered Newkirk's torn golf shirt, his cowed demeanor, the rings under his eyes. "But Corey never acted violent, did he, baby?"

"Neither did this other boy," Laura said.

"Did he ever hurt you?" Elgin said.

Carrie smoothed the sheet over her legs. "Yes," she said. "He hurt me. He's going to hurt me."

"When did he hurt you?"

"He scared me."

"That's right," Laura said. "And nobody knows what he's capable of."

"I wish he was dead," Carrie said. "So he couldn't hurt anyone else."

After they left her room, with the light on, Laura said, "You can see the kind of progress she's making after only two sessions with Pat. She's starting to feel it."

"Yeah," Elgin said. "Three days ago, she didn't want Corey in jail. Now she wants him dead."

"Isn't it amazing?" Laura said. "Karen said that Carrie is the best witness she's ever seen for a child her age."

Elgin couldn't bear to look at her.

"Daddy," Carrie called out. "Daddy!"

Elgin ran to her room, where she was sitting up in bed, shaking and crying hysterically. "I heard him!" she said. "He's outside the window! I heard him!"

"No, no," Elgin said, holding her in his arms. "Nobody's going to hurt you. I promise."

Laura stood in the doorway, then turned and walked away. After Elgin calmed Carrie, he found Laura waiting in their room, the gleam of a zealot in her eyes. "We're going to win this thing," she said. "Pat says she started to break down today; it's like a paralytic just beginning to feel the slightest sensations. I just feel so confident now that we can help her heal."

She looked up at him, studying his face. "Do you see the evolution?" she said.

"Yeah," Elgin said. He saw that she was being taught a depth of fear she had never experienced before, that she was being educated in terror. He felt so far out to sea now that there was no point in even trying to fight his way back in—might as well just let the current pull him out to drown.

And the next day at the hearing, when Pat Connoly testified that Carrie was only just now coming into her fear, Elgin wondered at the depths of terror Pat intended to pull her through. He sat by Laura, who sniffled throughout, tears streaming down her face occasionally, which she dramatically wiped with a lacy hanky, embroidered with violets. The Newkirk family sat on the other side of the aisle—like at a wedding—groom's side, bride's side. Corey mumbled denials throughout his testimony, showing defiance and fear, but mostly deep withdrawal. Pat Connoly testified that Carrie's ignorance of the gravity of the abuse inflicted upon her by Corey made him all the more of a threat. Karen tried to tear him apart like a TV prosecutor, but he just mumbled and looked at the floor, or at something on the back wall over their heads, denying everything. It was difficult to hate him, even with his denials, until Carrie testified through a closed circuit television, with Liz, the prosecutor's child advocate beside her. Karen led her through the entire story again, but this time it was colored with threats and deep shame and convulsive crying. And her fear was absolutely real, Elgin could see that. The abuse apparatus had done its job. There was no question that Carrie was a victim, damaged plenty by the skinny predator doodling on a legal pad next to his attorney. And afterward, after the judge had pronounced that Corey was to be detained until trial in August, and they had all assembled in the remote location from which Carrie had testified, Pat Connoly and Jervac and Hearn and Karen and Liz, and even Wolffson himself, who merely nodded at Elgin, marking his appearance, and then left, Laura crying, Pat beaming, Karen grinning, all of them encircling Carrie, who was crying and smiling, flushed with victory and fear, the center of this ring of adults, Elgin could see that she had been elevated, that the most painful part of all this might very well become her fall from celebrity status, that once the abuse apparatus spit her out, she would be merely the damaged, tragic kid into which it had transformed her. He watched her celebrating, and felt the pull of the current, but maybe it was them, Carrie and Laura, who were being pulled away from him; it seemed that they were already so far out of his reach as to be hopelessly lost. He stood outside the circle, waiting to touch Carrie, to pull her toward him. Laura cried into her hanky. She seemed like an imposter of the woman he had once known, the woman he could hardly now remember. Elgin wondered if he would ever feel close to her again. He wondered if he would ever even want to.

SEVEN

NOVEMBER/DECEMBER

W hich way?" Carla asked.
            "I don't know," Elgin said. "I've never driven in the city."

"No," Carla said, "I mean which way do you want to go, what direction?" She had the atlas propped against the steering wheel, opened to the map of the entire country. "Your choices are northeast, meaning, you know, New England, Canada, etcetera, or west, meaning everything else." She threw the atlas in the backseat. "South means Staten Island, and ultimately, of course, the South, so that's out of the question." She started the engine and let it run for a few seconds before turning to him. "So which way?"

"Everything else," Elgin said.

"Right," Carla said. She pulled out of the parking garage and headed for the Lincoln Tunnel.

When they emerged on the Jersey side, Elgin said, "Is it true what they say about New Jersey—that it's the land of plenty?"

"Yes," Carla said. "Weehawken was Joseph Smith's first choice for the Mormons. Had they stayed, you'd have Chemical Dump City here in Jersey instead of Salt Lake City out in Utah."

"Is it true that life's just a little better in Jersey?"

"Yes," Carla said. "It is true."

"Let's go to Salt Lake and see what the filthy Mormons have done to it."

"All right," Carla said. "Perhaps we can spoil it."

"Isn't it pretty to think so?"

She smiled at him.

"Let me know when you get tired," he said, "when you want to switch."

"I've only been driving for fifteen minutes."

"I'm just saying."

"You want to drive now, don't you?"

He did. The previous morning, down at the DMV, he'd used Carla's Subaru for the driving test, and when he was finally awarded an official New York license, he was as thrilled as when he'd gotten his first license at sixteen, and it seemed to have the same implications. Now, finally, he was free. He could go wherever he wanted, whenever he wanted. He was an official motorist.

She pulled onto the shoulder. "This isn't some kind of macho bull-shit, is it?" she asked. "You're not thinking that the man drives while the little lady sits in the passenger seat and knits, are you?"

"No," he said. He opened his door, walked around the front of the car and opened Carla's door. "I just really want to drive," he said. "It's been a long time," longer it seemed than the first sixteen years of his life.

"All right," she said. "Maybe we'll switch every fifteen minutes."

He pulled into traffic. "Don't mess with me," he said. "I am licensed to drive!"

Carla studied the map. Elgin fiddled with the radio. "Not fucking classic rock," she said when he stopped on a station playing "Gimme Shelter."

"This is the Stones," he said.

"Yeah, and the next song will be Jackson Brown or The Eagles."

Elgin did his Jagger imitation, pushing his bottom lip out and wagging his finger as he sang with the radio.

The next song was Lynyrd Skynyrd's "Free Bird." Carla turned the radio off. "See what I mean?" she said.

"I can live with that song," Elgin said, and Carla said, "I'm trying to study this map."

Elgin quoted another Skynyrd song in a sort of sad, serious, dra-matic reading voice, with long Jesse Jackson–inspired pauses and inflections: "Tyu-iz-day iyuz gone," he said. "Mah buy-bee iyuz gone. Mah buy-bee iyuz gaw-hawn . . . like the wee-hund." He pulled into the left lane, pushing the Subaru up to ninety to pass a string of semis. It was what getting out of prison must feel like.

"Hey," Carla said, looking up from the atlas. "Watch your speed."

"Whatever for?" Elgin said.

"Because I've got weed."

"You've got weed?" Elgin said. He hadn't smoked in years. The thrills were running into each other, piling up on top of him. He eased back into the right lane, slowing down to seventy. Weed.

"We'll stay on 78 until it hooks up with the Pennsylvania Turnpike," Carla said. "Then take 70 all the way through to Denver."

"What about small roads?" Elgin said. "Is that something we want to explore, you know, discovering America off the interstate?" and Carla said, "Absolutely not."

"Good," Elgin said. "Thank God. That would have sucked."

"And we'll only eat in national franchises. And only fried food."

"No," Elgin said, "that's too much," and Carla said, "I'm kidding," but that night in Zanesville, Ohio, they ate at the Applebee's across the parking lot from their Holiday Inn. They'd counted seventeen dead deer on the side of the interstate in Pennsylvania. "Hoofed rats, my dad always called them," Carla said. Elgin had wanted to stop in Wheeling, a fear creeping up on him at the prospect of entering Ohio, one state away from home, but Carla had insisted on pushing forward, and he shook off the fear. After the waitress had listed the specials and taken their drink orders, Elgin said, "So, what's the hurry? Why the rush to Zanesville?"

Carla shrugged. She was wearing a short, silver-studded suede jacket, the kind that naughty Barbie might wear. "It just feels good to move," Carla said, "to get away. I think the river should be our psychological relief boundary. Once we cross into Missouri, we'll be officially free."

"The gateway to the West. Have you ever heard anything good about St. Louis?"

"No," Carla said.

"Let's stay there tomorrow night. There'll be a good hotel. We'll discover St. Louis. We'll come home to St. Louis. We'll wander St. Louis. We'll find ourselves in St. Louis."

"We'll eat slabs of ribs in St. Louis. Drink fifteen martinis in St. Louis."

"We'll wage a war on drugs in St. Louis."

"End welfare as we know it in St. Louis."

"Right centuries of wrongs in St. Louis."

The waitress arrived with their drinks. "What is it about St. Louis?" Elgin asked her.

She smiled. She was young and clean and corn-fed. "I don't know," she said.

"Why is everyone talking about St. Louis?" Carla asked her.

The color was coming up on the waitress's cheeks, her smile tight and radiant.

"And just what are they saying about it?" Elgin said.

"And why?" Carla said.

"I don't know," the waitress said. "I've never been there."

"But what do you hear about it?" Elgin said.

"Honestly," the waitress said. "Nothing."

"So there's nothing in St. Louis?" Carla asked.

"No," she said. "I don't know."

"But you're saying that you've either heard nothing," Elgin said, "or are unwilling to tell us what you've heard?"

"No," she said. "It's a long ways off."

"It sounds like St. Louis sucks," Carla said.

"No," she said, laughing along to protect her tip. "I don't know."

Elgin presented a serious face to the waitress, read her name tag. "Lisa," he said, "my wife would like the veal-fed-chicken-fried steak."

"Uh," Lisa said. "We don't have that."

"And I don't want it," Carla said. "My father, however, would like the salad bar."

"You're not ready to order?"

"We're really not," Elgin said. "Give us five minutes."

They drank their drinks. "I love these kinds of shitty places on the road," Carla said. "Denny's, Stuckey's, Bob Evans. It means you're on a trip."

"Yeah," Elgin said. "I never really appreciated them until I had kids."

"What about when you *were* a kid?"

"Yeah," Elgin said. "Those were the places we stopped." He hadn't thought about the kids in days, had allowed himself to forget about them, and these had been the best days in a long time, maybe ever. He wasn't going to lose that. "Maybe we should buy a camper," he said. "A big old box on wheels we could drive around the West, irritating all the other drivers, staying in shitty campgrounds. Talk about freedom. Would that be fun or would that be stupid?"

"I don't know," Carla said. "I think stupid. I like hotels."

"And cabins," Elgin said. "Let's get a cabin in the redwoods for a month."

"But not a dumpy cabin," Carla said. "Not a rustic cabin. More like a luxury cabin."

"With servants," Elgin said, and Carla said, "Exactly."

=

The Holiday Inn lounge is like *the* spot in Zanesville on a Saturday night and we stop in for drinks and we're like celebrities in this nowhere town, not because of where we're from or who we are, but because of who we are together, the newness of it, or the potential, and it's like we've been smeared with gold dust. There's a disco ball and a DJ and bad music and Robert orders us whiskey sours for some bizarre reason, and he's so funny and not really noticeably mean or mocking to the locals, asking them about Zanesville and what they do, and making up lies about pre-scouting an Amway convention, and how we're looking for a spot in America where we can raise children, where you don't have to lock your door at night, where you can go to pie-eating contests and 4-H fairs and the people are God fearing and law abiding, yucking it up, drinks and laughing, and then half retarded jerking to the bad music, Robert dancing with other women, and me with other men, before coming back together, no jealousy or possession, but just the gold dust smeared all over us, everyone wanting to be a part of it, to touch it, to feel it, if only for a minute, and we're right in the middle of it, the darlings, the beloved, the blessed.

=

Carla woke him at 7:30 and insisted on hitting the road. They were in adjoining rooms, his door open, hers still closed. She called him on the phone. "Why?" he said. "What's the hurry?" and Carla said, "We're not on the other side of the river yet," so Elgin showered and got dressed.

West of Columbus, he said, "But once we are on the other side of the river, then we can sleep in if we go out dancing all night at Holiday Inn?"

"Yes," she said.

She talked about her family, the trips they took growing up, driving from Flint straight through to LA, fifty hours, the old man popping caffeine pills and drinking thermos after thermos of coffee, smoking cigarettes and listening to western swing and evangelicals in the middle of the black western night with nobody else on the road hardly. And he wanted to know about it, asked pointed questions, and she was so animated as she told her stories, so alive in them, that he wanted her to just keep talking, but then she wanted him to talk, and he found her enthusiasm rubbing off as he told her about the Dead tours, which she laughed about. "Not a fucking Deadhead," she said, and he laughed, too, told her about driving around the country, selling sandwiches at shows, taking acid, and goofing on all the important freak dealers who had to make stops at Western Union to wire funds back home for more sheets of acid, and meeting women at various shows. He didn't mention Laura and she didn't ask. He didn't mention the kids and she didn't ask. All the stories took place before those times.

≡

You have to be careful, I know that much. But it's hard with him. It's different on the road, away. The conspiracy feels deeper and I don't want to fight it. What you can do is drive and drive and drive. And go places and when you get sick of them, pick up and go someplace else. Until you've driven somewhere, it doesn't exist, and once you arrive, it starts using itself up, shrinking, reducing itself to what it is. But there's always somewhere else to go. St. Louis leading to Kansas City leading to Denver leading to Salt Lake City, Las Vegas, Los Angeles, San Francisco, Portland, Seattle, and on and on and on. And that's what you can do. That's what you can do forever.

≡

They got a two-room suite in St. Louis, with a bedroom and a pull-out bed. After dinner, she came out of the bathroom in a T-shirt and sat beside him on the couch. He ran through the channels on the TV, not wanting to look at her legs, the skin of her arms, the shape of her breasts through the T-shirt. She leaned her head on his shoulder. He put his arm around her and she leaned into him. He hadn't touched her since that night in New York when they kissed, except once down in Washington Square, when he touched her hair and she moved his hand away. He didn't want to be like all of the others, tried to concentrate on the TV, counted backward from a hundred in French, but his hard-on wouldn't go away; he was mister concrete dick. And he didn't want to be a fucking eunuch, either, a brother to her.

"I'm pretty tired," she said. "Are you going to watch TV?"

"Just for a little while."

"Do you mind if I take the bedroom?"

"No," he said. "Do."

After she closed the door, he went into the bathroom and jerked off, something he hadn't done in a long time. What did she expect of him? She certainly must have realized the power she had. And to come out in that T-shirt, what, did she think he was indifferent to her, to all that skin? Was she just teasing him, fucking with him, getting off on torturing him, some kind of payback against all the dirty johns?

≡

St. Louis sucks and I know if I don't cut the sexual tension something's going to explode, and he's trying so hard, I know, and I don't even want him to be like that; I mean I want to be normal, too, and I know that's part of it, but once you've turned part of yourself into a machine it's hard to figure out how to undo it. We walk the city, holding hands, so fucking corny, but, then, I like it, too, like I'm trying to let go, and I know he's trying, his erection last night making me feel like some kind of bitch, like in that Susan Minot story, "Lust," when the girl thinks that the worst thing anyone could call you is a cock teaser. So after dinner, I sit by him on the couch and we start kissing, real nice, soft, and I can feel how hard he's trying to hold back, to keep from devouring me, and it feels good, nice, but then the machine kicks in, and I'm like, "Ohh, yeah," and I see myself doing it, and I see in his eyes that he sees it, his hand on my breast and he sort of pulls back, and I say, "Come on, baby," and I reach down to rub him through his pants. I bring his head down to my breast and he licks and sucks, but I can't stop the machine. "Yes, baby," I say, unzipping his fly, pulling him out of his boxers, "That's right," I say, and he pulls away a little, that look in his eyes, like, "Who are you; why are you doing this?" and I just shake my head and say, "Don't, just don't," as I lower my head into his lap.

And afterward, when he wants to talk, I say, "Please don't say a word; just don't say one fucking word. And don't look hurt. Come on," I say, "let's sleep in the bedroom," but I wear a T-shirt and underwear, so he does the same. He stays on his side of the bed, waits for me. I slide next to him, put my hand on his chest. He puts his arm around me, my head on his shoulder, and pets my hair. Later, when he moves his hand down toward my ass, I lay still and quiet. He rubs my ass over the material of my underwear for a few minutes while I lie still and stiff as a corpse, thinking nothing, nothing, nothing, nothing, nothing. Eventually, he gives up. Eventually, I fall asleep.

=

The first Slaughterhouse Museum billboard was a hundred miles east of Kansas City. "We have to go there," Elgin said. St. Louis had been exhausted in one full day, two nights. In the morning, he had woken first, her back to him; he looked at her hair, the skin of her shoulder. He felt like a complete asshole. He wanted to touch her, but didn't dare. When he came out of the shower, the suitcases were lined up by the door. "I just have to brush my teeth," she said. "Why don't you get the car." She met him out front with two cups of coffee. Elgin pulled onto the interstate. "There'll be a cool old hotel in Kansas City," he said, "The Cattleman's would be my guess."

"You said that about St. Louis," Carla said.

"The Hilton was all right."

"Average."

They hadn't talked about a plan yet, but they were west of the river now, officially free. It was forty degrees, gray. "I don't know about this sky," Elgin said. "We need to think about where we'll be wintering. The quality, of course, winters in Palm Beach or Palm Springs. Anyplace with a 'palm' in its name."

"Yeah?" Carla said. "What about the trash?"

"I don't know," Elgin said. "San Diego? Orlando? Anyplace that ends with an 'o'?"

"Let's not make a plan, okay? I mean, I hate too much fucking planning."

"No," Elgin said. "We'll do whatever we want."

"Let's pull over, then," she said. "I want to drive."

He sat in the passenger seat while she drove, smoked cigarettes, and he knew that what had happened last night was her trying to do something for him, fulfilling some kind of expectation or obligation, which he did not want to impose upon her. He could have stopped it. He'd watched her head in his lap, what he should have wanted and did, but the image of Corey Newkirk's cock forced its way into his mind, his daughter's mouth. Oral fucking sodomy. And Carla making whore noises. Laura left to do all the work. Even all the shit raining down on him, he'd still reached for Carla in bed. She played dead. He was such an asshole.

Outside his window the land had become less monotonous, rolling prairie or what had once been prairie, now given over to corn, wheat, soy. So now he was nothing more than a fucking john.

"You know," he said, "the thing about last night," and she said, "Please, don't; not right now," and they fell back to silence. Later, he asked her a few questions, which she answered in one word, or with a nod, letting him know that she wanted the silence to continue, that she was pissed or bored or sick of him. He hadn't told her anything yet.

Maybe they were just tired.

Approaching Kansas City, Carla said, "And I don't want to just drive around until we find a place." It had started to rain. "And it has to be a good place this time. A really good place."

"All right," Elgin said. "Why don't you pull off and I'll look through the phone book—see if there's a visitor's bureau or something." Elgin called the Chamber of Commerce, a little desperate, but got exactly what he needed, a big, old, turn-of-the-century hotel, expensive as hell, with one of the best restaurants in the city, littered with stained glass and white-coated waiters and an enormous dark-stained bar.

Twenty minutes later, they pulled up to the Regent and a valet relieved them of the car immediately. "This is it," he said, ushering Carla through the grand, marbled lobby. "This is it." She still wasn't talking. He placed her in an overstuffed chair at the rim of a gilded fountain and got them the best room in the joint, a three-room suite up on the top floor. There were two bathrooms, one with the toilet, a shower, and sinks, and one with a jacuzzi that would fit a half-dozen people, surrounded on two sides by enormous windows and a view of the city. Elgin counted seven phones.

Carla said, "I'm taking a bath now."

"Okay," he said. "I'll go for a walk."

$$\equiv$$

I run the water as hot as it will go and lower myself by degrees into the heat. And I just have to burn through this somehow, undo whatever it was that was done—not to me, because I never let that happen, but by me. You put on a costume, you play a role. You get paid. You take off the costume and then you're yourself again. It's very simple. You just burn through it—burn through it and undo it. Because the weak shall inherit nothing.

$$\equiv$$

Outside in the drizzle he concentrated on being an observer, a tourist. It was too soon for the good feeling to die, too soon to go back to the obsessive review of who he was or what he had become. The city had a western feel, broader streets and more spread out, a few men wearing cowboy hats, for Christ's sake. He walked and his guts turned over a little, like he knew he was losing her, when, in fact, he'd never even had her, and if she was taking him for a ride, planning on stealing the money, leaving him dead somewhere, it was just what he deserved. But he wanted her—every bit of her, and not just as a fucking rental. But he was a liar. He wanted to fuck her in an alley, too, and he wanted her to want it, and didn't that mean that he was coming back to life, or was he merely sinking deeper into the muck? But he didn't want to whorify her, either. Christ, he was running away with her. And to what? She could have killed him in New York if that was her plan. And everything she'd been through.

His hair was soaked and he focused on the street, filled his mind with language, with idiotic self-evident commentary on his observations: "That woman must be ninety years old; that black kid should be in school; that must be the old fat-rendering plant," and he walked faster to burn off the uneasiness growing out of his guts. It was cold, and he didn't have a winter coat. He needed some jeans and a few pearl-snapped cowboy shirts and something warm that wasn't an overcoat.

There were people all over Kansas City who were not so much doing the right thing as not doing the wrong thing. They were going to the dentist or picking up the kids from soccer practice, or just doing what they always did, which would ultimately result in their returning home, though of course several were knocking off convenience marts or committing adultery with their secretaries or assembling meth labs in trailers or beating the hell out of their kids. God only knew how many were having old-fashioned heart attacks.

And Elgin thought that if there was a God, this would be His perfect opportunity to get even with Elgin, to lay down a little justice, a little righteous punishment, right here in Kansas City, on the other side of the river, where he was supposed to be free. Build him up a little by giving him something to live for, and then yank it away in Kansas City. Strand him in the West like one of those bleached long-horned cattle skulls out in the desert.

But he didn't believe in that shit, though he was reminded of Carrie's fear of ghosts and monsters, and how he'd tell her, rationally, that those things didn't exist, and how she'd say, "I don't *believe* in ghosts, Daddy, but I'm still afraid of them."

He was cold and wet. Before returning he got them coffee and a couple of Moe's Famous barbecued pork sandwiches.

Back at the hotel, the suite was empty, deep carpet silent, exactly what he'd expected, no note, nothing. Then she called out to him from the bedroom. "I'm in here," she said. "Aren't you going to come and find me?"

And she was on the bed, not yet dressed from her bath, waiting for him, the first time he had seen her naked. "Come on," she said. "You can take a bath first or I can give you one after."

He had to be very careful. "It doesn't have to be like this," he said, "I mean—"

"No," she said. "Come on."

"I don't want to do anything you don't want to do," he said. "I don't want to make you feel shitty in any way."

"You're making me feel shitty now," she said. "Come on," she said; "let's fuck."

$$\equiv$$

I always hated when people differentiated between making love and fucking, but I know I need a switch, some kind of mechanism, so I think, this is it, this will be the device, and I look straight into his eyes, and I say, "I want to make love," and I don't know if that's at all true, or what it even means, and I feel pretty stupid saying it, like a character in a romance novel, but I need the switch, and I think it probably means I want you to know just a little bit of who I am, or I want you to care about me, and it's a terrifying thought, the potential for damage enormous, and I start to choke up a little, I mean I almost start to cry a little, and he's kissing me and we're on the bed, and he says, "What? What is it?" and I just shake my head, and say, "Don't, just please don't," and pull him toward me, trying to kill the fuck-me-Daddy voice that's pushing to come out, closing my eyes tight, and opening them and looking at him looking at me, and the Fuck-me-Daddy voice competing with the This-is-who-I-am voice, and he kisses me all over my face, and I try so hard to surrender, to let him make me feel good, and then I just concentrate on his skin against mine, all the places where the skin meets, and I think, it's his skin, it's my skin, it's the places where they come together, and we both want to be doing this, and it does feel okay, and I say, "Come on; put it in," and I shut down, and I say, "Fuck me." And he does, but when I look up at him on top of me, pushing and pulling and pumping, he looks back, looks me right in the eyes, and I'm like okay, I'm not going to look away, you can see me if you want, you can look right into me if you want, and he keeps looking, and I'm like come, come on, go ahead, let's go, okay.

≡

She got out of bed when they were through. "I'm just going to take a shower," she said.

"No, don't," he said. "I got us some Famous Moe's barbecued pork sandwiches."

"Let me just shower first," she said.

"No," he said. "We need to eat these sandwiches. Come here. We're going to eat them in bed."

She stood at the door, looking at him. She smiled. "I just want to get cleaned up."

"No," he said. "Don't treat me like a fucking john."

"Fuck you," she said. "What do you know about that?"

"Nothing," he said. "And I don't care about it."

"Well, neither do I."

"Good," he said. He got out of bed, walked to her. She let him take her hand and lead her back. He stopped in the middle of the room, turned to her, put his arms around her, ran his hands through her hair, along her jaw, over her face and skull. He kissed her. She turned away.

"What is this, some kind of therapy bullshit?" she said.

"No," he said. He led her to the bed. "I'll get the sandwiches," he said, "and a bottle of champagne from room service. Maybe a fruit platter."

"A fruit platter?" she said.

"Yes," he said. "A fruit platter."

≡

People talk about how you can't run away, and I'm always like, Well, why the hell not? Why wouldn't you run away? What pain or punishment is it that you are so desperate to "confront"? It's all just another excuse for suffering.

He buys some idiotic cowboy clothes to wear to the Slaughterhouse Museum, a calico shirt for him, and a fringed leather skirt for me, and hats, of course, for both of us, which we actually wear. Something was certainly wrong in St. Louis, but Kansas City is like Zanesville again, with the gold dust, and that feeling you get when you know that something good is happening to you. In bars or restaurants, on the street or in jazz clubs people want to talk to us, to be near us. We're ambassadors from the land of not-miserable.

And at moments it feels better than anything I deserve to hope for. There was one guy in college whom I was stupid enough to get engaged to senior year. It seemed real for a while, and then it died. I don't know, I just got bored or something. He was heartbroken, wrote me nauseating poetry, called at all hours, showed up at the door, *crying,* until I finally had to become such a monster that he stopped bugging me. Clark was his name, and I can't think of it now without wanting to puke.

And the way you know it's real is when you consider the wearing of cowboy hats together to the Slaughterhouse Museum. Or when you don't consider it. When you actually do it. I mean, that's worse than having your names tattooed on each other's asses.

Which is why I have to be so fucking careful. I know I'm a goner, though, at Dooley's one night. The place is foul with happy-hour lawyers, the alpha lawyer right behind us in the packed bar talking loud enough to his cronies so that we—so that the entire bar—can't help overhearing his day's exploits. "Ripped Carson's fucking lungs out," he says. Robert swivels on his barstool so that he's facing me. The alpha pig in the two-thousand-dollar suit has been bumping up against us for half an hour. Robert lights a cigarette and props it in his hand on his knee facing alpha swine, who bumps up against it now and then as he gestures and pushes against it, until the cherry finally dislodges in the fabric. Robert looks at me and smiles. We watch the cherry burn a quarter-size hole in the worsted wool, and Robert says, "Let's get the fuck out of here." And it feels like payback, somehow, even though I was always paid well, for all the fucking pigs I wasted my time on. Or, worse, it feels like something I would do. And it's better and more dangerous than anything. But I'm not planning. No past. No future. No nothing.

≡

Kansas City was the papers in the morning over coffee—the *Times,* the *Star,* the *Journal,* the *Tribune*—then walking and lunch and the bookstores or a movie. Good bars, good restaurants, lots of music, plenty to say to each other and everybody else. Sometimes in the middle of the night he'd reach for her, and then he'd remember and bring his hands back to himself. Sometimes she'd put a hand over his, help him move it over her body. "Go ahead," she'd say. "I want to. Do it." Sometimes he did. Or they'd kiss on the couch. He tried to keep his hands to himself. It was when they wandered that she started to talk: "Go ahead," she'd say. "Come on." And she was somebody else on the couch with him, and he didn't know her at all.

He'd forgotten about the weed until she pulled out a joint one night after dinner. They smoked and it was funny for a while, laughing and telling stories, but then the paranoia started blooming, the protective bubble somehow suddenly gone. He relocked the door several times, thinking that Kansas City seemed like the kind of place where you'd be shot or garroted by one of Klister's hired goons, looked under the bed and in the bathrooms, wandering around the suite, sweating a little and not really listening to Carla's story.

"What is with you?" she said from the couch. "You're pacing."

And though he certainly hadn't planned it, he said, "I've been meaning to tell you something. About what happened, I mean."

"Okay," she said. "Why don't you sit down."

He poured them wine and sat next to her on the couch. He didn't know how or where to start. She waited. He said, "My little girl is such a sweet little girl. And my son . . ." He looked at the ceiling, didn't know how to *explain,* if that was what he was trying to do, which seemed inadequate—reprehensible, even.

"Why don't you tell me about them?" she said. "Your kids."

And then he talked about his kids, not what had happened, but just about his kids, who they were, what they did. For a long time, he talked about them, then he sort of woke up and said, "God, is this boring as hell to you? I mean, I'm practically forcing you to look at family pictures or something."

"No," she said. "I want to know. Go ahead."

He was propped on the edge of the couch. She slid behind him, put her arms around him. He leaned against her, then slid down so that his head was in her lap, and she petted him, as he told her about Laura, about the Department of Labor and McCabe and the Printer and corruption and falling out of love, and "How does that happen?" and Carla shook her head and kept petting him. Then he told her the rest, about Corey Newkirk and the cops and how it wasn't a designated felony because it wasn't forcible sodomy, but merely sodomy first degree, which meant family court instead of criminal court, all the deadening language he had acquired, and the depth of hatred Laura had cultivated, surpassing anything else in the house, certainly surpassing his own hatred or anger or rage, and her implicitly blaming him for that, his despicable lack of murderous intent, almost suggesting, it seemed, that he should tear Corey's limbs off, even after the kid was convicted and made to stay in Children's Village, especially after that, and the disintegration of his family, all the crippling therapy and then church, all the people who seemed to thrive and feed on the loss, masking their gluttony for his suffering with sympathy. And then the money again—the crime—and the flight, the running away. "I just want you to know," he said, "that they've got to be after me, looking for me. The cops or worse."

"I do know," she said.

"But I don't want you to get caught up in that."

"I don't care about that," she said.

"I care about it," he said.

"Don't be an idiot," she said. "I'm not interested in that kind of talk. It seems phony. Cheap. So you landed in New York," she said.

"Yeah," he said. He lay back against her. "It's just—I mean, I just abandoned them, pulled myself out of this shitty situation and left them there." And then he was back at the beginning again, telling stories, trying to make Carrie and Tommy real to her. She let him talk for a long time like that, running her hands through his hair, over his chest, until he ran out of words. "It's okay," she said finally. "You'll figure something out, and I'll help you. Come on," she said. "We'll take a bath."

She lit candles while the water filled the tub, helped him out of his clothes. "I have to do something for them," he said.

"You will," she said.

"I can't just disappear. I have to figure out a way to see them. I don't know how, though." She sat behind him, washing his back. "And you," he said. "It doesn't seem right that I should be in Kansas City with you while they're trapped in church and therapy."

"Don't be an ass," Carla said. "If you want to jones for guilt and suffering, when you have the rest of eternity to be dead, go ahead, but I want nothing to do with it. If you turn down one moment of happiness that you're lucky enough to run across just to chase misery, then you're a goddamn idiot."

They stayed in the tub a long time, not talking anymore. He washed her hair, her feet, her body. He couldn't help the erection, but he tried to keep it to himself. When she touched him, he moved her hand away. "Don't," he said. "Just leave it alone."

"I can take care of it for you," she said. "It's all right. Come on."

"No," he said.

"I really want to," she said.

He didn't believe her. She sat on top of him, her chin on his shoulder and didn't say anything as they pushed against each other, looking at opposite walls, holding on, as close as they could get. And then, after they were finished, he held on to her, wouldn't let her go. They didn't talk. They sat in the tub like that for a long time. When they came out of the bathroom, dawn was breaking. They slept all day.

≡

This suite is like our sanctuary, our home, the place we were born, so when the manager lets us know that our time's run out, that there's a reservation, that we can have another room, another, smaller suite, I'm like, No fucking way, and the last day in Kansas City is entirely ruined. It snows a little, flurries. We mope around, watch fucking television, order dinner from room service. And Robert's like, "Our last night; are you sure you don't want to go out?" but now I hate Kansas City, want nothing to do with it, though I do allow myself one last bath in the royal tub, and I ask Robert to join me and he does and we fuck, or whatever you call it, and hold on to each other, and it's starting to feel like far too much to have. I wake up at four o'clock so pissed that they're taking this away from us that I shake Robert awake and insist on hitting the road immediately.

Driving in the dark feels good, like escape, and at sunrise, the rolling Kansas prairie is stark and beautiful for a while until it becomes monotonous and redundant and boring and desolate. We don't talk much. Now I'm just logging the miles to Denver. I want a crippling snowstorm that closes the interstate. The sky is gray, a few flurries, but nothing good is going to come out of it.

And Robert doesn't even try to cheer me up, which means he's thinking about his kids. I know I can't really understand what that must feel like, and I'm even a little pissed that I can't obliterate the pain. The craziest fucking sick thing is that I stopped taking my pill in Kansas City, thinking, what—that I'd replace his fucking kids? I really didn't even think about it, just failed to fill the prescription, some kind of bullshit saintly selfish gesture or something, or maybe just wondering if I didn't need it anymore.

But what scares me so much is that I *didn't* think about it, that some part of me was like longing to breed or something, as if I were surrendering to the fairy-tale lie about spending my life with him, raising a family together or some such bullshit. Or worse, wondering if pregnancy would slam the door on the past forever. As if I give a fuck. It's only been a week, though, and my first stop in Denver will be a pharmacy.

He sleeps while I drive through the morning, through the miles of fields and farms and truck stops and more fields and farms and not one person outside of a car. I don't know how people live in this emptiness. I don't know what the hell they do.

=

After Denver there was Salt Lake City, where the snow finally came. The city seemed big and empty with the church at its center and everything radiating out from there, and the statue of Brigham Young, and the crazy Visitor's Center with enormous paintings of Roman-looking guys hanging out with North American Indians, and Mormons holed up in a basement somewhere as surrogate baptizees for their dead ancestors and anyone else, these volunteers dunked repeatedly to save the souls of the dead they'd never met or dreamt of, and lousy beer and not a drink to be had and the two mountain chains hemming in the city and the big dead lake out at the end of town. It snowed six inches and was fifty degrees the next day. They drove south to Capitol Reef, away from all the cities, into the big empty. It was Western movie country, with high plateaus, enormous sandstone outcroppings that changed color minute by minute, brown, pink, orange, purple, every color at once, or every shade of every color at once, more colors than you could name. He dragged Carla on a few long hikes, where there were no people and no signs that people had ever existed, except for an occasional airplane overhead. They saw Anasazi petroglyphs, thousand-year-old gang tags, Carla called them. It was the most empty and beautiful country Elgin had ever seen.

They had a little cabin in Torrey, right on the empty road, from which they could see the enormous humped rocks change colors, and the million stars at night. He got up early and walked and walked in the desolate rocky wilderness. He had never felt so powerful in his insignificance. Everything he had ever done was tiny, irrelevant, swept away in the indifferent wind that had spent thousands of years carelessly shaping the rock towers all around him. On a riverbed hike he'd taken twice before, he overtook a family, mother, father, twin girls about seven. It was a tricky part of the trail that demanded a climb along a shelf around a boulder and then a ten-foot drop back to the riverbed. "Hey," Elgin said, "are you stuck?"

"Are there footholds to get down the other side?" the father said.

"I can show you," Elgin said. "You can hand the kids down to me, halfway."

Elgin positioned himself, and the father handed him the girls, one at a time, and he lowered them. Holding them, helping them, touching them, he felt such a depth of longing for his daughter and son that he thought he would be overcome—struck down dead—with grief and self-loathing.

"Thank the nice man," the mother said, and the girls said, "Thank you," and Elgin waved them on because he didn't trust his voice, and then sat under the shelf and held his face in his hands. Who's helping your kids? he thought. Nobody. Not you. Nobody. You bastard. You asshole. He remembered holding Tommy after that last seizure, how horribly weak and vulnerable his son had been, both of them, how Elgin would have done anything to protect him, to bring him back from wherever he'd been. He remembered the morning Carrie was born, after Laura's sixty hours of labor: the night before, after hours of stalled dilation, Laura had finally gotten an epidural and lay sleeping in her hospital bed, Elgin beside her on a chair that opened into a bed, his stomach knotting up, cramping, all the coffee and cigarettes and two days without sleep doing him in, and at four in the morning he knew that he wasn't going to make it, Laura sleeping peacefully, drugged, he knew he was going to have to go home, that Laura would have to do this alone, but when the first light came he was okay, somehow, and then Laura couldn't push the baby out, Carrie's hand against her face in the birth canal, presenting, the midwife said, a compound presentation. Were they going to cut her out? Were they going to kill his wife with the knife to get to the baby? But then Laura said, "I'm going to push her out," and she pushed like hell through seven, ten, twenty contractions and Carrie's bloody head came out, and then her long, bloody body, and the midwife put the baby up on Laura's chest, the cord still attached, and she was alive, a tiny animal, all that blond hair plastered against her skull, and the midwife had Elgin cut the cord, and he watched the nurses prick the baby's foot for blood and clean her up, while the midwife took care of the placenta, Laura resting for a minute, and then they held Carrie in recovery for an hour or so, their baby, touching her hands, her face, her soft hair, and he had never felt such an outpouring of love for anyone or anything in his life, and he knew that he would gladly trade his own life for hers if she was ever in danger, and he had never not felt that way about her, or Tommy, so how did it happen that they were so far away from him, that he had just walked away?

"I don't know," he said to the river. "How do I know?" He stood and ran his hands over the wall of the canyon, pressed his forehead against it. He didn't know anything.

And they were always there at night, in fragments of dreams. He was with them and they were eating ice cream. They were in a canoe. They were camping. Birthday parties, with Klister and McCabe present.

The next morning he left before first light and walked and walked, and when he came back to the room Carla was still in bed, reading.

"It's so clean here," he said to her. "So pure, or something."

"You're being romantic," she said.

"I'm not kidding," he said. "I mean, I think this is where I could stay, where we should be."

She put her book down and scooted up in the bed. "What?" she said. "There's nothing here."

"That's what I like, though."

"I'd go out of my mind here. No way," she said, going back to her book. "Not me."

He sat beside her on the bed. What was he doing? Creating an impossible salvation? But on the morning's hike it had seemed clear to him that they would stay, buy a house and find jobs and exist in the enormous emptiness. Nothing would ever find him here. And alone in the emptiness he could reward and punish himself with memories of his children, filling himself with a false, noble emotion he didn't deserve, tasting the loss out in the dead empty desert.

He took one more day, a vertical hike, and up near the top a storm blew over, the sky turning black fast. He sat under a sandstone overhang and watched the lightning strike, the sheets of rain blurring everything. And as quickly as it came it was gone. For a second as the rain was abruptly dying, he knew that he was going to go back. He didn't know when or what would come of it, but he knew that it was only a matter of time. He didn't turn the thought over or examine it, but there was an inevitability now, a certainty to his future that had not been there before. Walking down the mountain to tell Carla they were leaving, he thought that whatever he could squeeze out of their time together would be entirely earned now. Now that he knew he was going back, it didn't really matter when or what the outcome would be.

≡

There's a certain hilarity to Las Vegas—the naked greed, the false promise of something for nothing, the corpulence and pretense of good clean family fun while Mommy and Daddy gamble their heads off and consume mildly naughty floor shows—something so purely American, a gambling theme park, sanitized on the outside, but filthy on the inside, an encapsulation of America that fascinates and entertains for about three hundred and seventy minutes, at which point it becomes merely boring and desperate, and then you might think that Los Angeles will wash the taste of Las Vegas out of your mouth, cleanse the palate, but you'd be wrong there because Los Angeles is even more idiotic. I mean Venice is entertaining in a sort of cheap carnival-like way, but after that it seems that there's really nothing to do but sit in traffic, waiting to get to the next nothing, like the whole place is a suburb without a center, which you keep expecting to find, everybody waiting around for something to happen. At Venice and the hotel, people keep asking if we're new to the area, if we're visiting, and don't we just love it here? Aside from the weather and the beaches and the health food and the people straining to be casual, sure.

I can't get settled, can't get comfortable. At the beach I follow Robert's eyes to the bronzed muscular ass of a fluffy blonde, switching her hips as she walks the shoreline, and I actually feel a tiny prick of jealousy, and I'm like, wait a minute, this is just not who I am. I look out over the water, feeling the old American tragedy, the end of the continent, nowhere else to go, and I know that at some point I'm going to have to figure out what I'm supposed to do. We head north to San Francisco on the coastal highway, get a suite at the Hyatt, and Robert takes me over to the Haight, dirty hippy Deadhead central, telling stories about shows at The Greek or the Shoreline, and I just could not care less. The whole tribal nature of the Deadhead phenomenon always struck me as asinine, and I tell him as much, but he says that, no, that was the beauty of it, that there was something you could belong to in the world, that you could surrender to, and I'm like, "All institutions are corrupt bloodsuckers, if you ask me," and he says, "But this was one institution where you could sort of drop the cynicism and just *belong*," and I say, "Yeah, and you needed handfuls of acid to accomplish that," and then he doesn't want to talk about it anymore.

Later, I walk through the Presidio by myself, sit on a bench and look out over the bay, the fog heavy over the water, wrapping itself around the reddish-brown—not golden—gate bridge, which will carry us north to Portland and Seattle, and then I don't know where else, and for absolutely no reason I start to cry. There aren't any people around, it's raw and wet out, but, still, I'm a little embarrassed, crying in my own presence, something I just don't ever do, and then I let go and bawl for a while. I've been off balance since Kansas City, especially since Capitol Reef, where Robert seemed most at ease or strong or something. I felt like a whining bitch. And it just seems so unfair that we don't have any kind of real chance, with his kids and somebody after him, and the money not enough to last forever, and somewhere down the road, however far we get, a fight erupts and he pulls out the weapon, the deepest insult he can find—"Whore"—not that it would hurt me, just that it would make me hate him so much. But I know how hard he tries, and I'll be goddamned if I'll care what someone else thinks, even if it is him. Then I'm like, Snap the fuck out of it. I walk over to the binocular machines trained on Alcatraz out in the middle of the bay somewhere under the fog, and I wonder why somebody hasn't blown that up, wonder how people can get off on this shrine to cruelty and suffering, riding ferryboats out to gawk, and then I'm like, What the fuck do I care?

When I get back to the room, Robert's in the shower. I sit on the toilet and tell him that I found out what we should do, that we should blow up Alcatraz. He turns off the shower. "What's the matter?" he says, toweling off.

"Nothing," I say. "People aren't happy all the time, you know."

Later that night, when I think he's asleep, I say, "Where are we going?"

He rolls over. "Where do you want to go?"

"I don't know," I say. He pulls me toward him, props my head on his shoulder. When he starts to snore, I extricate myself from his hold, get out of bed and dial my machine. I don't know why. I've been cut loose for weeks, nobody knowing where I am, and suddenly it's like I just want the tether.

There are only twenty-five messages, a lot from Teddy early on, and then he fades away, and I'm like, Good riddance, you fuck. Raisa from school calls twice, wondering where I am. My mother calls, wondering about Thanksgiving, and I'm not even sure where we were for Thanksgiving, Capitol Reef, I think, where the holiday passed unnoticed. "So we'd like to hear from you," she says. "We're wondering if everything's okay." I should have called them, of course, and let them know I'd be on the road, but they would have been so disappointed at the thought of my dropping out of school, and then how to explain that? She calls again on Thanksgiving Day: "We're getting a little concerned." I pick up a newspaper from the coffee table, December 12. Then my father's voice: "Stacey," he says, "sweetie, you gotta call home. Mom's in the hospital. Mom's sick. It's Tuesday, honey. You gotta call home." And I'm like what Tuesday, which Tuesday? Two days ago or two weeks ago? "Sweetie, it's Dad," he says in the last message. "It's Wednesday, honey. Mom's in the hospital and I don't know where you are. I called the police, but they won't do nothing. Where are you, honey? You're scaring me, and Mom's in the hospital. Joe's here. Michael's coming. I love you honey. Please. Call home, now. Come on."

I don't care that it's four o'clock in the morning in Michigan. Nothing's ever happened to us that wasn't supposed to happen, no fatal childhood illness or accidents, no deaths before old age; fuck, I've never even been to a funeral. But maybe this is old age, the beginning of it. Shit, she's only sixty. And, I've been such a perfect bitch, haven't even seen them since spring, before I started working, hardly ever even called them, never answering the newsy letters. A hundred years ago, she'd be dead already. Bitch. Stupid selfish bitch. And now nobody's home because she's dying in the hospital, but then he answers, after the third ring, a gravely, dopey hello. "Dad," I say, "Dad, it's me. How's Mom? What's going on?"

"Oh, Stacey," he says, "oh, honey, she's okay. Heart attack, but she's okay. I was so worried about you."

I feel all the air go out of me, like, All right, I dodged that one, and I say, "No, I'm okay. I'm in San Francisco; it's a long story. Is she still in the hospital?"

"Yeah, she's still there, but she's gonna be okay. You think you can get home for Christmas?"

"No," I say. "I mean, of course. Yes. I was planning on it. I should have let you know."

"What's in San Diego?"

"San Francisco."

"Right."

"It's a long story."

"Are you okay?"

"Yeah, I'm good. What happened?"

"I found her on the floor," he says through a deep sigh, "down the basement. They came right away, thank God. I just think if I hadn't of been there."

There's a long pause. "But she's okay, now?"

"She's okay, honey. Let me give you the number. She wants to hear from you."

There's a long empty buzz on the line as I envision him pulling himself out of bed and walking downstairs to the bulletin board over the phone, where he's tacked her number, and I'm like, He can't live without her, this isn't fair, and then he picks up downstairs and says, "Are you there, honey?" and he gives me the number.

"Okay," I say. "I'll let you get back to sleep. You need rest, too. I'll be home in a few days, four or five days, okay? I'll call when I know."

"Okay, honey," he says. "I'm just glad you called."

"Okay, Dad. Just take it easy, okay?"

"Okay, honey," he says. "Okay. Good-bye."

I hang up the phone, and on my way to the bedroom to wake Robert, I decide instead to let him sleep. I feel lucky and stupid and selfish and magnanimous. One day, of course, the call will go the other way, but not this time. I brew a pot of coffee and wait for morning. The feeling of relief bleeds out, replaced by a sort of vague anxiety. But she's okay and I'm not the parent yet, and I'm going to see her and erase my silence, and this doesn't have to be the end of anything, goddammit. For her or for me. This is just checking in is all it is. This is just coming up for air.

$$=$$

"You don't have to go," Carla said. "I could fly back and you could stay here or go down to Capitol Reef or anywhere else you want to go, and then I'll be back."

"No," he said. "I do have to go. I've known for a while."

"But what if they catch you?"

"They won't catch me."

"But what if they do?"

"They won't."

"Fine. Whatever."

They drove east through Reno, back through Salt Lake City, all the way through to Cheyenne, where they stopped for two days because of snow and exhaustion. And then two more days because they didn't want to leave.

Until they got east of the river, he wasn't going to quite directly think about what was coming or what his plan should be. She tried as hard as he did, it seemed, to ignore the pall that had fallen over them; she was chatty, tried to keep him occupied with banter and stories. In Chicago, they stayed at the Drake for three nights, and as they walked down Michigan Avenue or through the galleries of the Art Institute, he was certain that he would encounter someone he knew from Oakland County. Chicago, far more than Detroit, was the city you came to from Oakland. And his sister right up in Arlington Heights.

And east of the river, he still didn't know exactly what he was going to do, except see his kids and get Laura some money. And apologize. And try—somehow—to let his kids know that he loved them, which, of course, they had no reason to believe. And which, of course, they never would believe again. But, really, until he established contact and determined what was going on and how everyone was doing, it was pointless to plan. Or even to think about it too much.

On their last night, they got good and drunk, and Elgin said, "Should I get a disguise or something? Should I shave my head or get a wig?"

Carla laughed. They were eating in their room. "A beard," she said. "You should get a fake beard and glasses and maybe a nose job, and some other time-consuming surgery."

"No, really," he said.

"No, really," Carla said.

They went down to Kingston Mines and drank beer and listened to the blues, and she was right with him the whole time, as physically close to him as she could be, laying a claim to ownership on him for the whole bar to see, touching his face, a hand on his shoulder or rubbing his neck, grinding into him as they danced to "Rollin' and Tumblin'." They stayed for the sunrise set, the joint still packed on a Saturday night, a Sunday morning. She held his hand in her lap, squeezed it. He looked at her. She smiled. He smiled back. They looked at each other, smiling like a couple of idiots.

EIGHT

AUGUST

He had chaired only one board meeting of the Benefit Fund before he stumbled onto the scam. In late July, after McCabe had appointed him chairman, Elgin asked the fund administrator to route all the outgoing checks through his office for a month. He didn't know why. He was in way over his head with this thing, a $70 million fund, covering medical, prescription, dental, legal, optical, life insurance, every single benefit, except pension, for every single employee of the county, and, officially at least, he was in charge, the chairman of the board of trustees. So he sat at his desk, flipping through checks, hundreds of them, thinking, what, that he'd fulfill his fiduciary responsibility by merely touching these documents? The trial was two weeks away, and, according to the prosecutor's office, Corey would likely be convicted, and would likely do at least a few more months at Children's Village. The Newkirks had sold their house and moved. Marriage counseling was set to begin immediately after the trial, after, Laura said, that trauma was put behind them. He hadn't agreed to it so much as failed to disagree, more floating with the current of the sexual abuse apparatus, more of the ongoing erosion all around him. Two checks in a row caught his eye, one to an oncologist, one to radiology services at the county hospital, and the statement listed the covered employee as Susan Rajakowski, his own secretary. Jesus Christ, he thought, she has cancer.

And she hadn't even told him. Had he become so selfish, so consumed with his own mostly self-imposed disintegration, that a co-worker, a person he genuinely liked and respected, would know not to bother him with news of cancer? God, or worse, did she fear for her job? Did she honestly think that they would fire her because she was dying? It was too sick to imagine.

He picked up the checks and walked to Pearson's office, smiling at Susan as he passed her, hoping she couldn't see through him. "Everything good?" he asked her, the big smile hurting his face.

"Great," she said.

Elgin closed Pearson's door behind him, placed the checks—still attached by perforated seams to the statements—on Stan's desk, and sat in one of the leather chairs across from him. Pearson put on his granny glasses and scanned the documents quickly, then pushed them aside. "Don't look at these," he said.

"What do you mean, 'Don't look at these?' Do you know about this?"

Pearson handed the documents across his desk. "Don't know, don't want to know," he said.

"You don't *want* to know?"

Pearson took off his glasses, sucked on one of the bows, and squinted at Elgin. "That's right," he said. "You don't want to know, either. Get smart. What the hell are you doing with these anyway?"

"She's got a three-year-old," Elgin said. "How about that?"

Pearson's negotiating pose melted into what appeared to be genuine confusion, at least a face that Elgin had never seen used as a ploy before. "What?" Pearson said, shaking his head. "What are you talking about?"

Elgin waved the statements toward him. "Susan's got cancer and you don't want to know about it?"

"Wait a minute," Pearson said. "Wait just a minute here."

"No, I'm not going to wait a minute. If she's afraid to tell us that she has cancer—I mean, after everything that's happened in the last few months, I highly doubt that this is, like, a privacy issue—if she's afraid, if she thinks she's going to lose her job, then there's something wrong here. There is something really wrong here."

"Listen to me," Pearson said, holding up a finger, pointing it at Elgin, and emphasizing his words as he pointed to the ceiling, then right to the center of Elgin's chest, up and down: "You listen to *me*. A half year ago I saw something similar to this, something I wasn't supposed to see, something I blundered across like you blundered across this. Of course, I didn't know, and I still don't know—don't want to know—what was going on, but I asked some questions, naively trying to figure it out. And then I learned to shut up. Don't go down this path. You don't want to know about this."

"Now you listen," Elgin said: "I want to know if she's okay."

Pearson tore the statements out of Elgin's hand and placed them facedown on his desk, then pointed again. "Just keep your mouth shut and listen. If I call her in here, do not mention these documents," he said, tapping them with his pointer. "Okay?"

"Fine," Elgin said.

Pearson buzzed Susan and asked her to come in. He turned on the grandfather smile when she appeared in the doorway. Elgin craned his neck to watch her face. "Everything okay, Susan?" Pearson asked.

"Yes," she said, blushing a little, confused and then worried. "Fine. Is something wrong?"

"Nothing. Robert was just talking about what great work you've been doing," and Elgin said, "With everything I've been going through, you've had to pick up a lot of slack. I was just wondering about, you know, stress."

"No," Susan said. "No stress." She smiled, but the worry showed underneath.

"But, physically," Pearson said, "you're okay?"

"As far as I know," she said, blushing more deeply. She looked at the floor, then back up. "What is this?"

"No," Elgin said, "just that stress can sort of wear you down."

"Have I done something wrong?"

"No!" Elgin and Pearson said together. "In fact," Elgin said, "we were just talking about a raise. I know you're not up for review, but you've been pulling so much of the load that Stan and I have decided that a raise is in order. Ten percent. Three steps, whatever it is. Draw up the paperwork for payroll today. Stan'll sign it this afternoon."

Pearson cleared his throat. Fuck him.

"Great," Susan said. "Thanks."

"No problem," Elgin said. "But you're sure you're feeling okay?"

"Really. I'm fine."

"You're not sick?"

"I'm perfectly healthy."

"Robert's just been worried is all," Pearson said. "Feels like he hasn't been paying enough attention. He went through the same routine with me."

Susan laughed a little, looked at the floor.

"Go ahead and line up the paperwork for payroll," Pearson said.

"And keep up the good work," Elgin called as she closed the door. He turned back to Pearson, who handed the fraudulent checks over his desk. "Take these," he said. "And don't look at them."

"What the hell is going on?" Elgin said.

"I told you," Pearson said. "I don't know. Don't want to know. And neither do you. I'm going to tell you one more thing, though." He waited for Elgin to look him in the eye, then continued: "Don't trust anyone," he said. "Do you hear me? Do not trust *any*one."

"How about you?" Elgin said. "Should I trust you?"

"No," Pearson said. "I'll say it again. Do not trust *any*one. Do not dig around. Keep your head down and your hands off of everything. I'm not going to talk about this again."

"Well," Elgin said, "this is just bullshit."

"Listen to me," Pearson said. "How's your new car? Or, how about this: have you approached Artie Lynch yet?"

"You know I have." The week before, Elgin had sat at Sportsman's with Artie and explained over beers how the fixed arbitration would work, how the cops would agree to a new contract, and how, in two years, when McCabe was in the heat of the governor's race, an arbitrator would award agency shop to Artie's union, guaranteeing that every employee they represented would pay dues, through payroll deduction no less, whether they wanted to or not. The union's income would grow and become stable. The union local and the state umbrella would endorse McCabe for governor and aggressively get out the vote, bringing in the UAW, as well. Artie agreed. The wheel was turning. Elgin informed McCabe. It was such a petty crime, such a petty fraud, hell, it hadn't even happened yet, not the outcome anyway.

Sitting across from Pearson, Elgin felt the walls closing in. What a fool he had been, to sell himself so cheaply to them. "I understand what you're saying, Stan," he said. "I'll keep my hands to myself." But he dug around anyway, did a little detective work, and with full access to the fund's internal documents, and a few innocent phone calls to specific employees regarding alleged services they had received, he put it together, a lot of it anyway, and he never tipped his hand.

Carrie's birthday was six days before the trial and Laura wanted to have a party, Sasha, Donnie, and Nicole flying in from California, Ed and Joyce over from the lake house. Lou was there, Karen, Liz, Pat, the new therapy family, more abuse professionals in attendance than children. The night before, after leaving the kids with Laura's mother and father, who seemed to spend more time in his house now than Elgin did, he and Laura drove to the airport to pick up Donnie and Nicole, a rare moment alone together, which was uncomfortable, until Laura brought up the marriage counseling again, and then it seemed unbearable.

"I met Leah Goldstein this morning," she said just east of Ann Arbor, after a chatty rundown of the next day's party plans, "during Carrie's session with Pat. Leah," she said. "You know, the therapist? The marriage counselor?"

"I remember the name," Elgin said, wishing they could talk about anything but therapy—corruption, say, or crime, selling out. He had told Laura nothing.

"She said—and I think this will really interest you—she said that it was important to understand that *I* would not be her client." She paused. Elgin waited. "Also, that *you* would not be her client."

Even though Pat had recommended her to Laura, had indeed recommended the counseling in the first place, Laura would not be Goldstein's client. No, Goldstein would be impartial.

"Are you listening to me?"

"What if I got a different recommendation?" Elgin said. "What if I talked to somebody in the Department of Health and lined up another shrink?"

"Are you kidding me?" Laura said. "The Health Department? What do you want, a welfare therapist, someone not even good enough to have her own practice? Leah's probably the best counselor in the area. Why would you want less?"

"But how can you be sure?" Elgin said, knowing the answer, and Laura said, "Pat."

She leaned forward in her seat and turned her head to look at him,

gauging his reaction, looking for an opportunity to attack. He concentrated on the road.

"And I really don't want to get into this now," she said. "The
appointment's made, the whole thing is set up."

Elgin stared straight ahead. She sat back in her seat, looked out her
window.

She was worried about the trial, Elgin thought, worried that her
life would lose focus, become meaningless after all the intense preparation and anticipation was behind her. At the end of July, Pat had told
Laura that Carrie's *real* therapy wouldn't even begin until after the
trial. The weekly sessions, it seemed, had been nothing more than
preparation for that event: the testimony, the display of damage, the
parade of wounds. Laura had seemed relieved, had told Elgin that she
herself was also going to go into therapy, and when Elgin asked her
why, she shook her head and walked away from him. "I, for one," she
mumbled, "want to get over this."

But she didn't. It had become her religion, her reason to live.

"Do you want to know what Leah Goldstein said?" Laura asked.
"Or not?"

"Sure." And Carrie waking from nightmares almost every single
night: "He's there; no, in the closet, under the window, under the bed,"
Elgin holding her, then showing her the empty closet, leading her to the
window and looking out into the yard. Or, in her effort to be a good victim, pointing out kids at the playground or the grocery store, and saying,
"He could be one. You don't know. That one might be. You can't tell."
The potential molesters were everywhere for Carrie now, surrounding
her, and who was Elgin to say otherwise? Still, he wished that some part
of her could remain untouched by all this, though, at the moment, gearing up for the trial, it didn't seem possible.

"Anyway," Laura said, "she told me that *you* wouldn't be the client
and that *I* wouldn't be the client. She said we had to understand that.
The *marriage* is the client, she said."

"Oh," Elgin said. "Do we have to make it a victim first? I mean to
create the survivor?"

Laura shook her head, folded her arms across her chest. "Pathetic,"
she said.

"What's that?"

She shook her head.

They defaulted to silence.

The flight was late. They didn't speak, but the therapy hung between them, waiting to be discussed further, pored over, handled, as it always did. "If you don't want to do this, that's fine," Laura said. "I thought we agreed."

They sat in a row of attached chairs at the gate, waiting. "No," Elgin said. "We did. We agreed." When Laura had started attending the New Life Community Church a month before, she had dragged Elgin along a couple of times, and on the third Sunday, when he refused to go, she said, "But this is something we can do together, as a family. Come on," she said. "Let's go."

He sat at the kitchen table in his underwear, with the paper and a cup of coffee. After the previous week's service, the minister, Reverend Dykstra, had held on to Elgin's hand as he shook it at the back of the church, and said, "Always here to listen; always here to help." Elgin smiled back, finally managed to pull himself free, and vowed never to return.

"I can't stand that guy," Elgin said. "There's something nauseating about him."

"At least he wants to help," Laura said. "And even if you don't like him, just going is something we can do as a family." She was standing over him. "Come on. You have to hurry."

"We can go to the lake as a family," Elgin said.

"But this is ritualized," she said. "And spiritual. It's good for Carrie. For all of us."

No, it wasn't. It wasn't good for anybody. "The house is revolving too much around Carrie," he said. "Everything is Carrie. Everything is abuse. It's not good for her or anybody else."

"Oh," Laura said. "I see. Would you say the same thing about a heart attack victim, someone lying on the floor dying?"

"I don't think it's comparable."

Carrie had started using the "incidents" and the "post-traumatic stress" as leverage, which Laura allowed. Carrie couldn't go to swimming lessons because she was afraid of the male instructors. If she spoke, and didn't get an immediate response, her every desire met, she wailed about Corey. Any confrontation with Tommy was Tommy's fault. Laura bought it all, claiming it was temporary.

"You're not getting enough attention," Laura said, "is that it?"

"Yes," he said. "That must be it."

"'Bye," she said, and she loaded up the kids and drove off to Jesus.

That night, after the kids were in bed, after a day spent carefully avoiding any inflammatory issue, which meant not talking, Laura said, "I've been thinking about this quite a bit, especially after this morning, and your failure to participate. I think we need counseling," she said. "Pat agrees."

"I'm not going to church," he said.

"I said counseling." She sat next to him on the couch. "Look at us," she said.

He turned to face her, the woman he had fallen in love with, the woman he had married and had children with, the woman he no longer wanted to know or be associated with in any way. He couldn't remember the last time he had touched her or she had touched him. He couldn't remember the last time he had wanted to do something for her, or even to be in her presence. He looked at her looking at him, waiting, imploring him with her eyes, it seemed, to come back to her. He took her hand. "Okay," he said. "You're right," he said.

"Good," she said. She squeezed his hand.

"But I'm not going to church," he said.

"All right," she said, and it seemed as if they'd reached a tenuous settlement.

Passengers started filing up the ramp to the waiting area. "If you're not going to try, though," Laura said, "it's pointless."

He saw Donnie's big balding head above the crowd. "I am going to try," he said. "I promise," though it seemed more than likely that his effort would be inadequate. He put his arm around her mannequin's shoulder. She shuffled a step closer to him. They were trying. Or were they just putting up a front? When Laura saw Nicole, she ran into her arms, and Elgin could see that she was crying, allowing her sister to comfort her, something it seemed that he could no longer offer.

"Hey, Sasha," he said, kneeling down to his niece. Donnie kept his hand on her shoulder. "It's good to see you," Elgin said. She leaned against her father's leg. Donnie put his hand across her chest, worried, probably, that she would be next. Donnie went to Harvard. Donnie was a thief. Donnie came to my house and stole a leg of beef. Elgin stood and shook his hand.

"I'm sorry," Donnie said, looking at the top of his daughter's head and then up to Elgin. "I really am."

"I know," Elgin said. "Thanks. We all are."

They looked at each other. There was nothing else to say. Elgin watched Laura cry and take comfort in her sister's arms.

The birthday party the next day was interminable. Carrie ignored the three little girls she had invited and spent her time with the abuse professionals. After the games, after the cake, after all the strained pretending that she was a normal little girl, that this was a normal little birthday party, attended by cops and prosecutors and therapists, she began attacking the pile of gifts on the picnic table. She opened a present from one of her friends, a new Barbie, then dropped it and said, "I already have this one."

The adults hovered around the table. Carrie reached for another present. Elgin said, "What do you say, Carrie?"

Laura shook her head at him, shot him a warning glare. "It's okay," she said.

"What do you say, Carrie?" Elgin said.

Carrie looked at the table.

One of her friends, Taylor, picked up the Barbie box. "I'll take it," she said, and Carrie said, "Okay," and Elgin put his hand on her shoulder, and said, "Carrie, what do you say?"

"I already have that one," Carrie said.

"It looks like a good one," Lou said. "Maybe it's a lost twin or something."

Sasha said, "Can I have it?" and Donnie said, "No," and Laura handed Carrie another present. "This one's from Pat," she said.

Carrie took the box. Elgin put his face close to hers, and whispered in her ear: "I don't like the way you're acting," he said, aware of all the eyes upon them. "It's snotty. We're not going to open another present until you thank Emily."

Carrie didn't move.

"It's okay," Laura said. "Go ahead and open this one." Carrie opened the present, but Elgin didn't see what it was. Tommy had picked up the Barbie box and run. Elgin ran after him, grateful for the chance to escape. "Hey," he said, scooping up Tommy as he ran. "What do you have there, little man?"

"It's Barbie," Tommy said. "It's mean Barbie."

"Why's it so mean?"

Tommy made his mean-guy face: brow lowered, nose wrinkled, teeth bared. He growled. "It's a mean guy," he said.

"Oh," Elgin said, lowering him to the grass and resuming the chase. He played with Tommy at the party's periphery, until the guests began to leave, at which point he returned to shake hands and smile and say good-bye.

That night, while Elgin was giving Tommy a bath, Carrie walked into the bathroom, holding the new Barbie and its duplicate.

"Look, Daddy," she said. "It is a lost twin."

"Mean twin," Tommy growled in the tub.

"Maybe she ran away," Carrie said, "or was sold to pirates."

"Maybe," Elgin said.

"I really do like her," Carrie said, and Elgin said, "You don't have to like her, baby. You just don't want to be rude when someone gives you a gift. You just have to pretend to like her."

"Oh," Carrie said. "But I do like her."

"Good," he said.

"Pirate twin," Tommy growled.

"Do you like her?" Carrie said.

"Yes," Elgin said, rinsing the shampoo off Tommy's head.

"Well, good night," Carrie said.

"Wait a minute," Elgin said. He finished rinsing Tommy, then turned to Carrie. "Come here," he said.

She leaned into him. He pulled her tight. "Happy birthday," he said. "I love you," he said, and she said, "I love you," and he pulled her closer and finally let her go. "Good night," he called after her, and Tommy said, "Pirate Barbie."

After putting Tommy in his crib, Elgin stood by Carrie's partially opened door. "You don't have to play with both of them, honey," Laura said.

"No, I want to," Carrie said. "They're lost twins."

"Okay," Laura said. She paused. "You want to talk about anything else?"

Elgin walked away.

Later, after Donnie and Nicole returned to their hotel, and Ed and Joyce were put away in the den, Laura said, "Nice job, publicly embarrassing Carrie like that. Just what she needs right now." She climbed into bed next to him, careful to keep to her side.

"Maybe it is just what she needs," he said.

"Oh, yeah," Laura said. "More humiliation is definitely what she needs."

There was no point in going down this path. They would argue, trade barbs, until they became tired or bored. Nothing would be resolved. Nothing would be settled. Nothing would change. He turned off the light.

"I don't believe you're consciously trying to hurt her," Laura said. "Are you just not thinking?"

Elgin stared at his wall. It sounded like a good idea—not thinking. Eventually, they would fall asleep, the tension between them seeping out the open window, wafting out over the lawn, over the neighborhood, dissipating until it was nothing. But then they'd have to wake up.

The trial was a replay of the probable cause hearing, Corey bored, indifferent, a little gaunt, and Carrie hysterical. That morning, getting ready, it occurred to Elgin that Laura was like the mother of a beauty pageant child, primping the little marionette, adjusting her hair, coaching her on the talent part of the pageant, when she was to break down describing the rape. The trial reminded him of his father's funeral, when he was seventeen, a formal event seemingly unconnected to himself, a rite of passage to be endured, but not acutely observed or absorbed. The preacher and the mourners and the entire choreography of the event had seemed robotic, all of the people in attendance, even his dead father, merely players fulfilling roles. His own role was to be numb, far away, underwater. It was the same at Corey's trial. Actors appeared, spoke their lines, and disappeared. Laura cried on cue. The little bastard Corey mumbled denials. Liz ripped him to shreds. Pat helped. Carrie seemed ruined. It lasted four hours, Elgin's mind drifting away throughout. Corey was sentenced to three more months in Children's Village, which was to include intensive therapy, just as Liz had predicted, though, of course, she knew the script, having starred in countless performances of her role. They went out to dinner with the abuse crowd, the last time, Elgin hoped, that he'd have to be in their presence. Laura glowed. It seemed that her little girl had won the contest, had been named the new Miss Raped. Elgin smiled hard at the table, thanked them all. "We couldn't have done it," Karen said, putting her hand on Carrie's head, "without this one." Carrie beamed, like a good little victim.

Laura started her therapy; Carrie started going twice a week. The judge ordered the Newkirks to pay for all of it, including the marriage counseling. Laura talked about finding closure, needing closure, building closure. There was no closure. She contacted Carrie's school and met with the woman who would be her first-grade teacher in September, to go over Carrie's special needs, her fear of boys, her sensitivity to discipline. At home, when Elgin said, "No," Laura said, "It's all right. Go ahead." Sometimes they fought it out to stalemate. Mostly they tried to stay away from each other.

In their first session of marriage counseling, Laura reported that Carrie was now afraid of him, that, according to Pat, therapy had revealed an "association problem with her father." Most likely temporary.

How nice.

They sat in chairs across from Leah Goldstein, who had the couch to herself.

"And how do you feel about that?" Goldstein asked him.

"I'm not surprised," he said. He felt numb, half dead, not really a part of these proceedings, just as he had felt at the trial, though, now, he was almost relieved that they were moving toward an inevitable, inescapable conclusion beyond his or anyone's power to avoid, the freedom of surrender.

"Have you been led to believe that that's a normal response to this type of victimization?" Goldstein asked.

"No," he said.

"He doesn't like Pat," Laura said.

"Let's not put words in each other's mouths," Goldstein said. She turned back to Elgin. "How does it make you feel—that your daughter is afraid of you?"

"It makes me feel like shit," Elgin said. "What do you think? It makes me think she's been manipulated. It makes me think the whole thing is a sham."

"Okay," Leah said. "That's valid," and Laura said, "Valid?" and Leah said, "All feelings are valid," and Laura said, "Well, let me tell you about my feelings, because according to Pat, we're in real danger of backsliding here because of what's going on at home. I'm talking about permanent damage. I mean we don't agree on anything with how to approach this— if we ever even talk—so Carrie's getting all kinds of conflicting messages, which are getting in the way of recovery."

Goldstein nodded. Laura sat up straight in her chair. Fifteen seconds passed. "Robert?" Goldstein said.

He looked at her. He wondered if he could kill her with one punch to the head.

"Do you agree that there's a lack of coordination on your approach to Carrie's recovery?"

"Yes," Elgin said. Maybe two punches. Or six.

"Okay," Goldstein said. "That's good; that's a point of agreement. Let me ask you both this: we've talked a little bit about Carrie and the impact her trauma and recovery are having on your marriage; do you disagree on other things?"

Elgin looked at Laura. Her lips were drawn tight and she looked back at him, a staring contest. "What other things?" he said to Laura. "There aren't any other things. That's all we are, the entire family: grease for the therapy machine."

"That's just what I mean," Laura said. "And I wanted to wait until after the trial, but at this point, for Carrie, I think the most important thing is to get a little space, to get a little perspective."

"Oh," Elgin said. They looked only at each other. He was vaguely aware of an audience, but not of Goldstein specifically. "What, so you want to split up?" he said. "Boy, this therapy does work."

"Trial separation," Laura said. "For perspective. For Carrie." The hate in her eyes, the same hatred he must have been showing her, was an almost palpable thing, invisible, like electricity, but locking them together in opposition, the only thing connecting them.

"And is that what you want, Robert?" Goldstein asked.

"Yes," Elgin said. "For Carrie."

They told the children that Mommy and Daddy just needed a little time away from each other to think, that they still loved each other very much, and that the whole situation was temporary. Carrie cried. He held on to her. "I'm going to see you on Wednesday," he told her. "And Friday and Saturday and Sunday. Really, baby," he said, petting her hair, "this is not a big deal." Eventually, she believed him, or exhausted herself. Tommy cried because Carrie cried, and stopped when Carrie stopped. He held both children, kissed them several times. For a few hours after leaving, he felt a deep relief to be away, as if he could feel his body lightening up, letting go. His hotel room seemed like a refuge. And then it started to feel like a hole he would never manage to crawl out of.

He'd never considered taking the money, never considered flight, at least not seriously, not consciously; he'd never really considered anything beyond serving out whatever sentence was handed to him. When he called the dentist over in Sterling Heights, Dr. Lawrence, he was bored, fishing for information on the Benefit Fund scam after vowing to himself to leave it alone. It was dumb luck, good or bad. But, Christ, he'd been living in a hotel in Pontiac for almost two weeks, his family more or less lost to him. There was no way he could stay with Laura, especially after the second day of marriage counseling and the final revelation it had brought. Goldstein had given them a little home-work assignment. "Where do you see yourself in ten years?" she'd said. "Where do you want to be? What do you want to be? If you woke up tomorrow morning and a miracle had occurred, what would it be like, what would it look like? Jot down your thoughts," she said. And so Elgin sat in his hotel room, trying to *jot down his thoughts,* trying to envision himself in ten years, trying to figure out what he wanted. And there was nothing. Absolutely nothing. He didn't want anything and he couldn't see anything or imagine any kind of life in ten years. He couldn't envision anything miraculous, except getting away, being away from everything, which felt like suicide. He wanted his children, yes, but Laura was nowhere in the picture. She was the one who'd sent him to live in this hotel, away from his children. Though, of course, he was the one who'd surrendered. Long ago, he'd surrendered. But, regardless of that, his miracle was merely a negation, the absence of Laura. That was it. So divorce would lead to weekend visitation, and he would sink by degrees out of his children's lives, until he was finally entirely irrelevant to them, or worse, an irritant, something to be endured. What more could be taken away?

On that last day, the day after the last marriage counseling, he sat in his office, putting off work, wondering how or when he'd lost the ability even to hope for a way out, for a better life, and, finally, he called the dentist, Dr. Lawrence, who was so stupid and afraid, so wed to the same script Elgin was reading from, that he seemed to beg to be intimidated. "We're missing a payment," Elgin said on the phone, like a mobster in a bad movie, or like Klister himself. "Buddy's not happy."

"What payment?" the dentist said, and Elgin could practically hear him sweating. "I took care of it last week."

"Yeah," Elgin said, "well, maybe you fucked it up."

"I didn't fuck it up."

"We're not seeing it."

"I'm telling you I didn't fuck it up. Come on."

"Maybe you made a mistake, is all."

"I didn't make a mistake. I did just like I always do."

"Let's just be real clear about it, okay?"

"What?"

"Just tell me exactly what you did."

And then he told Elgin how he wired the money.

"Yeah, but maybe you got the number wrong," Elgin said. He felt great, better than he had in months. It was all so easy, and such a relief—like kicking a dog after a bad day. "We've seen that before," he said. "Too many times in fact, and then it's a mess."

"I didn't get the number wrong," the dentist said, and then he told Elgin the number.

Elgin didn't know where to go. He borrowed one of Pearson's negotiating tactics and hung ten seconds of silence.

The dentist said, "What?" and Elgin remained silent, and the dentist said, "If Buddy changed the password again, that's not my problem."

It was as if the money were being handed to him, as if he had set off a chain of events that would inevitably lead him out of this trap he was in, the words falling out of his mouth as if from a script, or as if by divine dictation. "No, it's all your problem," he said. "What do you know about the password? That's none of your fucking business."

"Hey, Buddy told me a long time ago, and now you're coming along and saying I can't be trusted?"

"What I'm saying is, if anything's missing, and it looks like it is, then I'll know where to go."

"He's changed it before," the dentist said. "I don't even know if it's the same. Come on."

Elgin stayed silent, letting out rope for the prick to hang himself with.

"Ask Buddy," the dentist said. "I'll call him right now," he said. "I've always been trusted. Christ, we grew up together."

"Calm down," Elgin said. "Buddy doesn't want to talk to you right now. Not until we locate the payment." In fact, Buddy was on vacation in Hawaii, unreachable. Everything was coming together. How often would this happen in his life, this kind of opportunity, this kind of convergence?

"I told you, I sent it. What am I supposed to do?"

"And this money that's missing," Elgin said, "like somebody's skimming. Somebody who knows the password."

"I told you, it might not even be the same. Please. Buddy's changed it before."

"Yeah, and you're the only one who knows and now there's something missing."

"I told you. We're like cousins."

"I gotta tell you, that's not what he's feeling. And McCabe is fucking furious."

"I didn't—"

"Shut up and let me think," Elgin said. He sighed deeply, grunted, counted to twelve. "All right," he said, through another deep sigh. "Which one did Buddy give you?"

"I've always been trusted."

"So let's clear the whole fucking thing up then. If you don't want to work with me, that's fine. If you want my help, then let's clear it up. Which one did he give you? And don't lie to me; don't make it worse."

"Okay," the dentist said. "Jesus. It was like five months ago."

"Which one?"

"Mariner623," he said, "okay?"

"Okay," Elgin said. "That's your luck," he said. "That's an old one. Still, you just sit tight and keep your mouth shut. I'm going to keep looking at this thing. But let me tell you, Buddy's ready to rip your fucking head off. McCabe's ready to rip Buddy's head off. And one more thing: the next time Buddy wants to tell you a secret when he's drinking, do yourself a favor. Don't listen."

He hung up the phone and contacted the bank. He was a machine now. This wasn't the man being pulled out to drown; this was someone fighting to stay alive. The account number and password gave him full access. It was all being handed to him. He did not have to think about what he was going to do. He was already doing it. He left a note for Pearson, saying he needed the rest of the week off to attend a therapy retreat with the family, then got out of the office, and packed a duffel bag. Before leaving his hotel for Detroit Metro and then Miami, before leaving forever, he called Dr. Lawrence back to buy a little time and to enjoy the role of chief tormentor, to torture the guy. "It was a fuckup with the bank," he said. "Not the first time. Don't worry about it. Just keep your mouth shut. Your ears, too. Buddy is pissed as hell. At everybody. Especially you."

"All right," he said. "I will. Jesus."

He parked the Jeep in short-term parking but took the keys with him. He unloaded the duffel bag, then ran the key along the paint job, up one side of the Jeep, down the other. He was running to the money. He was acting like a twelve-year-old. Everything in Michigan had been contaminated, used up, and now, in front of him, it seemed that there was limitless potential, virgin territory, new lands to be despoiled. He was a machine, but he felt a brief thrill of freedom, followed by the leaden weight of guilt, which would not serve him well at this point, which could only get in the way, which was pointless and meaningless because he was doing the only thing he could do. He was running away. Best not to think about the implications, especially with so much delicate work ahead. Best not to think at all. Everything would sort itself out later. He needed some space, "to get a little perspective," as Laura had said. He bought his ticket with a county credit card and boarded the plane, and the giddiness came in waves, always followed by the guilt, but he didn't even have the money yet, so he just had to control it somehow, turn himself off. He sat in his seat, waiting for takeoff. He was free. He was dead. He was alive. He was a machine.

NINE

DECEMBER

Carla rented a car for him at the Kalamazoo airport, a Dodge Stratus, since he didn't have a credit card and couldn't rent one himself. After he'd transferred his belongings from her car to the rental, Carla wrote down her parents' phone number and handed it to him. "I won't be able to call you," she said. "Whatever it is you're going to do, just be smart." He kissed her one last time. "And I'm not going to wait here forever," she said.

He followed her up to 94, honking and waving when she turned to get on the interstate, then drove up Portage Road and into Kalamazoo. He drove around for three hours. He was a hundred miles from home, fifty miles from where he'd grown up outside of Grand Rapids, where his mother still lived. Corey's sentence would be up by now, but Elgin didn't know where the Newkirks had landed after they'd sold the house in August. Nearly four months had passed since he'd seen his children, more than a tenth of Tommy's life. He had no idea what he would say to them. He finally stopped at the Sleepy Time Motor Lodge, not five miles outside of Kalamazoo, where he got a mildewy little cabin. At this rate it would take him a month to get home. He could walk it faster. Hell, he could crawl.

After unloading the car, he resolved to count the money, something he hadn't done since securing the safe deposit box in Manhattan. It was a Sunday afternoon, five days before Christmas. He turned on the Lions game, the duffel bag containing the money on the floor beside him. At halftime, he walked across the parking lot to watch the rest of the game in the lounge. A dozen or so fans were gathered there, groaning and cheering, Elgin right along with them. He ate dinner at the bar, then went back to his room, resolved to count the money in the morning.

But not until after breakfast, though this time he was at least smart enough to take the duffel bag with him. And then, with the Santa Clauses and reindeer and snowflakes and little miniature Christmas trees all around him, it seemed that a little Christmas shopping should probably be his first priority, which was just as good, or, hell, better than counting the money, because if he bought gifts, that surely suggested an intent to deliver them. He drove over to the Westmain Mall in town, and even at ten in the morning the place was jammed with Christmas shoppers. Since leaving the world of the employed so many months ago, Elgin had been repeatedly struck by how many people didn't work during the day. In his previous life, he had assumed that just about everybody lived the way he did: they got up, they went to work, they came home. At first he had been mildly offended by the realization that so many people did not live that way, practically muttering, "What are all of you people doing out on the street, in restaurants, at movies, in stores? Go to work." Now, he cheered them on. Don't go to work, fuck work, good for you. Still, today, he wished they were somewhere else, out of his way.

He wandered the mall, indecisive and inept. Laura had always bought the kids' presents, carefully budgeting and determining a gift limit sometime around September. She'd show him the purchases, and he would nod. It wasn't as if he was completely uninvolved: if she sent him to the toy store with a list, he usually managed to get the right thing. But it was Laura who determined just what the kids wanted or needed or would love. Now, walking through the packed mall, the Christmas music an attempt to soothe over the low, echoing roar, kids Tommy's and Carrie's ages lined up to see Santa, all the shoppers carrying packages and bags, Elgin, still empty-handed, fought with himself over just what to purchase, resisting the dad-of-divorce impulse to buy the most impossibly expensive and elaborate gift he could find, thus generating plenty of anxiety over finding if not the most expensive present, then the most thoughtful and absolutely perfect one. No matter what he chose, though, it seemed that the gift would be fraught

with political significance and hidden messages: either Daddy's trying
to buy your love, or Daddy doesn't really care about you. After several
hours of this paralysis, he finally settled on a china doll for Carrie (far
too fragile, Laura would say, but Carrie was old enough to be careful,
Elgin believed) and a wooden train set for Tommy. He'd found the
balance between too much and too little, and surely, these were gifts
that the kids would love. He hoped. He took the wrapped packages
out to the car, and drove back to the Sleepy Time, feeling pretty good
about his day's work.

Not that he was any closer to a plan, of course. He called Carla,
but nobody was home. What if she had inadvertently written down the
wrong phone number? What if she'd done it on purpose? No, that was
ridiculous. His room smelled like old sweat and mildew and ten million cigarettes. The bedspread was polyester, the pillows foam. He'd
gotten used to the good life. He turned on the TV, turned it off.
Carla's absence left him acutely sensitive to the hums and murmurs
over ordinary silence, the static of the picture tube, the baseboards
ticking as they cooled, the almost discernable buzz of a lightbulb burning. He sat on the dingy bedspread in his shitty room in the middle of
nowhere with nowhere left to go. The kids' presents sat atop the beat-
up dresser, a strip of veneer peeling up off one side. He'd forgotten
Laura, had not even considered a gift for her. Maybe a prayer book or
some bathroom art with a Jesus saying. What an asshole he was. And
what about Carla; wasn't he now obligated to buy her something?
Would she expect it, be hurt if he failed? But they weren't like that,
really, entangled by gift obligation and expectation, were they? He
watched a semi pull in through his lot view window. He got up and
closed the smelly drapes, then dumped the contents of the duffel bag
onto the bed.

The money was wrapped in a black garbage bag, still in packets of
hundreds, so it was easy to count. During the trip, he'd pulled out a
packet at a time, each containing ten thousand bucks, but he'd never
looked in the bag to determine his total. Before they'd left, he'd placed
ten packets in the safe deposit box, so the counting started at a hundred. There were twenty-two packets left, meaning he still had well
over a quarter million. In his previous life, back when there was still

income and the strong likelihood of income for most of the rest of his life, that would have seemed like a lot. Now, it was close to nothing. And he'd be giving Laura most of what he had with him. So figure a hundred grand. To last him forever.

He handled the money, smelled it. Even when he'd first arrived in New York, he'd never dumped the money out or rolled around in it like people did in movies. Nor did he think much about it, except as something that was his to use. It didn't talk, or, even as Dylan said, swear. It was his to use, but somehow, it seemed that it had never really belonged to anyone, especially coming out of a bank in Barbados. At one time, almost as an abstraction, it had belonged to the taxpayers of Oakland County. But, then, they had passively agreed to give it up as part of their tax bills, less than a dollar a person. And then it had found itself in the Employees' Benefit Fund. And then it had found itself stolen by Klister and McCabe, and then stolen again by Elgin. But, in a very real sense, he was the only person who had ever seen it. Most of this money had never been more than an electronic impulse. The taxpayers had certainly never seen it, nor had the county, except as numbers on a balance sheet. The people who stole it first—who created the complex web that facilitated its transfer from the County Benefit Fund to corrupted doctors and dentists and an insurance agency for work and services never provided, and then the transfer of the kickbacks from those same non-service providers into a separate, offshore account—they never saw it, at least not as dollars that could be handled and smelled. And when Elgin claimed it, it was all new money, never spent or touched by anyone but clerks. It was fresh, brand new, made just for him, it seemed. And now it was being redistributed, not that he had any illusions that he was Pretty Boy Floyd or Robin Hood.

So that would be Laura's present, two hundred and twenty grand, give or take. Convincing her to accept it would be another matter. Maybe it would wind up back with the county to be stolen and re-stolen again. Maybe that would be his gift to humanity, or to someone as lucky or unlucky as himself, who would walk away with it. He hoped it would turn into coats and shoes for his kids, toys and books and music lessons and candy. But he doubted it. He'd have to give that some thought, figure out a way to get it into their hands—just what they wanted: Daddy's stolen money.

He tried Carla again, and was a little caught off guard when the phone was answered by her father or one of her brothers. It didn't seem possible that anyone was still alive outside of his shitty room. "Uh, hello," he said. "Can I speak to Carla, please?" He felt like he was in high school again, talking to the man whose daughter he was fucking or wanted to fuck.

"Wrong number," the man said, and he hung up.

So she *had* given him the wrong number. Then he realized that they didn't know her as Carla. Only he did. Carla was entirely his. He wrapped the packets of money back in the garbage bag and redialed the phone, asking for Stacey this time. The man didn't answer, just moved the phone away from his face and shouted her name.

=

My pretty pink room where I grew up is once again intact, jammed with stuffed animals and my princess phone, and a poster of two darling puppies, a shrine to my girlhood, certainly not how I left it when I went to college, the last time I truly occupied it. Then it was posters of indie bands and a Job box in a drawer filled with roaches and a green double-chambered U.S. Bong on the shelf in my closet wrapped in a sweater, and lots of books. I was the baby, the last one to leave, so maybe that's why I got away with murder.

My father is tired. My mother is tired. I am not tired, except when I have to explain myself, but as I weave my story, the lies building a plausible truth, it becomes easier to entrench myself for the siege, however long it will be until I get the fuck out of here. Not that it's so bad seeing my family. Everyone is here, Joe in from Battle Creek, with his wife and kids, Michael up from Miami, and Rachel and her husband and kids across town. My father hovers over my mother, admonishing her to take it easy if she so much as stands from a chair or sits up on the couch. I settle into the female role of cook and house slave, dusting, vacuuming, cleaning and organizing the shelves in the pantry. Not that I have to, just that it gives me something to do, and helps erase my previous silence. And, of course, I can't tell them about Robert, at least not yet, because I don't know how to or even what he is to me. He's a former trick, I could say, a john, who abandoned his wife and kids after ripping off some dirty politicians down in Oakland County. He's currently on the run. I think you'll really like him.

Joe's wife, Tammy, cooks the first night, and Mom and Dad tell the story of the heart attack over dinner. When my mother asks about school, knowing full well that something went wrong, I tell her it's great. Fantastic. Michael and I smoke a joint after everyone goes to bed, and he says, "So what's going on? Mom said you dropped out of school."

"I don't know," I tell him. "I'm on sabbatical."

I shove the stuffed animals piled over my pillow onto the floor, and crawl into my narrow childhood bed. Stopping feels like a huge mistake. I can't help thinking something horrible is going to happen, and I even fear his wife and children, the pull they'll have on him, and I hate myself for this jealousy. Stopping is the problem. If we were just on the road, moving, everything would be fine.

When he calls, I talk to him in my room, pretending to be happy. He's trying, too—to sound upbeat and to be funny, so I laugh in the right places. I tell him to be careful, to call as often as he feels like it, which sounds just a little bit desperate. And at dinner my mother says, "Who was that boy that called?"

"A friend," I tell her. The only friend I have, it feels like.

Though I visit Amy Schumacher over in Burton the next afternoon. It's only been a year since I've seen her, but she has a baby now, and a house, and doesn't work anymore. We get stoned and play with the baby. "I shouldn't do this," she says, taking an enormous hit. "Jimmy'd kill me." We reminisce about our high school days, which feels like mourning, but funny, too. Her three-month-old daughter is beautiful, a wonder. I watch her breast-feed and am struck by how profound it is that Amy's body has served as a lunch wagon for this tiny human being from the moment of its conception. Profound and terrifying—to be the constant fulfiller of need. I even hold the baby and don't feel freaked out that I'm going to drop her or break her. After she goes down for a nap, Amy makes us tea, and says, "It's a lot of work, but I like it, too. The whole motherhood thing, though, I mean, it totally changes your life. You're tired all the time, and you don't really do anything. I mean, compared to your life, in New York and everything."

"Yeah," I say, "that has ups and downs, too." The diaper pail, the changing table, mobiles and various bouncing seats and other baby appliances seem to fill the entire house.

"But just to get out of the house," she says. "Just to talk to adults."

"It's not all it's cracked up to be," I say, though I'm thinking that anything must be better than this, trapped in a house with a baby, under the thumb of some moron who won't even let you get stoned.

"But you're doing well," she says.

It's a question.

"Oh, yeah," I say, "really, really well."

Driving back to my parents' house, I think that I'll probably never see her again.

My father has not been to work since my mother's heart attack, several weeks ago, and does not plan on returning until the new year. "More than thirty-five years in," he says over a can of beer. "Hell, I could quit now, the pension I've got."

Joe and Michael are out doing all of their Christmas shopping, as they do every Christmas Eve that they're together, stoned to the bone, I'm sure, and Tammy and Rachel have taken the five kids sledding. Mom's asleep in the living room, so it's just Dad and me at the kitchen table. I get us each another can of beer. "Well, why don't you retire?" I say, but I can't imagine what he would do with himself if he did. In the few days I've been here he seems out of place in his own house, fidgety, waiting for an opportunity to get away or to make himself useful. This morning he spent two hours sweeping the driveway of the half inch of fresh snow that fell overnight.

"I don't know," he says. "Maybe I will, maybe I won't. The funny thing is, the amount I've bitched about it, I think I'd miss going in. A lot of the guys who retire end up coming back to lead the tours. They just can't let go."

"What about travel?" I say. "You and Mom could drive around the country like you've always talked about doing."

"Yeah," he says, "but how long can you do that?" and I think, Forever.

He turns the conversation to me, to school, to how I'm doing. "I'm all right," I tell him. "Just taking a little time off." I feel like a fool or an ingrate for making such a remark to a man who worked as much overtime as he could get to put us through college. "I'm just trying to figure some stuff out," I say, feeling more stupid still, but my father says, "That's all right. You take your time with it. Do you have enough money?"

"Yeah," I say, and then I surprise myself when I tell him that I've met someone, that we spent the last seven weeks on the road, just driving from place to place, and my father says, "That's absolutely perfect. That's exactly what you should do. Most people put it off until they don't want to do it anymore. Good." He clears his throat, takes a drink of beer. "Now, what's his name?" he says.

"Robert," I tell him.

"Oh," he says. "Robert," he says. "Not Bob?"

"I don't think he cares," I say. "Sure, Bob."

"What's he do?"

"He's in labor relations," I say, resurrecting his old self.

"The right side," my father says, "I hope."

"Of course," I say.

"Who's he work for?"

"Oh," I say, "one of those big labor things in New York. I'm not that sure."

The back door flies open and the kids pour in, puffing and screaming. I help them out of their snowsuits. "Santa's already in the air over China!" Jill screams into my face, and I say, "That's right."

When the phone rings during dinner and I run to the kitchen to answer it, I hear my mother say, "I believe Stacey has a boyfriend. Who else would call on Christmas Eve?"

After asking Rachel to hang up the phone in the kitchen, I talk to Robert in my room. He's all the way over in Ludington, alone on Christmas Eve. He's moved farther away from his family. "That's good," I say. "Just stay there. I'll come up in a few days."

"No," he says, "I have to see them."

"My mother thinks you're my boyfriend," I tell him.

He laughs. "Well, I am, aren't I?" he says.

Boyfriend, I think later that night. Puppy dogs and class rings. A milkshake with two straws. Matching Winnie the Pooh sweatshirts. Anal sex by candlelight.

≡

The Loving Cup, Elgin's hotel in Ludington, featured a heart-shaped tub for two, a mirror over the bed, and piped-in porn. He hadn't realized it was that kind of place, and then decided that he didn't care. He'd been driving around the state for two days, never getting closer to home than Lansing. Just being in the car, on the road, felt good for a little while, and then became stupid and oppressive. Outside of Grand Rapids, he drove through his old neighborhood, the woods he'd explored as a child, which had seemed endless, filled with any possibility imaginable—buried treasure, arrowheads or cannon balls, the ruins of an old fort or Indian village—chewed up by development. There was really nobody he wanted to see, though for some insane reason, he stopped at the Majic Market, not three miles from his mother's new condo, and called her. "Where are you?" she said.

"Out of town," he said.

"Whatever it is you think you're doing," she said, "drop it and go home. Do you hear me? Those babies need you. Go home. Laura's hysterical."

No kidding, he thought.

"Do you hear me?" she said. "Whatever it is that's happened, you can come clean and make a new start."

"You're absolutely right," he said.

"Don't patronize me."

"I'm not."

"And about Carrie," she said. "Yes, it's hard, but it's certainly not harder on you than it is on her. Stop acting like a crybaby."

So Laura had told her. Good. Something else he wouldn't have to do. This was what dying was like. Letting go, slipping away.

He ended the conversation promising to go home, then wandered the state, wondering if and when the car would decide to lead him into Oakland County, but getting farther and farther away. He stayed in Ludington Christmas Eve and Christmas, fifty or so miles down the lake from Laura's parents' place. It seemed appropriate to keep the porn on twenty-four hours a day and to smoke as much as possible, wallowing in the mire until he became so sick of himself that he would be forced to go home.

He went out to Ludington State Park on Christmas Day and wandered the empty beach, the sky gray and low, spitting a few flurries into the lake. Laura's parents were probably at his place, maybe Sasha and Nicole and Uncle Donnie as well. Just last summer they'd been right up the beach and had buried a dead fish. Elgin had always loved being by the lake in the winter, when it was lonely and cold and almost colorless, infinite shades of gray, the sand, water, and sky smeared together. He sat in the sand and looked out over the water. Maybe he could give the money back. He still had more than half. Maybe he could cook up some kind of insurance scheme wherein Klister and McCabe's theft and corruption would be automatically revealed if they ever came after him. Yeah, and they'd just let him be.

He'd been duped, stupid, thinking that the minor corruption, the deal with the cops, was all they were after, when, in fact, they just needed another puppet, someone who owed them something to chair the Benefit Fund, which they were busy milking. Pearson had been getting too close, so they'd cleverly ensnared Elgin in a minor corruption to keep him scared and quiet and off balance, and then installed him as the chair, so that the enormous corruption, the skimming of the fund, could occur right under his nose, on his watch, his fingerprints all over it, implicating him in the crime. He'd be the one to go up in flames, while they rode on to the governor's mansion and a bigger pond to drain. But it hadn't gone that way. He'd been played all right, but he'd gotten the last laugh. Maybe.

He could still go to the attorney general and blow the whistle. If he only cared about it that's what he would do, but he didn't care. Their corruption was entirely irrelevant to him. Though making them suffer, revealing them for the pigs that they were, did have appeal. But, really, none if it had anything to do with him anymore.

On Christmas Day Laura always made a big roast of beef tenderloin, Carrie and Elgin's favorite, and they were probably around the table now, the kids suffering gift OD and letdown, probably worse than ever this year, everybody heaping the presents on Carrie, and then Tommy so there wouldn't be hard feelings and envy. Elgin would sit on the floor with Tommy, setting up the new train set, the scene one of domestic bliss and security, and the mommy and the daddy would love each other and protect the children, who would grow into stable healthy adults with families of their own for the still loving grandparents to dote upon.

If the only problem was the money, the crime, the solution would be easy. He'd pick up his family and move, run, settle somewhere near Capitol Reef, and they'd live out their lives. Or he'd blow the whistle, do his time, or maybe get some kind of immunity, and then return to his family.

But the crime was just one of the problems, the smaller one. He got up and walked on the packed sand down near the waterline. He'd come clean with his wife and his kids before the year was out. But, God, Klister was capable of anything, especially with his ass and McCabe's on the line. And there were probably others involved. Who knew how deep this shit went? He couldn't let them hurt his kids. Or, shitheel that he was, even Laura.

He'd have to stake the place out, determine the right opportunity for making his appearance. And then he could see his kids, touch his kids, apologize, make promises. Laura, too.

He went back to his room and called Carla, who was, she said, feeling a little trapped, a little antsy. "When are you going?" she said. "Do you know?"

"Soon," he said.

"Why don't you come here first," she said.

It seemed like a good idea.

≡

The deal is to meet in the lobby at the Econo Lodge out on Bristol Road. He's there when I arrive, thank God; I couldn't bear to sit waiting, on display, not that I give a fuck about the people of Flint, whom we always called the Flintstones. And I'm so happy to see him that I feel like part of a bad movie, slow motion and everything, him standing when he sees me, then the both of us rushing toward each other to embrace. "How you doing?" we ask each other. "Fine, fine," we answer.

The room of course sucks, but I don't care.

"Let's get out of here," I say. "I'll give you an insider's tour of Buick City."

We get Halo burgers and I drive him around, pointing out the landmarks of my childhood, most of downtown entirely boarded up now.

"Why would anyone willingly stay here?" I say, and he says, "Maybe they don't have anywhere else to go."

"That's ridiculous," I say. "Every road leads out of here."

"I drove through this town this morning," he tells me, "when I was coming over from Ludington . . ."

"Yeah," I say.

"I'd been through it before," he says, "a couple years ago, no, more than that, before we had kids, I don't know, seven years ago."

He's talking to the windshield, staring at the ruins of Flint.

"So?" I say, pissed at his need for prompting.

"We were coming back from Laura's parents' place up at Bear Lake," he says, starting to roll, but still staring straight ahead, "and we decided to take small roads. It was a Sunday in April, maybe Easter, in the morning, and we came upon this town, just a collection of faded shacks in the woods, pine woods, maybe twenty or thirty beat-up shacks and one cinder-block church, all mud, and these black people standing out in it, up to their knees it seemed like, a few sitting on crumbling old porches and a few standing on the concrete in front of the church, but their legs covered in mud, and they all stopped and watched us drive by on the blacktop, most of them stuck in the mud, sinking for all I knew, but the weirdest part was all these blue and pink balloons attached to the railing of the church steps and the porches of some of the shacks, all these cheerful balloons, the only color there, among the deepest, dirtiest poverty I'd ever seen in my life, poor people planted in the mud watching us go by."

He clears his throat. I refuse to look at him.

"Anyway," he says, "I happened upon it this morning, the same place—and, I mean, what are the odds of that?—though there wasn't any mud, of course, or balloons, but I slowed down, practically stopped, and looked to see if the people were still there, covered in snow now and aged and weathered, maybe crumbling or frozen, cracked and broken, but there weren't any people outside. Smoke rose from most of the shacks through stovepipes and cinderblock chimneys, and I had this bizarre feeling of elation that they were all warm inside, that they'd gotten out of the mud. It was just so weird."

"Yeah," I say, "horrible," and I drive us back to the motel in silence.

"There's no use putting this off any longer," he says, after he pours the wine.

He's dead again, that's what it is.

"And when it's done," I say, "then we'll be happy like before."

"Why not?" he says.

"So don't act like this."

"Like what?"

"Like you're beaten. Like you're out of chances."

He rubs his chin, staring at the motel wall.

"Snap out of it," I tell him.

"No," he says, "I just have to do this thing."

"So, do it," I say, "and then we go. We're not the people in the mud."

"You're right," he says, looking at me, smiling a little, climbing out of the casket.

And I think, It only feels like we are.

≡

He stayed in Flint through the end of the year, fifty miles up 23 from home. It felt like a grace period. On the second morning, when Carla arrived at his hotel, he asked if he could meet her family. "I didn't even tell them you were here," she said. "But sure." She told him the lie about being some kind of labor guy with an organization in New York, and he said he could come up with a story.

"Will you be staying at the house?" she asked.

"Do I have to?"

"No," she said. "Why don't you get out of this shithole, though. Move over to the Holidome, invite the kids over to go swimming."

They went out to lunch, then moved to the Holidome and planned their story for the next day. They lay in bed and watched TV and talked, and it felt like the last day in hiding.

The next day he met the family as Robert Oliver, drank a beer with the old man, talked labor—the Triangle Shirtwaist fire, the great sit-down strike in Flint, Homestead. Carla, whom he was careful to call Stacey, was proud of him, he could tell, the proprietary hand on his shoulder, the way she smiled at him from across the room. He passed all the tests. The siblings and in-laws came over to his hotel so the kids could go swimming. He and Carla played with them in the water while the adults sat poolside on indoor lawn furniture. Carla was clearly the favorite among the children, and playing with them made him anxious and nervous to see Carrie and Tommy. After swimming and dropping the kids with the grandparents, Elgin took the adults out to dinner. Later, he had another beer with the old man, and when everyone went to bed, he and Carla sat on the couch in the family room in the basement, kissing.

After he did what he had to do down in Oakland County, whatever that was, it seemed likely that Carla would be waiting for him. It was almost too much to hope for, but the way she was bringing him in, it seemed that they were preparing to be together at least for a while—a day, a week, a month. Whether or not he deserved it was beside the point. And he didn't want to think like that. He just wanted to do what he had to do, find out what he had to do, and knowing that Carla might wait for him, that a whole life might be waiting, seemed to make action possible, as if now, finally, there was a chance to move forward. He just had to figure out a way to bring his kids back into his life, that was all, or, more accurately, to bring himself back into their lives. And, somehow, to stay there. And, hopefully, to stay alive.

=

The night before he leaves, I stay with him at his hotel. My parents don't approve of this kind of thing, but they like him so much that they don't bother to say anything. I know I'll be on edge, ready to move, after he's gone, but we seem like normal people now, out of hiding, and when we're together it doesn't seem like anything bad could ever get to us. I know it's a lie, but I don't care. We stay up most of the night. I don't want to let him go, but I know he'll be back. I know he loves his children and needs to see them. There's a lot I know and some things I pretend not to know, or am afraid to know, or am afraid to let him know. I don't want him to be influenced by it, when I haven't even taken the test yet and so don't really know for sure. I think it happened in Wyoming, in Cheyenne, if it happened at all. I've been reading about it, and I'm pretty sure that what I felt in Nebraska was implantation cramping, or maybe not. But, I feel better about it now, the way he's acting, healthy, human—if it's even true, if it's even viable, if I even want it, which, more and more, and especially after this week and all the other stuff we've been through, it seems like I do. Except when I question my motives. Except when I think about the trap it could be. And it might be wrong not to tell him, but how can I tell him something I don't even know for sure myself?

In the morning, the first day of the new year, we order breakfast from room service, and lounge around, clawing time. "I have to go," he finally says. I don't want to walk him out. I don't want to watch him get into the car. "So go," I tell him. I kiss him by the door, but don't cling, don't hold on too tight. And then he's gone.

TEN

JANUARY

Pearson was dead by his own hand, which turned the key, which started the engine, which filled his closed garage with carbon monoxide, which killed him. The autopsy had revealed nothing of the coercion or fear or guilt or whatever it was that those motherfuckers had held over him, the threats that Elgin couldn't guess at directed toward Pearson's wife, children, grandchildren, or, and he hoped not, Pearson's own good name, his dignity, his ability to hold his head high. But it couldn't be that. You wouldn't leave your shit- and piss-smeared body in the garage for your wife to find if you were trying to preserve dignity. What Elgin had hoped would be a means to propel him further forward—calling Pearson to feel out the terrain—had instead locked him into a paralytic fear for his children's safety, a spiral of deepening paranoia. Not that he was going to quit or give up. He'd come this far. But he had to be more careful now than ever. Maybe he needed a gun. Maybe the thing to do was to drive over to Klister's house, grab him by the scalp, stick the gun in his mouth, and blow a large hole in the back of his skull, through which his atomized brains could spray out. Same for McCabe. But he didn't know what they'd had on Pearson or how deep he'd been in or what any of this was really about. It would be a mistake to sanctify the man. There was just too much Elgin didn't know.

Except in his guts.

And he believed that as long as he was not physically associated with his children, as long as he was still missing, whereabouts unknown, they would be safe. The kids would only hold value if Klister could get to Elgin, could locate Elgin and talk to Elgin and threaten Elgin. And that had not occurred.

Besides, Laura's father's connections to the party and the Printer would certainly protect his grandchildren. Christ, this was just crazy paranoia. For all Elgin knew, Pearson's suicide, his lonely desperation, was as tawdry and cheap and common as a thousand others, connected to some woman he'd had on the side, maybe, or gambling debts. Not that Elgin had ever seen evidence of anything like that. But there was plenty you never knew about people.

He sat in a wing chair in his hotel room, another hotel room— how many hotel rooms had there been?—the paranoia a shadow chamber ringed by infinite doors leading out into endless scenarios of what had and what might occur, none of them less than horrific. God, they could already be dead. But he'd seen the house. It hadn't burned down or exploded. Though he hadn't seen any signs of life there, either. But, no, they were fine. He just had to settle down, keep a cool head.

Driving down 23 from Flint, his confidence and excitement had built to such a degree that when he reached the 11 Mile Road exit, he took it, as he had a million times before, as if he were merely returning from the hardware store. Daddy's home! Though he quickly realized that it wouldn't be right to just show up. He had to at least call Laura, prepare her for his arrival. And, also, he certainly didn't want Klister or McCabe or anyone else who was after him to know of his presence in the county. And so, the first thing he had to know was the spin they'd put on his disappearance, which meant a discussion with Pearson, the person he distrusted the least.

He drove past the house, then turned around and drove past it again. The Christmas lights were strung over the bushes out front, one of his many neglected jobs that Laura must have performed. Snowflake shapes cut from white paper decorated the front windows; Carrie had certainly made those. And Tommy running around the dining room table, his blanket held high over his head, trailing him as he chased Carrie or she chased him, probably not shouting "Bunge!" anymore, but another private word or phrase which Elgin wouldn't know about. His throat tightened with guilt and tenderness. The garage door was open, but the car was gone, which meant, perhaps, that they would be home shortly. Or maybe not. It was New Year's Day, a holiday. Maybe they were at a party. Maybe not. Their business was no longer his. He had to get this thing moving so he could see them, touch them, talk to them. He had to start making things right or better.

He drove down to Ann Arbor and checked into the Sheraton off State, between the mall and the airport, and called Pearson. It had been over four months, and now he couldn't wait five more minutes to see them. When Doris picked up the phone, Elgin could hear the grandchildren screaming in the background. "Robert!" she said. "My goodness! Where are you? What happened?"

He told her it was too much to explain, complicated, but he was all right, in Florida, and how was she? And the grandkids? Good, good, and was Stan available?

"Stan?" she said, as if she'd never heard the name. "Oh," she said. "You don't know, do you?"

And then he did know, even before she told him about the body in the garage, the car still running on a Sunday morning when she'd discovered his corpse and a note that said, "I love you," and, "I'm sorry."

"I didn't know he was depressed," she said. "There weren't any signs. Maybe a little tension, maybe his upcoming retirement, but he never talked too much about his work. You keep asking yourself what you could have done. You keep wondering—"

"No," he said. "Doris, there was nothing you could have done."

"But is there anything you know," she said, "that could somehow help explain this? I mean, one day everything's fine, and the next day you kill yourself?" She was crying now. "Or did I not know him at all?"

"No," Elgin said. "Doris, no. Of course you knew him. I don't think that's it."

"Well, then what? It happened right after you disappeared, a week, two weeks, I don't know. And Buddy and Don were so good, over here that afternoon. They arranged everything. You should have seen the flowers, everything catered so beautifully. Every department was there at the funeral, and Buddy and Don and the boys were pallbearers."

"I'm so sorry I wasn't there," Elgin said, panic breeding and mutating and multiplying in his mind like bacteria. McCabe and Klister carrying the box containing the corpse they had made.

"But what happened to *you?*" Doris said. "I knew about Carrie and all; Stan had told me. I hope you don't mind."

"No, no."

"He said maybe you cracked or something. That it was just too much, even after the conviction. If someone had ever touched Marcie like that, he said—"

"Right," Elgin said. "Things were falling apart."

"But just to leave them?"

"Right," Elgin said; "it was a bad move. Cowardly."

A moment of silence hung between them. Elgin didn't know how to take back the word.

"Like Stan, right?" Pearson's wife said.

"Doris, that's not what I meant."

"I know," she said, crying again. "It's just that you want to know why. Not that you ever would or could, I guess, but that you want to."

"Things were getting a little weird at work," Elgin said. "Did Stan mention anything?"

"What do you mean, *weird?* It was always *weird.*"

"Well, with McCabe planning a run for Lansing and everything."

"Oh, that. Yeah. Stan just said he was done, time to quit."

"And after I left," Elgin said, "what did Stan say then?"

"Well, he was worried."

"About what?"

"About *you.* Everybody was. Buddy and Don. Everyone. Laura was there at the funeral, and I have to tell you, Robert, she looked a mess. We all tried to help."

All? Klister, McCabe, with his wife, his family, comforting, calming, what? But he had to push forward, had to get as much out of her as he could, as selfish as it was. "I know," he said. "It was wrong of me. Like Stan said, I was messed up. But what about the papers, the *Free Press* or the *News?*"

"Oh, God. They both ran such beautiful obituaries."

"Of me?"

"Of you? No. Stan."

"I mean, was there a sort of official explanation for why I left?"

"Certainly nothing in the papers. Not that I saw."

"Well, I guess what I mean is, what was the official word in the office, or with Klister or McCabe? People like that."

"Like I said. Everybody thought you had cracked. That you'd be found dead somewhere."

"Yeah," Elgin said.

"I'm glad you're okay, Robert," she said. "Come back and take care of those children, now, all right?"

"I will," he said. "And Doris, I'm so sorry about Stan. He was a good man."

"Yes, he was," she said through more tears. "He was a good man."

Elgin hung up the phone. So they were trying to contain it, trying to hold on to the scam. He had always figured they would have fingered him for the whole thing and washed their hands of it once he disappeared. But there were too many players involved for that, maybe, though all of them were tightly connected to the party: a couple of doctors, the life insurance agency, somebody at the county hospital, a handful of dentists. If somebody got fingered, they'd all go down, or a lot of them. So the public didn't know anything. And poor dead Pearson, and poor Doris, and Elgin's own kids out on the line, vulnerable. And Laura.

He called home and got the machine, Laura's recorded voice a monotone, bringing on another jolt of guilt. He couldn't tell if his position was strengthened or weakened by the ongoing cover-up. He was the one who could bring them all down, which of course put him at risk, but at the same time, it gave him something to hold over them, a bargaining chip. And the cops and the prosecutor's office wouldn't be involved, at least not officially.

What a fool he was, what an imposter. Stan was the genuine article. Stan was dead. The dentist over in Sterling Heights as well, probably, the guy Elgin had squeezed for the final piece of the puzzle, the information that had set him in motion: the offshore account number, and how the money was moved. Dr. Lawrence. And, now, if he was dead, like Pearson, if McCabe and Klister had figured it out, which they probably had, Elgin hoped his death had been slow and painful, the dirty fuck. And then he felt ashamed for having such a thought. The poor bastard probably had kids. And what had they ever done to deserve a dead father?

$$\equiv$$

It's only been a few days but everything feels different now. I don't want to read about it too much, but then I can't help it and feel like a fool, sneaking around the library, paging through one and then another of the five thousand books on the subject. As if we need help with this. As if we'll become extinct without all of these words and theories and advice. Most of it's just guilt on my part. I never thought much about the abortion I had, which I never even told Clark about, what finally probably undid us, thank God. As if the whole thing had been his fault, which, in a way, of course, it was. But looking back, that was when I started to hate him. I even feel sorry for him now, pity him a little for not knowing, for not having the chance to voice an opinion, which is not, of course, a very generous emotion—pity, that is. But the guilt and the fear come from thinking that maybe the abortion damaged me somehow physically, or that maybe I'm due for retribution, some sort of cosmic justice in the form of a miscarriage or one of the horrible anomalies the various books articulate in excruciating detail: tails and horns and jellied spines. And then I don't want to think about it too much. Then I want to try to trick whoever or whatever it is that might administer the justice. It won't be worth anything if I don't care; if I don't care there won't be anything of value to take away. Not that I believe in any of that. But the way you're brought up and everything, religion and all that bullshit, some of it sort of seeps in. And it's not like I'm so thrilled or sure about this thing all the time. It's not like I've made any kind of decision.

It's not like I even know for sure. I threw up after Robert left, but it seemed like a normal reaction, and I haven't puked since. Eat crackers, the books advise, so I do. And then there's the tenderness in my breasts. With Clark, before the abortion, it felt like an invasion, a cancer inside of me, and I resented every cell. This time it's like something I have to be very careful to protect. And something I'm afraid of as well. Afraid that it won't work out and afraid that it will. Afraid of hurting it later, or someone else hurting it. And I'm very careful to keep it an "it." And pissed off, too, that it forces me to consider the future and the past.

I watch Rachel with her kids over at her place off Dort Highway, Jill three, and Patty six, their drawings and paintings all over the walls of the kitchen, and I feel entirely off balance. Out of control almost. Three months ago, I would have viewed the walls of that kitchen with derision, contempt, the domestic suburban existence a nightmare into which I would have never willingly stepped. It all looked like sacrifice to me. Stupid sacrifice.

It still does. I mean, I really have no fucking idea. Mostly, it's a secret that I have, something to push me along, maybe a guarantee. But I think about money all the time. I sell myself as a daughter to my parents. Sold myself as a student to my teachers, as pussy to the johns. And while it might be a relief to slam that door shut, to guarantee that it's locked forever, it also pisses me off, the loss of choice or the thought that I need to save me from myself. And I don't know if I can sell myself as a mother to anyone. But, mainly, the hormones are all over the place, trying, it seems, to steal me away.

When Robert calls on the second night, waking me from a dead sleep, it's either good news or bad, I can't tell which. Something about the cops not knowing and his old boss being dead and a last chance. I try to follow it, but I'm so tired, I can hardly concentrate. "Just come home," I finally tell him, and he says, "I will," and I say, "Come on, enough with the drama," and he says, "I will."

He had to move before the paranoia made movement impossible. He drove out to Metro and got the first available flight out—to Dallas— and checked into a hotel at the airport. It was after nine and the Printer wouldn't be in his office on New Year's anyway. He had room service send up a bottle of scotch, but it didn't help. He resisted the urge to call Carla. Only last night, in the hotel room up in Flint—and, God, it seemed like a month ago—she'd seemed afraid, but had tried to hide it. It was in the way she looked at him, like she was trying to hold on to him with her eyes, to pull him back. He didn't want to scare her anymore, and there was no way he'd be able to hide his own fear and uncertainty. He drank the scotch, scheming, until he passed out on top of the bedspread.

At eight-thirty Michigan time, the Printer still wasn't in. Probably sleeping off a hangover. Or dead. Elgin made a pot of coffee and took a shower. His mind felt cold, numb, blank.

At nine-fifteen, the Printer answered the phone.

"So you killed him, huh?" Elgin said.

"Bobby!" the Printer said. "Very well, thanks, and how are you?"

"I'm still alive," he said.

"How nice."

"There's a person I call once a week," Elgin said, spilling it faster than he'd intended to. "If I don't call her," he said, "she mails one package to Lansing, to the attorney general, and one package to the FBI."

"Not bombs, I hope."

"No, just photocopies of fraudulent checks and some other documents, a list of names, a letter outlining the scam."

"Clever," the Printer said. "Sounds like a movie."

"Yeah," Elgin said. "That's where I got the idea."

"So, what do you want?"

"I want to be left alone."

"Nobody's touched you yet, have they?"

"Nobody's found me."

"Right."

"I want my family to be left alone."

"Come on," the Printer said. "They're fine. Who do you think you're talking to? It's not like that. It's never been like that. We took care of you."

"Yeah, and you took care of Pearson, too."

"No, you took care of Pearson."

"Oh, yeah?"

"Oh, yeah. He was the first person we suspected. Never thought you were smart enough."

"Thanks."

"And we did have something on him, sure. But we realized pretty quick it wasn't him. I mean, you used the office credit card for your flights down and out. And why would he stick around town?"

"Because he didn't do anything."

"Right. Why he would want to protect you I can't imagine."

"Protect me? He didn't know anything."

"Yeah, that's what he said. And that you didn't know anything, either; that he had no idea where you were; that you were just messed up because of what happened to your daughter. But that's not what your little secretary said. She told us you both knew, in so many words."

Elgin felt something twist in his guts. "What," he said, "so you killed her, too?"

"I have no idea what you're talking about. We all knew you were unstable, everything you'd gone through; I just wish we could have helped more."

"So what did you do with her?"

"Who?"

"Susan."

"I didn't do anything with her. Don promoted her into your old job. She knew the office better than anyone. Bryler took Stan's old job. The county *can* function without you, believe it or not."

Electricity danced around the periphery of Elgin's vision. This wasn't the way he'd imagined the phone call. He'd figured the Printer would be afraid or threatening or both. But, of course, as a negotiating pose, he wouldn't want to reveal anything more than a bored, detached nonchalance. Elgin focused his vision on the toes of his shoes, which the carpet blurred around, speckled with electricity. Susan was a big girl, a grown woman, but, still, he hoped she wasn't being sucked in. And he was not responsible for Pearson's death; he kept telling himself that, focused on the tips of his shoes and what he needed to get out of this conversation.

"You still there?" the Printer said.

"Yeah."

"I say let bygones be bygones."

"That's what I'm saying, too."

"Though you know Buddy. I mean, if something were to get out, you know, then I can't guarantee anyone's safety."

"That's just what I'm saying," Elgin said. "If I haven't leaked in four months, why would I now?"

"Well, at some point you'll run out of money, and then you'll think maybe there's a place to get some, but there won't be any more. You follow me? If there's some kind of blackmail thing that comes up in ten or twelve or twenty years, I just think Buddy will take it personally, go berserk, and maybe I won't even be around, or your father-in-law, and then, again, who knows what the man will do?"

"That's fine," Elgin said. "So we have an agreement?"

"It's a one-shot deal and you never appear again."

"That's what I'm saying."

"Where are you, anyway?"

"If you come after me, and I can't make a phone call, those packages get sent."

"Sure they do," the Printer said. "My caller ID says Dallas, but I guess you'd be smart enough to get the hell out of there. I've always hated that town."

"Right," Elgin said. "So we have an agreement?"

"And if something should happen to you, if you get in a car accident and fail to make that call, then, again, all bets are off. So you'd better think about that; find a way to make sure that those packages don't get sent for the wrong reason. You don't want people to get hurt."

"Fine," Elgin said.

"All right," the Printer said. "I'll pass the offer along."

"No," Elgin said. "You tell me right now. I'm not fucking calling again."

"Bobby, don't take that tone with me. I taught you everything you know."

"Right," Elgin said. "Klister and McCabe as well, which tells me you can close the deal right now."

"I don't see a problem. Unless you reappear, or something leaks, or you come begging for more."

"That's a definite yes, then?"

"I'll do everything I can."

"Is that a definite yes?"

"All right. Yes. I'll make it happen."

Elgin hung up the phone. His hands were shaking. It seemed that he'd won. But you never could tell with negotiations. Sometimes you got blinded by what you won, and didn't realize right away what you'd given up. His shirt was soaked through with sweat. He'd have to go over the conversation a thousand times. He poured a cup of coffee and lit a cigarette, paced a line at the foot of the beds. He wasn't responsible for Pearson's death. That was a ploy to throw him off balance. Pearson had his own toilet, and Elgin wasn't responsible for anything, except in the most indirect way. He'd have to contact Laura, and he'd have to go back, undetected by anyone but his family, to see them one last time. And it was sinking in now, what he had given away, but maybe he'd given that away a long time ago.

He'd planned on calling Laura from Dallas to prepare her, but he realized now that that was out of the question. There was too much risk in her knowing anything. He'd have to catch her by surprise, as unfair as it was, for her and the children's safety. He booked an early afternoon flight for Detroit and waited in his room in Dallas. He would not see his children grow up. After this last time, he would never see his children again. He sat at the foot of the bed and held his face in his hands. There was always more that could be taken away. He'd hold them and look at them, memorize their faces and touch, fixing them in his mind forever as the children they were now, as big a lie as a photograph. But that was what he had now. That was what he could get. He could have divorced and at least seen his children from time to time, could have quit his job, started something new. He could have done a lot of things. But he didn't. All of his life he'd heard people proudly proclaim that whatever mistakes they'd made, they had no regrets. What idiots they were. They were either liars or blessed or just plain stupid.

On the flight and at Metro, an almost palpable treachery poisoned the air, every face a potential spy's or informant's. He got out of the airport as fast as he could, head low, collar up, willing himself invisible, praying that no one would see him and report to the Printer or Klister, and drove to his hotel in Ann Arbor. He called Carla, told her as little as possible, but she was tired and spacey, and it seemed unfair to bring her any further into this mess. He lay in his bed waiting for sleep, struggling to find another way out, a scheme or solution, which would of course have to involve Laura's complicity. Once a year they could meet somewhere. Yeah, and the kids would love that, dragged off for the obligatory visit with fugitive Daddy, a man they could hardly remember, if at all. Or he could still go to the attorney general, and maybe he would. Except that what he knew, what he had to admit, was that even if it was indirect, he was responsible for Pearson's death. As sure as if he'd cut his throat, he had killed Pearson. The dentist, too, if he was dead. He would not handle the fates of his children so casually, so selfishly. He would never put them at risk again. One last time and this was the end of him in his children's lives, and the end of them in his. Forever.

$$\equiv$$

When I wake up I hear in my head the sound of his voice from last night and I know exactly what he's spiraling into, and could scream for my nearly narcotic drifting as he talked about his dead boss and the cops and whatever else he had said. I call his hotel. I want to remind him of the road, of the hotel in Kansas City, or whatever else he needs to hear. He said he would see the children today. He said it was almost over. The phone rings and rings. I see it on the nightstand in the empty hotel room, ringing and ringing. He's already gone. I rub my hands over my stomach. It's in there somewhere, the size of a walnut, the size of a pea, a tiny Napoleon. "You're going to wait with me," I say. "That's what we're going to do. And everything's going to be just fine, isn't it?" I say. "Yes, it is," I say. "Everything is going to be fine."

ELEVEN

Elgin packed up the car and pulled out of the parking garage before first light. If Laura had a job, it would likely start after Carrie got on the bus, and he wanted to at least give her a moment to digest his presence without Carrie being there. Lights were on in several of the houses in the new subdivision across from his place, his family's place, but no one was outside yet. He couldn't remember what time Carrie got the bus, but he was certain it was still far too early. He picked up a cup of coffee at the Dumpy's Doughnuts drive-thru, and swung by the house again. He'd run through a thousand possible scenarios, a thousand speeches, none of them more than a few words long before he'd hit a wall and realize that there was absolutely nothing he could say, and no way to plan the encounter. He couldn't park and watch, and he couldn't drive by too many times, so he drove various, expanding loops around the house, and finally, the buses were on the roads. He got behind one on 10 Mile Road, number 28, almost certain that it was Carrie's bus, and he followed it, waiting behind it at every stop. As they turned onto his street, he saw Carrie running across the front lawn to her stop a few hundred feet in front of him. His throat seemed to collapse. He crawled by the house, hung back a bit behind the bus when it stopped, and watched her scramble toward the open door and up the steps, so self-contained and clearly herself, her gait, the angle at which she held her head under the mouse hat that Laura had made her, so sweet, his daughter, his beautiful daughter.

But he wasn't about to grant himself the luxury of falling apart, of tasting the loss. Not today. Though the sight of her made him wish he were dead. What the hell did he think he was doing, anyway? Wouldn't this just make everything worse for them? And him? Just what did he hope to gain from this?

He followed the bus, straining for a glimpse of Carrie, but the windows were steamed up, and there was little hope of seeing her. And what good would it do if he did?

He turned around and headed back for the house. It would be Laura's decision as to whether or not he would see the kids, but he had to see her, had to make some kind of statement, had to give her the right to break a lamp over his head and tell him that no, he would not be seeing the children, that he no longer had the right to, that in fact he could go fuck himself. A car, coming from the other direction, signaled to turn into his driveway, so he drove by again, watching in the rearview mirror as Laura ran Tommy out of the house. He was bundled up in a new snowsuit, his arms sticking out like fixed wings. Elgin couldn't see his face, or Laura's as she handed him to a woman Elgin assumed was his sitter. But it was Tommy and it was Laura and they were all alive, all fine, it appeared. That was something. He turned around again, and watched the car pull out and drive away. The garage door was open, the Mazda inside warming up, emitting a cloud of exhaust that hung over the driveway in the cold morning air. He parked behind Laura's car in the cloud. He swallowed against an urge to vomit. Laura wasn't in the Mazda. He walked across the back porch, past a Radio Flyer sled he and Carrie had bought together, and a couple of child-size snow shovels he and Laura had given the kids last Christmas. It seemed that he could feel his blood moving, and that it was moving too fast, pushing at his heart to pump harder and harder. He didn't try the knob. It didn't seem right. He knocked.

Laura's face appeared in the window. When she saw him, she squeezed her eyes shut, her lips open, revealing two rows of teeth ground together in their clenched jaws. She opened her eyes and looked at him. He tried to absorb the hatred. He could hardly breathe. The air was forming ice crystals in his lungs, killing him. Laura swung the door open. She squinted, showing him her teeth between tightly drawn lips. He hung his head and waited, the heat from the house rushing out all around him, enveloping him.

"What do you want?" she said, her voice hoarse and low.

"I don't know," he said, wondering how he could possibly answer that question. "I want to apologize," he said. "I want to talk to you."

"You've got to be kidding."

The cold and the heat were mixing in the air around him, bringing on waves of nausea. "I'm not going to say I want to explain," he said, "because I know there's no explanation. I want to tell you what happened. I want to say I'm sorry and tell you what happened, and then I'll get out of your way, if that's what you want."

"If that's what I want," she said. She stood looking at him, holding the door in one hand, and covering her chin with the other, shaking her head in disgust. "If that's what *I* want?"

He waited.

She walked away from the open door.

He followed her into the house.

She stood at the sink, showing him her back. The kitchen felt familiar, but wrong somehow, a place he shouldn't be, the scene of a crime. He wanted to touch her, to put his hands on her shoulders, to cry in her arms, to be forgiven. He didn't dare move. He had to say something. Carrie's paintings covered the walls, a few he recognized, most of them new. Tommy's were all new. Maybe she'd let him take one of each. Laura's shoulders were tense, hunched up as she leaned against the edge of the sink. "I can smell that you're smoking again," she said. "That's nice."

"Laura," he said.

He saw that she was crying, the small jerks of her shoulders and back giving her away.

He moved toward her, then stopped in the middle of the kitchen.

"I thought you were dead," she said, "you fucker."

"No," he said. "Not dead. Not yet."

"Then what?" she said, turning quickly and hurling the bottle of dish soap at his head.

He didn't flinch. It sailed past him and bounced off the wall. She stood facing him, slightly crouched as if winded, her face red, showing him her clenched teeth.

"I—" he said. "Something happened. I—"

"Something happened?" She ran her hand through her hair. "A lot of shit happened."

"Let's sit down," he said. "Let's sit down at the table."

"All right," she said, walking past him. "Let's sit down at the table."

He pulled out a chair, his old place on the far side of the stove. He sat and finally looked across the table at her. She held her face in her hands, fingers at her temples, and squinted at him, the same look she'd trained on Corey throughout the trial, the hatred face.

"Laura," he said. "I'm sorry."

"You're sorry," she said. She smiled. "You walk away from a bad situation, a situation that was, thanks only to me, finally improving, and then you walk back in six months later to say you're sorry?"

"Four months," he said.

"Oh, excuse me. Four months."

"And it wasn't improving."

"It was for Carrie. But, of course, you didn't see that." She looked at her watch. "Is this going to take long?" she said. "I have to be at work."

"I was hoping we could talk," he said, though the way things were going so far, it didn't seem that there would be much more to say.

She ran her tongue over her teeth. "I'll call in," she said. "How about that? Then we can *talk*." She walked out of the kitchen, though there was a phone on the wall. He stood and walked to the cabinet where the coffee had always been kept. It felt like a minor victory that a can was there. He filled the pot with water.

"Do you have any idea how embarrassing this is," she said before she was even back in the kitchen, "how humiliating this has all been, to even be associated with a man so weak and pathetic that he runs away from his family when they need him most. Do you have any idea?"

He started the coffee brewing.

"Don't tell me it's another fucking woman. Were you fucking somebody else? Is that what this is? What happened? She got tired of you? Threw you out of her bed? Too weak for her, too?"

"No," he said, walking back to the table and sitting. "Let's sit down."

"Oh, yes," Laura said. "Let's sit down." She kept her eyes trained on his as she sat, and after she sat as she waited.

"Laura," he said, "it wasn't another woman," though, of course, he thought, there is one now, you fucking bastard. "It was nothing like that," he said.

"Oh. And what was it like?"

"You asked me to leave the house. I left the house. What was I supposed to think?"

The smell of coffee filled the kitchen.

"You were supposed to think that we were going to help Carrie, that we were going to help ourselves. You were supposed to *try.*"

"I did try," he said.

"No, you didn't," she said. "Two sessions of counseling is not trying."

"Are you telling me you thought we would stay together? Is that what you're saying?"

She looked down at the table, still squinting. "I was willing to try," she said.

"But it was always on your terms."

"What other terms were there? If it had been up to you, we would have ignored everything that happened to Carrie, and she would have sunk deeper and deeper—"

"That's not true."

"It is true."

"Do you want some coffee?"

She looked up at him, the tight-lipped smile smeared across her face. "That would be lovely," she said. He poured the coffee, his hands shaking a little as he walked their cups back to the table. Nothing had changed. They were right back where they'd been before he'd left, where they'd always be, blaming each other, hating each other. He took the sugar bowl from the cabinet, the milk from the refrigerator.

"But just to run away?" Laura said. "I mean, how fucking weak—"

"Right," Elgin said, placing the sugar and milk on the table. "I'm not going to defend myself. I know it was wrong."

She stirred milk and sugar into her coffee.

"And I was fucked up then, and I'm sure I still am."

"Uh-huh."

"Laura," he said.

She looked at him over the rim of her cup as she drank.

"Do you know that I love the children," he said, "that I have always loved the children and will always love the children?"

She put her cup down on the table in front of her and looked at it.

"Do you really believe—and I really want to know this—do you really believe we were going to stay together, that therapy or counseling was going to somehow make us okay?"

"I don't know," she said to the cup.

"When you asked me to leave the house, with the blessings of the various therapists, and when I agreed, didn't you know it was over?"

She looked at him. "I didn't know," she said. "It seemed like the right thing."

"But when we had to do that thing for Goldstein about the miracle, was I a part of yours? Was I a part of how you wanted your life to be?"

"The way it was," she said, "yes. The way it had been."

"But did you really believe that? You were the one who kept saying that nothing would ever be the same, for Carrie, and by implication, for any of us."

"And that's true. But that doesn't mean it couldn't have been different and still okay."

"But you knew I hated that stuff. The therapy, the church stuff; you said I was holding all of you back."

"Well, I don't know whose fault that was. And if you weren't willing to change for your daughter, for your family, for me—"

"Did you still love me?"

She took a drink of coffee. "I don't know," she said. "But for the kids, I would—"

"You said I was hurting the kids, that together we were hurting the kids, which was why I moved out."

She looked at the wall behind him. "I don't know," she said. "But just to leave? To just run away—"

"I know," he said. "That was wrong. I'll take all the blame, okay? I swear to God."

She blinked twice, slowly, studied him. "So what do you want?" she said, and the skin of her forehead twisted up and she put her face in her hands and she started to cry. "None of it was supposed to be this way," she said through her hands.

He reached across the table and touched her arm, her head, her hand over her face, and she let him touch her. At some point after this was over, right after, probably, he was going to fall apart completely. Now, they would negotiate terms, as he had with the Printer, and these would be the terms of his absence, the terms of his death to them.

"Okay," she said, "so you're sorry," she said. "I don't know what it is you want," she said, "or how you think you can just walk back in here."

"I'm not," he said. "I won't," he said. "That's what I have to tell you."

"You know, being around some of the time for them, helping out with money, at least, for God's sake." She shook her head, rubbed a thumb and index finger over her closed eyelids.

"I know," he said. "Something happened. Bad things happened. I got swept up in something and didn't know how to get out."

She was hunched up, rocking and shaking her head and still rubbing at her eyes.

And he realized that he couldn't tell her anything, that he had made a huge mistake in coming here, because he would have to tell her something, that just by showing up he had placed all of them in danger, again, that everything he touched was left smeared with his corruption. And now she would have to hold a dirty secret, and be contaminated by fear, simply as a result of having been in his presence again. "Laura," he said. "Just a minute, okay?"

She looked up at him from her hunched position and seemed to wake up. She sat up in her chair.

"I'll be right back," he said, "okay? I'm just going to get something from the car."

She nodded and he walked outside and got the presents for Carrie and Tommy. He turned off the Mazda's ignition. Carrie's bike was against the inside wall of the garage. He had taught her how to ride it, running beside her, holding her up, until she could finally do it herself. There were beach toys and a whiffle ball bat and a cheap plastic kiddie pool. He'd been selfish and stupid for coming back. They were all lost to him now forever, and had been for months. And now he knew, once and for all. The grief was physical, uncontainable, nearly blinding. He didn't deserve to let it out, but he couldn't hold it in, either. He quickly stepped around the side of the garage and vomited, the retching burning his throat, his mouth, his nose, his eyes, everything burning. He stood, and then doubled over and retched some more. He had given everything away. And now he had to minimize the damage to them and get away as fast as he could. He swallowed bile and walked into the house with the presents, and put them on the table. "These are for the kids," he said, clearing his throat. "Use them sometime, next birthdays, maybe. Don't tell them they're from me."

"Wait a minute," Laura said. "What are you talking about? You're walking away again?"

He didn't sit. "Laura," he said. "I did a lot of stupid things. I did something illegal, something worse than illegal, something that could hurt you and the kids. I don't want to tell you about it, because telling you will put it into your lap, will put you at risk, in one way or another."

"Wait a minute," she said. "You came here to tell me that? What are you talking about?"

He pulled out the chair next to hers and sat on its edge, leaning toward her. "Listen to me," he said. "Please. I shouldn't have come here. I wanted to see the kids. What I said before, about how I've always loved the kids, you believe that, right? Even after everything, you believe that, don't you?"

She closed her eyes. Five seconds passed. He waited. "Yes," she finally said, a whisper. "Which is why—"

"No," he said. "Please, please listen to me now. I didn't come here today. You didn't see me; you haven't seen me since I disappeared. Did you tell the police I was missing?"

She nodded.

"Okay," he said. "And did they give you some kind of timeline with the life insurance?"

"Yes," she said, "but—"

"Do you believe I love the kids?"

"Yes, but—"

"And that we loved each other?"

"Yes," she said, "but there has to be a way to—"

"You have to listen to me," he said. "I've done something that can't be cleaned up. It's not a matter of going to jail and serving my time. I've done something that will never be forgiven. Going away, being away is the only thing I can do now for the kids. Do you believe me?"

"How can I," she said, slapping her hands down on the table, "if I don't even know what you're talking about?"

"Laura," he said, "I'm asking for your trust. Telling you anything would hurt you, would hurt the kids. Will you please trust me?"

"I . . ." She folded her hands under her chin, squeezed her eyes together, her entire face clenched.

"And if you believe that I love the kids, and I know I don't deserve this, will you somehow let them know that?"

"I don't know what you want from me," she said, and she covered her face with her hands.

He crouched on the floor next to her, and put his arms around her. She leaned into him, hiding behind her hands.

"I shouldn't have come," he said. "I'm sorry. I'm sorry for everything. But now you can't tell anyone that I was here, not your father or your therapist or people in the church or anyone. Just another of my fuckups that you have to hide, and I know that's not fair to you, but that's all I can say."

She pulled away from him, ran an index finger under one eye, and then the other. "But what about the kids?" she said. "You're just gone? Forever?"

"Maybe I can figure something out," he said, though he knew he never would; he just had to keep talking, had to wrap this up and get away before anything else happened, and if he kept talking maybe it would keep him from throwing up all over the kitchen. "Someday. I don't know. And I don't know if that would be better for them. But you trust me, right?"

She nodded, sniffled, said, "But I don't know why I would."

"If you get an envelope of cash, use it for the kids, for yourself."

"I don't want your dirty money."

"It's not dirty," he said. "I earned it. And take the life insurance."

She looked toward the sink.

"Please," he said.

"All right," she said.

"And I didn't come here."

"Yes!"

"Laura," he said. "Can I have two of these pictures on the wall, one of Carrie's, one of Tommy's?"

She looked at the wall behind her. "Which ones?" she said.

He chose two, and she carefully took them down and rolled them up and taped them tight. They didn't look at each other.

She handed him the rolled-up pictures and they stood facing each other in the middle of the kitchen. "I'm sorry," he said again.

"Okay," she said. "I know." She walked toward him and fit herself into his embrace. "And if it can be worked out," she said, "they will want to see you. I'll make sure."

He held on to her, smelled her hair, felt the bones in her back, the bones in her shoulders.

She closed the door behind him. He walked to his car and pulled away, not wanting to look at the house, to study it, to try so hard to memorize it. Why couldn't they have been like this before, when everything had been falling apart, when there had still been something to save? Why would they trust each other now, when there was nothing left? Though, for Laura, of course, there was something left. Carrie running to the bus in her mouse hat, carrying her school bag, and running across the front lawn as fast as her legs would carry her. He pulled over and vomited again. He didn't bother to get out of the car, just pulled over, opened his door and leaned out over the shoulder and road, retching, the burning blinding him. He waited for his vision to clear as he stared down at the smear of road and gravel. And so it was done. And so it was fucking done.

TWELVE

Dead man calls at twelve-thirty from a gas station near Ann Arbor, says he's on the way to Kalamazoo, and can we meet there. I've been preparing my parents for my departure since he left earlier in the week; I kiss them good-bye, get in the car, and drive to him. We're going to be okay, I'm thinking; we're going to get back on the road and we're going to be okay. It starts to flurry before I hit Lansing, and it's coming down hard by Battle Creek. There are a million places you can go in the world. He has a right to feel this way, I tell myself, everything he's lost, whatever that might be. And he doesn't know yet what there is to gain.

I pull into the rental lot at the airport, and he's waiting in the Dodge by the booth. I park behind him and get out of the car. He doesn't open his door, doesn't see me. I knock on his window. He looks up and smiles a little, opens the door, and steps out to greet me. His face is drawn. It looks like he hasn't slept in days. I smell vomit on him. His skin is cold, rubbery. I hold on to him, try to squeeze some life into him. "I'll never see them again," he says into my hair, and I say, "Let's get out of here. We'll talk about it in the car."

He doesn't move, allows himself to be held. I lead him to the passenger door of my car and put him in the seat. It's going to take time. All of it. I know that. You have to be patient. I load his belongings into my car, handle the paperwork with the rental company, and pull out of there. And we're moving.

I put my hand on his leg, squeeze his knee. He manages a weak smile. He looks like hell, shell-shocked, half dead. The snow's coming down, big fluffy flakes.

"I love this kind of snow," I say. "Remember in Kansas, when we kept waiting for the snow?"

"Yes," he says.

"Well, now here it is," I say.

"Yes," he says.

As I approach the interstate, I say, "Which way? East or west?"

"I don't know," he says, and I say, "I was thinking east, back to New York."

"All right," he says.

"I mean, I've got my apartment, and we can sort of make a plan. If that's what you want."

I pull onto the eastbound ramp.

"Sure," he says.

"Okay," I say, "you can talk when you want to or you can take a nap or you can smoke a cigarette or you can listen to some bad classic rock," and I'm hearing the strain in my voice, the woman-trying-too-hard strain, the cheerful wife routine when Daddy's had a bad day, which I am just not accustomed to, I mean babying a man and that kind of bullshit, building him up, except of course in the world of my old job, and that thought is just too sickening to bear. So I shut up. Even with the plows out, the interstate is covered with snow. "Go to sleep," I say. "You need it. You'll feel better later and we can talk."

"Yeah," he says. "Okay."

It all feels very fragile right now, delicate and tenuous. And I can't talk him to death. I know that I just have to wait, and I should have grown accustomed to that by now, and even if I haven't I can at least shut up and hope that he sleeps. Which he does, almost immediately, slouched down in the seat, his mouth open a little, head thrown back. And I'm not supposed to want to nurture my husband, and he's not my husband, and what's wrong with trying to help each other, anyway? I have a right to that. To him. At least to some degree. And, anyway, I'll be okay no matter what.

He sleeps. I feel myself settling into my seat, calming down, relaxing. I head south on 69 toward 80 and Ohio and Pennsylvania, and the snow lets up and finally dies away, and there's not even any on the ground in Coldwater. Maybe we're not really going to be on the road again until I get rid of my apartment in New York. Maybe this is still part of the intermission. He sleeps and sleeps. I can't tell him yet, but I can't wait to tell him, either. Maybe that's just what he needs. Then again, maybe it will scare him. I'll know when the time is right. I don't want him to latch onto the idea as some kind of salvation, though. Not the way he is now.

The sun goes down behind us and I keep driving. He shifts his weight occasionally, coughs or clears his throat. I make it all the way to where 80 splits off the Turnpike, west of Youngstown, where I finally have to pull off and look for a hotel. He wakes up with a start. "What happened?" he says.

"You slept a long time," I say. "It's okay. Everything's good."

He shivers, cracks his window, lights a cigarette.

I follow the signs to the Ramada.

"Hungry," he says. "Jesus."

"Yeah, me too. We'll get room service. A bottle of wine."

Up in the room, he takes a shower while I order dinner. I just need to lie down for a minute, but then I wake to the smell of meat and I feel like I'm going to throw up. Robert tips the room service guy, and I just barely make it into the bathroom, locking the door behind me. When I come out, he's got the table set up, the wine open, and it feels a little like our old life.

Except there's nothing I can eat. He doesn't really eat, either, though he focuses on his food, on sawing the meat and pushing it around the plate. The smells are overwhelming. I manage to swallow a half piece of bread. He looks up from his plate. "I'm not hungry anymore," he says.

"Right," I say, pushing away from the table. "I'm not, either. Come on," I say. "Bring your wine. We'll lie down on the bed for a little while and talk." I hold his head against my shoulder, pet his hair, as he tells the story, tentatively at first, and then the words rushing out, painting the delusional picture that he is trapped, that there is no way out, that he has lost his children, that these people, Klister and McCabe and whoever else, have some kind of divine power, that they're omnipotent, omniscient, that they can't easily be brought to their knees, which is all too apparent to me. But I let him talk, running my hand over his head, his shoulders. He is fixated on the idea that he's responsible for the death of his boss, and I finally say, "You didn't kill him. They killed him and he killed himself."

"I can't take the risk," he says, his head on my ribs, and I wonder if he can hear it down there, or feel it somehow, though, of course, I can't, so why should he? "Not with my kids," he says. "You don't know these people."

"They're far more trapped than you are," I say. "You're holding all the cards. Get your family, hide them somewhere, then go to the attorney general or the FBI or both or someone else and take the fuckers down."

He shakes his head against my ribs.

And I don't want it to happen, either. Then he goes to jail or doesn't, but our lives will never be the same. And I'm not going to spend the rest of my life waiting. That's not who I am. That's not who I am going to become. Ever.

"Listen to me," I say. "It's not as bad as you think. Time will pass and you'll think of a way to get out of this. I promise."

But it's not what I want, a man brooding and scheming and spending all of his time trying to clean up a bad fucking mess he's made, and, really, it's just that I am so selfish, that I want him for myself, that I want us to have a chance, and a life together, and maybe part of it has to do with the running and hiding and secrets and loss holding us together. "Time will pass," I say stupidly. "Time will pass, and you'll find a way, and I can help you." And I will help you, I say to myself. And I will help you and time will pass.

He begins to move his hands over my body, and I think, even in this grief, yes, even in this grief. He's over me, tears open the top of my dress, handling my breasts, then one hand up between my legs, rough, and I push against him, pull his face down to my breasts, which are tender and already starting to swell, and he's biting and it hurts, and I pull at his hair even as I press his face down against the nipple in his teeth, and he pushes himself in around my underwear hard and I push right back against him, my teeth ground together waiting for a piece of skin to chew off, and he's all the way in now, we're bone to bone, and we fuck it all out, the only thing to do, it seems, and later, while he sleeps against me, I look up at the ceiling, feel his breathing, my breathing, my heart, everything slowed down, back to normal, and we're all together here in this room now forever, and if I could only have this, I think, if I could only have this.

THIRTEEN

JANUARY 6

She lived in Alphabet City, at the edge of the creeping East Village on Ninth and Avenue C. It wasn't totally gentrified yet; there were still soup kitchens next to the cafés and bistros that were rapidly encroaching. The only remaining squats were farther east. There were winos and poor people and students and families and a few pricks new to Wall Street. They'd been back for two days. They walked through Tompkins Square and saw more mothers with small children than junkies. "Can you imagine," Elgin said, "trying to raise kids here? God, the number of terrors. You'd have to be completely out of your mind."

She didn't answer.

He was back on the walking plan, trying to burn something off, trying to think, trying not to think. They walked Third Avenue all the way up to Sixtieth and then back down Second. She could still be taken away, and he knew he would lose her if he wasn't careful, but he didn't know how to be careful, and he was out of words. They walked. Sometimes she took his hand. Sometimes he took hers. He had to get out of the city, had to disappear into a life that didn't involve all of this movement, all of this running, some kind of normal life, with some kind of a normal job, because he had already sent most of the money to Laura and the kids. He knew that there was no way back to that world, that in fact that world didn't exist, had never existed. But he was creating a world in which raking the leaves was some kind of noble endeavor, and his kids were there with him and so was Carla, and Laura was okay, but somewhere else, and at night Carrie and Tommy would be on either side of him on his big bed and he would read them *Black Beauty* and *Robin Hood,* and during the day he would work in an insurance agency, a job which he would find entirely satisfactory.

He stopped walking. What a fool he was.

"What?" Carla said.

Last night she had called him delusional, and now he realized that she'd been right. He took her hand. "Come on," he said. He opened the door to Mick's Place, and ushered her in. They sat at the bar, down from two old men at the far end. "Little early, isn't it?" Carla said.

"No," he said. "I just realized how stupid I am," and Carla said, "About time," but she was smiling and it reminded him of Kansas City, how they'd be in bars or out on the street and how people would want to be around them, be close to them, though it was really Carla they wanted to be close to and maybe him just to try to figure out how he had gotten her.

He ordered scotch and she asked for ginger ale, and he said, "Come on, let's have a drink," and she said, "Go ahead," and after the drinks came he said, "I was thinking about this world of, like, junior high school recitals and family outings and picnics down by the lake or something, I mean just entirely insane, like nothing I would ever even want, and just longing for it, lost in it, like a television fantasy family world, and then I thought, 'Oops, look what happened the last time you tried that,' I mean just entirely fucked up, and I—"

"Knock it off," she said. "Stop it."

"What?" he said. He took a drink.

"All this crybaby bullshit. You fucked up and now we're going to move forward."

He picked up the pack of cigarettes from the bar, put it down, pushed it around. "I've got a lot of shit to bury," he said. "You don't know. You can't imagine."

"I'm pregnant," she said.

"No, you're not," he said.

"Yes, I am," she said. She turned away from him.

He put his face in his hands, his fingertips pressing against his eyes. He couldn't have this. It wouldn't be right or fair to the ones he'd left behind. He'd done so much damage already. Maybe some day, when he figured it all out, and had lost his taste for suffering, and had his real name back and wasn't hiding and running and ashamed, maybe if that day ever came, maybe then. But that day would never come. And Carrie in her mouse hat, running across the front lawn and Tommy screaming, "Bunge!" on top of the dining room table and Laura in her shorts and a T-shirt the day he asked her to marry him, the certainty they felt that they were untouchable, that they were somehow blessed and already leading a charmed life, that together they would be able to withstand anything life offered, and then for him to be given some kind of chance to try again, to fuck up again or not; he didn't deserve the chance. Nine months wasn't enough time. Nine years might not be enough time.

So what was he going to say to her? Get an abortion? Don't have the kid?

He opened his eyes and turned to her, but she was gone.

He left his cigarettes on the bar, his lighter, his wallet. He left his coat over the back of the barstool. He opened the door and ran out of the place. She was already across Second Avenue. They weren't going to take this away, not without a fight. He shouted her name and some other words. She didn't turn. She was walking away from him. He ran out into the street after her. The cold air tightened the skin over the bones of his face. He wasn't going to give up so easily this time. The sounds of horns and brakes blended together; he focused on her back, on her movement away from him. Nobody was ever going to take anything away from him again.

Acknowledgments

I am deeply indebted to the following professionals for insight into their occupations and the worlds in which they have worked: Robert Draffin, former deputy director of labor relations (Suffolk County, N.Y.); Thomas Eaton, deputy director of personnel (Oakland County, Mich.); Detective Lieutenant Robert Hoss (retired), former commanding officer, Suffolk County Police Sex Crimes Section; Delmae Ferrelli, LICSW; Laurel Ferrelli, staff attorney, Office of the Court Appointed Special Advocate (Providence, R.I.); Sergeant Artie Cliff, president, Superior Officers Association (Suffolk County Police); Professor Ellen Schuler Mauk, president, Faculty Association/Suffolk Community College; and N.S. "Pete" Pedersen.

Thanks also to Amy Williams, Alison Callahan, Kevin Peterman, Joyce Gabriele, Michele Aquino, and Fritzi Rohl, and to my readers: Paul Agostino, Lynn Trenning, and William Walsh.

Most emphatic thanks to Joseph Salvatore, who helped shape this book.